BEYOND THE
mountain
SKY

I0631373

MCBRIDE BROTHER
LUMBERJACKS

BOOK TWO

USA TODAY Bestselling Author
GWYN MCNAMEE

BEYOND THE MOUNTAIN SKY
© 2025 Gwyn McNamee

Cover Model: Jon; Photographer: Wander Aguiar

Cover Design: Y'all That Graphics

Editing: Encompass Press

To anyone who ever ran from the past and found a brighter future in the place you least expected it...

1

LIAM

The last trickle of daylight disappears behind the highest peak of McBride Mountain, taking with it any ability I had left to plaster on a fake smile and pretend I was actually enjoying the Memorial Day Festival this year.

It used to be my favorite time of year.

The start of summer.

When McBride Mountain truly comes alive again after making it through the cold, snowy winter that often feels never-ending.

Days grow longer and warmer.

The sun stays up well into the evening.

All the plants and animals wake up and begin relishing it all.

But the days of enjoying the beauty of this place and the traditions I grew up with are well behind me—irrevocably tainted by the ugly truth that looked back at me with the same eyes that day up on the mountain when my world came crashing down around me.

Now, as I pull away from the parking lot behind the church near town square, confident we've finished cleaning up from the crowd of locals and tourists who flocked downtown for the festivities today, I know there's only one place to go.

Home.

Up the mountain.

To the land the McBrides have lived on, worked, and protected for generation after generation.

The McBrides *did...*

A shudder rolls through me at the thought of going back there, to the only place I've ever called home, just as it has every day for the past nine months since I learned the truth about who I am, about where I came from, about the blood that runs through my veins.

My driver's license may say Liam McBride, but I know— and now, so does everyone else in town—that I'm a Byers. That my father brutally killed my mother after she risked her life to get me away from his abuse.

And they know what he did to Willow...

Something I can't help but see every time I look at her.

Those bruises, cuts and scrapes that marred her body when Killian dragged her from the river weren't merely caused by the rocks and logs in the water, and the emotional scars she now carries are far worse than anything physical she endured.

All because of the man who is my father.

My stomach turns violently, and I grip the steering wheel tighter, sitting at the single stop sign in town for far too long, unable to force myself to take the long, winding road past the falls and up the mountain to my cabin. Because as soon as I get there, I'll have to spend another night alone, with nothing but my thoughts that keep me awake and nightmares that attack the moment I do manage to fall asleep.

And I don't know if I can survive another night.

They've only gotten worse as the weeks have passed.

Each night, when I close my eyes, I see *his*.

The violence in the green orbs when he faced down Killian on the mountain. The way he looked at Willow and didn't see her at all, but rather, the woman who gave birth to me and then died to save me. The way he didn't even see her as a person but as something to possess, to control.

That's what I have to look forward to when I get home—those images, those realities.

But I don't have anywhere else to go.

I've never left the mountain.

I've never even left this town.

It's the only home I've ever known, and these people I can't seem to look in the eye anymore are the only friends or family I have—unless you count the Byers who are rotting in jail.

So, whether I like it or not, home it is.

I pull away from the stop sign at the corner and make my way down the narrow two-lane road that winds around McBride Mountain toward the turnoff that will take me up it to the homestead.

Each mile that passes, the darkness of the night envelops me even deeper. The trees rise higher on either side of the pavement, the mountain looming to my right.

The faint floodlights of the McBride Timber yard appear ahead on the left, and for a brief moment, I almost consider turning in, spending the night in the office, and just crashing there at my desk, but it wouldn't be any better there than at home in my own bed.

Not with the memory of Willow enduring that hypnotism there. Not with all the maps lining the walls, including the one Willow and the rest of us used to figure out where Earl must have taken her and where he had held her captive for a year. Where he forced her to give birth to Niall and run for her life afterward with a newborn in her arms and a prayer to a God who had failed her.

My eyes burn with unshed tears, but I try desperately not to let them fall.

I've wasted so many of them over the last nine months, spent too much time dwelling on what happened and my father's and aunt's roles in it, but no matter how much I tell myself to move on, to get over it, I can't.

Even as I watch Killian and Willow with Niall, finding their joy and moving past the pain to build the life they've always wanted together, I can't.

Because Earl's blood flows through me.

A man who was capable of that kind of devastating violence.

A man who was capable of murdering his wife.

A man who was capable of kidnapping an innocent woman and torturing her for a year.

A man who was prepared to kill anyone who got in his way.

A man who did God only knows what else over the past several decades that was hidden behind the veil of fog the mountain provides.

What does that make me?

The son of a monster...

As soon as I pass the lumberyard, the darkness that matches the feeling in my soul engulfs the truck again and I head toward the turnoff for the falls. I'm tempted to turn in there, too. To park in the small dirt lot and meander through the trees down the path to the waterfall that cascades off the face of the cliff and into the giant pool below.

I could strip off my clothes and slide into the still-icy waters. Let them wash away this constant feeling of being dirty. My soul tainted by what someone who shares my blood did to someone I love so much.

My headlights illuminate the narrow, two-lane road

bracketed by towering trees, providing the only break to the pitch-black of the mountain this time of night...

Until a flash of movement and something white cuts across the road.

"Shit!"

I slam on my brakes, the tires squealing as they search for purchase on the pavement, and the truck finally comes to a halt.

My heart thunders against my rib cage.

My breaths rush out hard, my chest aching as I try to see what darted out in front of me.

Out here, it could be just about anything—a rabbit, most likely, given the small size.

I could keep driving, just *go*, especially since I didn't feel a bump like I *hit* anything, but the way I'm shaking, I don't trust myself to head up the sometimes treacherous mountain trail to the McBride homestead right now.

Nor will my conscience allow me to do that.

I throw the truck into park, push open the door with a trembling hand, then climb from it onto shaky legs. My boots crunch over random bits of gravel in the road as I make my way toward the front of the truck, but I don't see anything until I fully round the headlight.

What the...?

A small French bulldog sits in the middle of the road, staring up at me with big, wide eyes with the bumper of the truck mere inches from going right over him.

"Shit." I scrub my hands across my stubbled cheeks. "Where the hell did you come from?"

I scan the woods on either side and the mountain towering behind him. There aren't any houses for dozens of miles, and I don't recognize the dog, which is odd since I know *all* the dogs in town.

He trembles violently, keeping his gaze locked on me.

I take a cautious step forward, and the dog flinches.

Crap.

If I'm not careful, I'll scare him off, and he might end up lost in the woods or worse.

I hold up my hands and slowly squat. "Hey, buddy. Where'd you come from?"

The pup tilts his head slightly, making the black patch covering his left eye shift over his wrinkled muzzle. Considering how white the rest of his fur is, he can't have been out here for very long. If he were out in the underbrush for any amount of time, he would be filthy by now.

I scan the darkness again, squinting for any hints of light from the pitch-black that surrounds us. "Where's your mom or dad?"

He continues to stare at me.

Interested.

But *not* barking.

Not snapping.

He doesn't display any signs of aggression.

That's a good sign...

I inch closer, extending my hand, and he shifts away slightly. "It's okay. I won't hurt you. But you gotta get off the road."

Almost everyone else left downtown hours ago, when the festival ended, except for me and a few others who volunteered to stay and clean up. So thankfully, there shouldn't be too many people out here, but truckers use this route at all hours of the day and night. It's only a matter of time before one comes barreling down this stretch and this tiny dog is no longer.

My chest aches at that thought, and I move closer still, risking my fingers as I reach for him, but he allows me to scratch under his chin as he sniffs me.

It's now or never...

I take the opportunity to quickly scoop him up before he

can bolt. He doesn't fight it, just snuggles into my hold and lifts his head, licking my face.

"Well, aren't you a sweet dog?" And very clearly someone's pet, given the thin red collar. I check for a tag but don't see one. "How did you get way out here?"

It's a pretty decent drive out this far, and on his tiny legs, there's no way he made it on his own.

I take a step toward the right side of the road where he came from and scan the darkness. "Hello?" My voice echoes through the otherwise silent night, but no response comes. I yell louder this time. "Hello? Is anyone there?"

Still nothing.

A light wind rustles the trees, and my engine rumbles on the road behind us, but there isn't any sign of where he might have come from or how to get him back to his owner.

Hell.

"Well, big guy, it looks like you're coming home with me tonight. We can go see Doc Lawson in the morning and see if you have a microchip. Try to find your owner."

I scratch behind his ear, and he licks me again excitedly, as if he's been alone and starved for attention for far too long. But he has clearly been well cared for, so he's likely just enjoying the scratches.

Despite how awful I've felt all day, watching the people in McBride Mountain enjoy the festival while I spent my time watching *them* and waiting for eyes to drift my way filled with concern and question, a grin pulls at my lips.

I climb back in the truck and pull the door shut. The dog immediately leaps onto the passenger seat, tongue hanging out, tail wagging, and I lean over and pop the glove compartment to pull out a bag of beef jerky.

"You want a treat, buddy?"

He pushes up on all four paws, practically bouncing in place.

"That's what I thought."

I open the bag and tear off a piece, letting him nibble it from my fingers excitedly. He nudges the bag for more, and I laugh as I pull it out and let him take it. "I guess I *won't* be going home alone tonight."

LUCKY

Panic seizes my chest, squeezing so tightly that it's all I can feel. The ache in my feet barely registers anymore as I rush down the shoulder of the narrow, winding mountain road before the sun even fully rises.

Where is he?

"Gizmo?"

My voice carries out across the pavement and disappears into the endless trees, swallowed up by the ominous mist hovering over everything.

It's eerie.

Yet, the way it clings to the ground and rolls up the trees, covering the mountain, gives it an almost ethereal quality—like I've stepped off Earth and arrived in some alternate realm.

But this isn't any realm I want to be in.

Not one where Gizmo is gone.

Despite how loudly I yell for him, I don't hear his scurrying paws or bark of response. Only chirping birds waking to a new, bright morning in North Carolina greet me.

I try to breathe through the anxiety threatening to drown me.

You'll find him, Lucky.

You. Will. Find. Him.

That's what I have to keep telling myself because from the moment I woke and found him gone, it has felt like my entire world had fallen apart—what was left of it in the first place. And in the last forty-five minutes since I realized he was missing and started my walk into town, it has only gotten worse as I near what passes as civilization out here.

It can't be much farther now.

At least, I hope not...

The straps of my backpack bite into my shoulders, weighed down with all the items I've dragged with me on this trek, and every part of my body screams for a break from hiking the desolate road under my feet, but I can't stop.

I can't.

Not until I find him.

He has to be okay...

I won't let myself consider what could have happened to him out in those woods in the dark.

I can't.

If I *actually* thought about it, I would lose my ability to think clearly, and that's when things go to shit—a lesson I've learned far too many times in too many painful ways.

The sign bearing the words *Welcome to McBride Mountain* looms on the side of the mountain in the distance, but rather than being welcoming, I tense up even more than I already was.

Towns are bad.

Towns mean people.

People mean questions.

Questions mean scrutiny.

And I can't afford that.

But I can't worry about the possible fallout of having to lie my way through McBride Mountain.

I'm on a mission—one far more important.

I have to find him.

For the millionth time this morning, I blink away the burn of unshed tears. The feeling is so foreign now. It's been so long since I've allowed myself to *feel* anything, and even longer since

I allowed myself to cry that my body forgot how—until I woke and found Gizmo gone.

He's all I have save for the items in my backpack, and I *cannot* lose him.

I won't.

The worn soles of my Chucks eat up the pavement as I make my way around the bend and spot the first buildings in the distance.

Thank God.

It feels like I've been walking forever, even though the sun is barely up. But maybe time just moves at a glacial pace when something so important is at stake.

Anything could have happened to him.

He could have wandered off and fallen into the water or some deep, dark ravine...

A wild animal could have gotten him—a coyote, a mountain lion, a bear...

No.

I shake my head to clear away those dark thoughts that could lead to a spiral I won't be able to get out of, and a car slows as it passes me, the driver leaning forward to glance out his window at me.

Wide eyes take me in before he speeds up again and drives into town.

Shit.

Wincing, I angle my head down, using my bright blue dyed hair to conceal my face.

It *seemed* like a good plan at the time I did it—change my appearance, do something that I normally *never* would so no one will recognize me, hide by being loud. But people always say hindsight is twenty-twenty, and now, the way it is going to draw attention to me seems like a *horrible* idea.

What the hell were you thinking?

Once the car is well past me, I tuck my locks behind my ear

and continue my hike into town, keeping my head dipped as a few people who are up at the asscrack of dawn start to trickle past in their vehicles.

I walk past a stop sign that seems so lonely and out of place on the empty road and almost laugh, scanning all directions of zero traffic to search for any sign of a vet's office.

If someone found him, that's where they would have brought him to get scanned for a microchip. At least, that's what anyone with any human decency would do, but I've experienced the worst of human nature and know not all people are good.

Some are inherently evil and get off on the pain and suffering of others.

Unfortunately, that's *most* people.

Hopefully, someone found him and is one of the few good ones...

That's the thought I cling to as I proceed onto Main Street.

Directly in front of me on the sidewalk, a massive wood carving of an eagle holding what looks to be a croissant stands in front of one of the cute shops. A light breeze picks up, and an incredible smell hits me. My mouth waters instantly, my stomach churning, reminding me I haven't eaten a real, sit-down, full meal in almost a week.

Chocolate.

Sugar.

Cookies.

I would know that smell anywhere.

A memory flashes through my head, one of the very few good ones that resides there, of baking chocolate chip cookies in a small kitchen with flour on my cheeks and joy filling my heart.

With it, a smile starts to pull at my lips.

But it quickly vanishes, replaced by the reality of the situation.

There isn't any time to stop for a snack. There isn't any time to stop for *anything*.

If I don't find him...

That burn returns to my eyes, blurring the sidewalk under my feet as I keep my head dipped slightly.

Don't even think that way, Lucky.

You will.

He isn't gone.

I know that, deep in my gut, but I haven't been able to stop wondering if some wild animal got him in the night. Or if he could have run out onto the road and got hit and whoever did it grabbed his little body and took it with them.

A door opens to my right, and I jerk at the sound, spinning toward an older woman with her white hair tied back in a bun. She offers me a friendly smile, stepping out from below a sign that says "Claire's Bakery" in hand-painted letters. "Hello, dear. You're up early."

Holy hell.

I press my hand over my chest, trying to calm my thudding heart as I force myself to smile back at her. "Hello. I, um...lost my dog. I'm wondering if you might have seen him, or if there's a vet's office where someone might have brought him to get scanned for a microchip?"

Her brow furrows. "A dog? What does he look like?"

"He's a French bulldog. Mostly white with a dark patch over his left eye."

The woman's eyes brighten. "He sounds adorable, but I'm sorry, I haven't seen him. Where did you lose him?"

Shit.

I am not about to delve into where I spent last night with anyone in McBride Mountain—or anywhere, for that matter—and the way she's assessing me, sizing me up, I can already tell more questions are coming if I don't get on my way. "Um... thank you for your help."

She smiles, still watching me carefully as I take my first steps to move on down Main Street. "If you want to check with the vet, he's all the way down and over a block north, but he isn't open this early."

Crap.

"You could wait at the diner just up the street. It's near the vet's office. Or you could step in here and have a cookie." She motions back toward her bakery. "They'll be done in a few minutes."

My stomach grumbles again.

A cookie does sound nice, but I want to be as close to the vet as possible so I can get there first thing when he opens. And I can already tell Claire isn't going to stop asking questions if I step into her place. "Thank you, I appreciate your help. I'll head over to the diner now and wait."

She nods. "No problem, dear. I hope you find him."

Her eyes follow me as I walk away.

They always do.

In these types of towns, strangers get a lot of attention. Which means I need to find Gizmo and get out of McBride Mountain as soon as possible.

I glance up at a sign draped across the road, announcing a Memorial Day Festival that must have happened yesterday, so I might be in luck. Maybe there are enough tourists here for the festivities that no one will notice me too much. Just one more stranger lingering after the long weekend to enjoy the North Carolina scenery.

If I'm lucky.

But the irony of my name is that I never have been.

I hustle down Main Street, lined with more carvings of animals in front of various businesses as it starts to come more alive—a few more cars and trucks, several people coming out of the shops that line the sidewalk to set out signs and brush off the areas in front with brooms, but every single set of eyes watches me as I move past them.

"You haven't seen a French bulldog have you?"

Each person I ask shakes their head and offers me luck in finding him, and the irony is not lost on me.

My skin crawls at all the attention focused on me the longer I'm out here on Main Street, and I tip my head down slightly while keeping my attention focused on my target: the small diner that's just ahead on the right.

I glance at my watch and find it's not even seven yet, which means the vet is unlikely to open for at least another hour, perhaps later.

Shit.

That means killing time.

A lot of it.

I pause at the small parking lot for Wilson's Diner. A carved bear holding a picnic basket stands directly outside the front door, and only one truck sits in the dozen or so spots, so at least there won't be very many people in there while I wait.

Gathering my nerves, I approach the front door and tug it open.

A bell jingles over my head, and I step in.

The smells of breakfast hit me instantly.

Oh, my God.

Bacon.

Eggs.

Pancakes.

Toast.

My stomach rumbles even harder, and I place my hand over it in a useless attempt to quiet the sound before anyone hears it.

A woman with dark hair graying at her temples stands behind the counter, wiping it down. She smiles at me. "Can I help you, honey?"

"Hi, I, um...just need to sit for a little while, while I wait for the vet to open."

Her brow furrows. "The vet?"

"I lost my dog. You haven't seen him, have you? He's—"

"I have him."

The deep voice rumbles through me like an avalanche charging down the mountain about to engulf me completely, raising goosebumps on my skin as it somehow simultaneously heats it.

I freeze on the spot, slowly turning my head toward the man seated in the corner booth with a half-eaten breakfast plate in front of him. Mossy green eyes lock squarely on me, but I tear my gaze away and down to a very familiar dog curled up in his lap who doesn't seem at all concerned about the fact that he hasn't seen me since last night.

"Gizmo!" I rush across the restaurant toward the booth, and Gizmo finally lifts his head and tilts it, as if he's surprised I'm there. "Oh, my God, I was so worried!"

Without even considering the huge stranger sitting on the bench seat, I bend down and scoop Giz up into my arms from the man's lap. I clutch him to me as the man assesses me with an intensity that raises the hair on the back of my neck.

Retreating a step, I examine him the same way he is me.

Heavily tattooed, muscled arms encased in a tight t-shirt are crossed over his barrel chest beneath his broad shoulders as he reclines slightly against the back of the booth.

The man with the dark coppery-red hair screams danger and would be intimidating to anyone, and given how Gizmo usually reacts to strangers, let alone *men*, there's only *one* way this guy could have him.

I straighten my spine and glare at him. "Why the hell did you steal my dog?"

2

LIAM

W *ait, what?*

It takes a few seconds for me to process her words.

Maybe I was too focused on the stunningly beautiful woman standing next to my table to actually *hear* her right.

I shake my head in an attempt to clear it and ensure I'm processing properly, then climb from the booth and approach the breathtaking stranger with hair the color of the bluebells that grow on the mountain and a dusting of freckles that spread across her peachy skin. Icy eyes that match the locks spiraling around her face meet mine and don't look away.

And I have to hand it to her, she doesn't appear at all fazed by the fact that she just accused a McBride of theft.

Stopping a few steps short of her, I tilt my head, examining her even more intensely now that we're this close. And I can't miss the slight blush that pinkens her cheeks the longer I assess her. "Did you just accuse me of *stealing* your dog?"

She clutches him tighter, like I'm some sort of villain who is going to snatch him straight out of her arms, and even though she's clearly distraught about her missing pup, a laugh bubbles up from my chest that I can't contain at the absurdity of the accusation.

The woman seems startled by my laughter for a moment, and her wide eyes that match the sky over the mountain on a crystal-clear day lock on me as I struggle to contain my reaction.

It takes a few seconds before she seemingly realizes how ludicrous the allegation is, and she finally cringes and shakes her head, sending those brightly colored locks floating around her face.

She releases a deep sigh, glancing down at the dog. "Shit. I'm sorry."

That ache in her voice and how deeply she obviously cares about the dog make it impossible for me to be mad—not that I was in the first place.

I incline my head toward the little fur ball who is snuggled deeply against her as if he never left. "I found him on the road west of town in the pitch-black last night. What were you doing out there?"

Her shoulders tense at my question, and she clears her throat, glancing out the windows toward the street. "I, uh...I'm not sure how he got away from me."

That wasn't what I asked, and her avoidance to my real question seems intentional.

There's absolutely nothing out that way except the lumber yard and the falls, and they're both several miles from where I found her dog. If he was with her and they somehow got separated, he either trekked pretty damn far by himself or this woman was on the base of the mountain alone, at night, somewhere she definitely shouldn't have been.

The business owner in me bristles at the possibility that she might have been trying to do something illegal at McBride

Timber. The product and millions of dollars of equipment sitting in the yard could certainly bring someone a lot of money if they sold it to the right people, but this woman doesn't seem like the type to hop a fence to steal a sawmill.

Which leaves the falls as the other possibility, and that's just as strange because it's closed after dark due to the drowning danger.

What were you doing out there, Bluebell?

She clearly doesn't want me to know, and I won't push.

"It's all right. No harm done." I tip my head toward the tiny animal in her arms. "At least, I don't think. I was going to take him to see Doc as soon as he opens to have him checked out, but he was with me all night and seemed completely fine."

Her head whips back up, her soft brow now deeply furrowed as her eyes meet mine. "You had him that long?" I nod. "And he...behaved?"

I narrow my gaze on her and the dog, then reach out and run my hand over his head and scratch him behind the ear in a spot that I found that he likes so much. "Yeah. Me and my little buddy. He snuggled with me all night."

And somehow managed to keep the nightmares at bay and give me the best night of sleep I've had in nine months.

"Really?" Her focus darts down to him, then back to me. "I'm surprised. He normally doesn't like other people. Especially men."

I raise a brow and shrug. "Well, he sure seemed to like me."

Her lips purse slightly. "Apparently so."

She sounds almost *annoyed* that her dog didn't put up more of a fuss when I found him.

I fight a smirk. "What's his name?"

The corners of her lips twitch, like she too is fighting the pull of humor. "Gizmo."

"Gizmo?"

Her head bobs, sending her blue hair cascading over her

shoulder. "Because he kind of reminded me of a gremlin when I got him from the pound. A little nuts, especially if you feed him after midnight. And you better not get him wet."

My bark of laughter echoes around the diner, drawing the attention of a few people who have wandered in since we started our conversation, as well as Elaine, who gives me a look from her usual perch behind the counter. "Well, he didn't cause me any trouble."

If anything, he was exactly what I needed last night to distract me from the darkness that seems to settle around me as soon as the sun goes down. His warmth pressed along my side as I slept did something no amount of alcohol ever could. Something I didn't know was possible.

His owner gives me a tight smile. "Good…"

An awkward silence falls between us, and I rub the back of my neck just for something to do with my hands. "Are you in town for the festival?"

She pulls her plump bottom lip between her teeth, chewing on it slightly as she shifts, drawing my attention down her over the straps of a backpack on her shoulders, the long-sleeve t-shirt that exposes one collar bone, ripped jeans that hug her thick hips, and finally to the worn Chuck Taylor's on her feet. "Uh, yeah."

That wasn't very convincing.

Plus, I would have noticed a woman like her around town the past several days.

She's impossible to miss, and not just because of her shocking hair color.

The woman standing in front of me somehow heats my blood despite the fact that she's icing me out right now—and clearly lying about why she's in McBride Mountain.

For the first time in a long time, she managed to get me to laugh and smile and really mean it.

I hold out my hand. "I'm Liam McBride."

Her eyes flare slightly at the mention of my last name.

Shit.

People don't typically have that reaction, but that's because everyone here *knows* me and has my entire life. But this woman clearly doesn't have any knowledge about our small town or the people in it—including how I got the McBride name or what it means.

She might be the only person in a hundred miles who doesn't know every single detail of the sordid history I learned about my biological parents and the blood that flows through my veins.

After a few seconds of hesitation, she holds out her hand and slides her smaller palm against mine. A little zap of electricity shoots up my arm at the contact, spreading through me with a warmth I relish and want to cling to. And she seems to feel it too, jerking her hand away quickly as if she's afraid to maintain any sort of physical connection between us.

"Lucky."

"Your name is Lucky?"

She nods.

Well, how about that...

I grin. "Well, I think Gizmo was the lucky one, that *I* was the one out on the road last night. If it had been anyone else who wasn't paying attention..."

A little shiver rolls through me, and she shudders at the same time, clutching him close.

"Thank you. Really." She smiles, and the genuineness of it only flares that heat to a raging inferno. "And I am *so* sorry for accusing you of stealing him. I just don't understand how he got away or why he was on the road."

Neither do I.

"There isn't really anything out there." I watch her carefully as I press to figure out where they were before she lost him, to learn *anything* about this woman and why she's here. "He must've traveled a long way from town on those tiny little legs..."

She must hear the disbelief in my voice that she was in town for the festival and the question there because she glances away again, toward the kitchen, where the smell of all the breakfast food being cooked emanates from.

And I know better than to push.

People have been pushing me for months, trying to get me to talk about what happened with my biological father and Willow and what I learned, but all they've managed to do is poke at me in a way that has left me feeling raw and exposed. Like I'm bleeding from a thousand tiny cuts and every question directed at me is like a knife being driven into a gaping wound.

So, I won't force Lucky to reveal what she's not ready to give me.

At least, not yet.

"Are you staying in town for a while?"

I do a shitty job of concealing the hope in my voice, but in twenty-four years in McBride Mountain, no woman has ever affected me the way this one has in less than five minutes.

She glances back toward me and shakes her head. "Wasn't planning on it."

"So...heading home today?"

Real subtle, Liam...

Lucky offers another restless shift, averting her gaze again and focusing on the door as if my simple questions are an inquisition she has to escape at all costs. "Uhh..."

I know what that feels like.

For the past nine months, I've felt as if I were being raked across the coals by the inquisitor, with my very life in jeopardy depending on the answers I provided. And the questions came from all sides—Killian, Connor, Willow, Raven. Not to mention how just about every person in town has been giving me those looks of pity and concern and asking how I'm doing, most without directly flat-out asking how it feels to learn my father's a murderer, a kidnapper and a rapist.

The small bit of my breakfast I ate before Lucky came in threatens to come up my throat, but I swallow it and watch the way *she* watches the room, always keeping her eyes on the door, never putting her back to it for very long.

She's nervous about something, and her story about Gizmo walking all the way out there from town is virtually impossible. Either someone drove him out onto the road and dumped him far from anything or anyone, or she was out there, which makes even *less* sense.

And that mystery, as much as the strange way I'm drawn to this woman, makes me take a massive leap I shouldn't.

"Would you...like to join me for breakfast?"

Her eyes dart back to me, then to my table, and she chews on her lip again.

I can see the debate in her eyes, the way she assesses me to see if I'm a threat or to determine what I might expect in return for the meal.

It's easy to recognize that look.

It's the same one Willow had after she returned, when she didn't know who she could trust or what she should be doing.

Whoever Lucky is, whatever brought her here, it's definitely not something she wants to discuss, and given how she's acting, I don't think she has the money to leave town or buy herself breakfast.

I motion toward the table. "My treat. You had a rough night worrying about Gizmo. You need a good meal."

She continues to worry her lip, glancing around at the various tables and Elaine bustling around them, delivering plates and cups of coffee and chatting as McBride Mountain wakes up and people make their way in.

Those blue eyes don't miss anything, and when they focus

back on me, that inexplicable heat bubbling under my skin flares under her assessment.

This woman is sizing me up, and I'm going to let her.

LUCKY

Liam McBride continues to watch me with green eyes that seem to see right through the thick walls I've built up so aggressively over the years, the ones that have allowed me to maintain my distance from people.

They served me well for a long time but feel as flimsy as butterfly wings under his assessment.

The longer he assesses me, waiting for me to decide about his offer, I can't help but let my own gaze travel over him again.

Standing at least six-two, he towers above me. In his perfectly fitted, worn jeans and t-shirt tugging at his muscled arms and chest each time he moves, my first impression that he would intimidate most people is certainly correct.

He is the picture of the rough, gruff mountain men this part of the world is known for. The kind of person to avoid at all costs.

Yet, there's something about his soft smile, the easy laugh, and the warmth in his mossy eyes that tells me he isn't exactly what he appears. Like me, the outside appearance doesn't match what's on the inside.

This blue hair screams that I'm confident, outgoing, ready to take on the world around me, while in reality, I'm trying to hide from it. I'm looking for anywhere to disappear, some way to become someone else before who I really am destroys me.

This isn't the place to hide.

Not with someone like this here, someone who so easily sees me. Plus, Gizmo likes him, and he doesn't like *any* men.

That makes it even more important that I don't stay here any longer. He's already asking too many questions I can't answer, and he's the type of man who could *get* me to answer them.

"Thank you for the offer...but I can't."

I don't want his charity or his attention.

All I need is somewhere to lay low for a little while. I hadn't intended to stay in McBride Mountain, and standing here, I can see moving on quickly is definitely in my best interest now that I have Gizmo.

These people are too nice, too inquisitive. They won't just let things go. This is the type of place where everyone knows everyone else's business, and I will quickly become a source of focus for the regulars who come to this diner.

That. Cannot. Happen.

It's hard to lie low when you're already drawing attention.

Which I definitely am.

Liam's brow furrows. "Are you sure you don't want to eat?"

It's almost like he can *see* how hungry I am. How long it's been since I sat down and had a *good* meal. And how damn *exhausted* I am after walking so much yesterday and practically running into town today.

His insistence tenses my shoulders—something I'm sure he notices too—and I give him a tight smile that I hope at least mildly appeases him.

"I'm good. Go back to your breakfast. Thank you for taking care of him."

I don't know what I would have done if Liam *hadn't* found Giz and kept him safe last night.

Would I have kept walking straight on through McBride Mountain alone?

Would I have been able to keep this up without my little sidekick and constant companion?

For as much self-confidence as I usually possess—or at least, I used to—I don't think I could. I would have been crushed under the weight of my loss and guilt that I let it happen. But thanks to this man, I don't ever have to suffer that fate.

Liam looks deeply disappointed in my final brush-off, and I can't draw my eyes away from the way his lips tip down slightly at the corners.

Why do I hate that so much?

I don't even know this man, and I can already tell the frown looks wrong on his face. Those lips were meant for laughing and smiling...and kissing.

And I need to get the hell out of here.

The older woman behind the counter watches us out of the corner of her eye, and I drag myself away from Liam and approach her with a smile. "Can I just get a cup of coffee to go?"

That's about all I can afford right now, and it will have to do to get me through however far we can make it today before the sun starts to go down.

Caffeine can work wonders, help me push through the long days on the road and handle the constant fear that keeps me looking over my shoulder.

I hope it's enough today.

She nods slowly as her eyes skim over me. "Of course, dear, but I have to ask..."

My back stiffens, bracing for another round of questions. "What?"

"Well, I know you told Liam that you weren't planning on staying, but I could use help here in the diner. One of my regular waitresses quit last week to stay at home with her granddaughter, and I thought we'd be able to handle it without her. But then, with the crowd that came in for the Memorial Day Festival and people likely staying for a few days after, I think it's going to get very busy, very quickly." She scans the diner, as if anticipating a massive rush even though it's relatively quiet this early. "Any chance you know how to waitress?"

The hopefulness in her voice tugs at my heart.

It weakens my resolve to walk away from this place so easily.

"Umm...I can."

Her warm eyes brighten, and she offers me a pleading look. "Would you want to stay, at least for a few days, to help? You could start right away. I'll pay you cash."

Cash.

That is what finally gets my attention away from the quickest route out of McBride Mountain.

No filling out paperwork.

No handing over IDs.

No government involvement.

Just cold hard cash I can stick in my pocket when I leave here.

"Of course, but"—I lift Gizmo slightly—"I have him and nowhere to leave him while I'm here."

Plus, the thought of being away from Gizmo after the terror of last night is too much for me at the moment...

Liam clears his throat. "I could hang out with him while you're working here today and bring him back when your shift is over."

That voice again.

That deep, rumbling, yet somehow soothing sound comes from the man standing behind me who has already unnerved me more than anyone has in a very long time.

I turn to face him again, and I allow myself to assess him one more time. From the dark coppery-red hair, the hard muscles, the exposed tattoos, and the large, calloused hands. Handing over Gizmo to him would mean I would have to see Liam McBride again, and staying very far away from this man seems like the safer option. "I..."

He holds up his hands, approaching slowly with heavy booted steps that seem almost tentative, like he's used to handling wild animals and doesn't want me to bolt. "I know you had a scare with him, and you just got him back, but I promise we'll be all right. We're buds."

I swallow thickly, glancing down at Gizmo, who stares up at Liam with his tongue lolling out of the side of his mouth happily. "Where would you take him?"

Liam offers me a half grin that makes me weak in the knees. "My brothers and I own the lumber yard just outside town, at the base of the mountain. I'll be there all day. I'll bring him back around closing time, and if you get done earlier, Elaine knows how to get ahold of me. He'll be fine. Killian and Connor will keep him busy if I have to do anything where he can't tag along."

"I told you, he doesn't usually do well with men."

At least, no men I've met since I got Giz...except *this* one.

He chuckles and reaches out to scratch the top of Gizmo's head. "Trust me, he'll be fine. Worst case scenario, he can trot around the lot with me all day if he doesn't want to stay in the office. It'll be fine, I promise."

Promises are nothing more than empty words.

That's a reality I've lived with for far too long.

But passing up any cash right now would be a massive mistake. I need it if I want to any farther north, if I want to put more space between me and my past.

I glance back at the kind woman behind the counter, who offers me another smile.

She nods toward Liam. "You can trust the McBrides."

For some reason, those simple words from someone I don't even know settle the anxiety I have about not having Gizmo with me.

Think about the money.

I'll need it to get out of McBride Mountain. Cash will help me do that.

Otherwise, I'll be hitting the road broke.

Stepping toward Liam slowly, my hands shake as I pass Gizmo over to him. Giz lifts his head immediately to lick Liam's jaw, apparently excited to see his new friend again.

Liam runs a large hand up and down his back. "See? We're good. I'll see you at close unless I hear otherwise?"

He raises a brow at me, and Christ, it shouldn't be so hot, but the way it arches above his emerald-green eyes makes my heart skip a beat. It takes a moment for me to process that he asked me a question and is expecting an answer.

I nod almost numbly. "Okay."

"Elaine, throw that on my tab?" He inclines his head toward the table, waits for her to nod her agreement, then moves to the door. Turning back toward me, he offers another bright smile. "Don't look so worried. We'll be fine."

Liam steps out of the diner with Gizmo in his arms and climbs into the truck parked in front of it. I watch him start it up and drive away, staring far too long out that window until a throat clears behind me and I whirl back around.

"I'm Elaine, by the way." The older woman extends a hand, and I take it and shake. "I own the diner. My husband passed away two years ago, but my son, Matt, is usually running the kitchen."

"Just let me know what you need me to do."

She grins, her eyes bright and welcoming. "That's the spirit. You said your name is Lucky?" I nod. "Well, let's hope you are, because I have a feeling as soon as that sun fully comes up, it's going to be a madhouse in here. Did you enjoy the festival?"

"The what?"

One of her brows rises. "The Memorial Day Festival. You said you were in town for it."

"Oh." I nod, smiling in a probably vain attempt to cover my lie. "Yeah, it was uhh...cool."

And if she asks me anything else about it, she will know for sure that I'm lying.

Thankfully, she just wipes her palms on her apron and moves over to the register, ushering me toward it with the wave of a hand. "Do you think you can work this?"

"Umm…" I stare at it, my hands trembling. "I'm not sure."

"Well, I'll stick you on the tables and whenever someone has to pay, I'll take care of it so you don't have to worry about it, okay?"

I nod, my throat suddenly dry.

This woman just met me, doesn't even know my full name, and has already offered me a job and access to her cash register without question. And I handed off my best friend in the world to a man I don't know.

Something about McBride Mountain is causing me to make very bad decisions.

3

LIAM

The office door swings open just as Gizmo goes careening across the wood floor, chasing the tennis ball I found for him, and almost slams into Killian's leg.

Killian freezes and glances down as Gizmo snags the ball that ricochets off the wall and races back to me, then sits and drops it at my feet. One of Killian's blond brows rises, and he offers an incredulous look. "You got a *dog*?"

I scoop up the ball, bounce it a few times. Gizmo watches intently, waiting and prancing on his paws until I fire it across the small space again, letting it bounce off the wall while Gizmo goes charging for it. "No." I shake my head. "Dog-sitting. It's a long story."

And not one I particularly want to get into because big brother will have endless questions about *why* in the *world* I would offer to watch the dog of a woman I don't know at all.

Nudging the door the rest of the way open, Killian walks in and Willow follows, with Niall sleeping in her arms.

Her warm gray gaze lights up even more the moment she sees Gizmo. "Ooh, a puppy!"

I watch him chew on the ball, trying desperately to pull the bright yellow felt off the outside. "I actually don't know how old he is."

She rolls her eyes. "All dogs are puppies to me. Age is completely irrelevant."

Killian offers a snort of laughter at that, and Willow hands the baby off to him, then bends down to say hi to Gizmo.

The dog immediately rolls onto his back for her, offering his stomach for a belly rub.

Willow doesn't waste a second complying. "Well, aren't you just the cutest thing ever?" She glances up at me. "Where did he come from?"

I sigh and scrub my hands over my face.

There goes any chance of getting away with simply saying it's a long story and leaving it at that...

"I almost hit him with my truck last night."

Willow gapes at me. "You *what*?"

Killian moves over to his desk, uses his foot to pull the chair back, then sits, cradling Niall against his chest. "Sounds like there's a story there."

I shrug, leaning back in my chair until the old thing creaks. "Not really. He darted out in front of the truck as I made the turn around the mountain. It's a miracle I didn't hit him."

My brother's blue gaze travels to the pup who is enjoying endless attention from his wife. "What was he doing out there?"

I offer another shrug because that's precisely what I still want to know, but if I express that interest to either of them, they will latch onto Lucky and probe at me even harder than they already do. "Who the hell knows?"

Willow rubs Gizmo's head as he leans into her touch. "What about his owner?"

Lucky flashes through my mind, that blue hair and

matching eyes that assessed me so cooly at the diner when her brief touch somehow offered such a strange warmth. "A woman named Lucky."

Killian shakes his head. "I don't know anyone by that name."

Anywhere else, it might seem odd for someone to automatically assume they're acquainted with every single person in the community, but it's not for Killian, Connor, or me. Mom was the rock of McBride Mountain, and that meant we all stepped into roles as her little helpers, even when we were very young.

Anything anyone needed, we helped provide it or found someone else who could.

We facilitated, and that meant getting to know *literally* every face and name in and around McBride Mountain.

"She isn't from around here."

And she certainly wasn't in town for the festival like she claimed.

The way she tensed up every time I asked her a question felt all too familiar, and it wasn't hard to tell she was lying. Elaine saw what was happening from her perch behind the counter, stepping in with her offer to help the woman, even if she was reluctant to take it.

Elaine certainly could use help at the diner for a few days after the festival for any stranglers leftover in town, but she's been running that place mostly alone for the past two years anyway with only a few part-time waitresses who came in for a shift or two to give her a little breather.

That woman saw Lucky needed money and maybe a place to stay and made sure she couldn't say no by offering it in the only way she *knew* Lucky would accept—as a favor to *her*.

And ultimately, it doesn't matter *why* Lucky is staying, just that she is.

Because something tells me she does need somewhere soft and safe to land, and McBride Mountain is exactly that place.

As long as you aren't me.

"And why isn't the dog with her now?" Willow scoops him up, snuggling him like he's her baby rather than the infant in Killian's arms. "Not that I'm complaining."

Killian chuckles, pointing to their son. "You know, we have a baby right here."

She grins at him. "I know, but this one has fur."

He rolls his eyes and leans forward to search for something on his desk. "So, where is this Lucky?"

"Working at the diner, actually. Elaine needed help, and Lucky was there. And it seemed like she could use the money, so I offered to take him so she could work a shift."

Willow and Killian share a look, and she sets the dog back on the floor. He immediately snatches the ball again and runs over to me, dropping it near my feet.

The little guy definitely has energy to burn today, and it gives me an excuse not to work for a while.

I toss the ball for him, but instead of following it, my gaze drifts to the maps of the mountain on the wall, drawn over centuries by various McBrides to show what areas have been felled and where we've replanted.

Our current project on the far side of the mountain, beyond the gorge, was well-intentioned.

Killian thought destroying all the evidence of what my father did to Willow would help both of us, so he set to work ensuring that cabin where she was held was razed, and now that the trees in that area are all large enough, we can finally log it all again. Giving the land a fresh start the same way he had hoped to give Willow and me one.

And it seems to be working for her.

Watching the way she lights up around her husband and son—and even this little white dog—demonstrates how resilient she really is.

Nothing happened *to me.*

Not really.

Yet, there are days it feels like I can't even *breathe*.

Willow wanders over to lean on the edge of Killian's desk, giving me more room to re-throw the ball once I drag my gaze off the map. "That's very nice of you to offer to help her."

I shrug again, trying to be nonchalant about it. "It seemed like..."

Her brow furrows. "Like what?"

For a second, I consider how much to tell them. Of course, if Lucky's working at the diner, they'll eventually see and meet her, but that doesn't mean I have to offer them the little information I do have on her, or the speculations I've had since the moment she walked in that door and the bells jingled above her.

But they also see a lot, and if they *can* help her, they would want to.

"It seemed like...maybe she needed the money and doesn't have anywhere to go."

"Oh." Willow's face falls, the good mood she had while playing with Gizmo suddenly disappearing as easily as it appeared. "Well, maybe she'll stick around a while. I know they definitely need a good waitress."

"For sure."

Elaine works too hard and should be looking to cut *back* on her hours rather than taking more on, but she kept insisting she could handle it when Maryann "retired" to stay home with her new grandbaby.

Willow watches Gizmo bring me the ball again. "So, you're going to drop him off back there later today?"

I nod and throw the toy. Gizmo's little paws shoot out across the room, and he snags it when it hits the wall and brings it right back.

Killian watches us play fetch for a minute. "He seems well trained."

"He is a very sweet dog, which is funny"—I release a little laugh—"because Lucky said he generally doesn't like men."

With a snort, Killian raises a brow. "Really?"

He hands the baby off to Willow and comes across the office and squats near us. Cautiously, he reaches a hand out toward Gizmo where he sits near my feet, and a low growl sounds in the back of the dog's throat that I haven't heard from him before.

I can't help my grin. "Apparently, he's a good judge of character."

Killian offers me a dirty look. "Ha fucking ha." He's smart enough to pull his hand back before he gets bitten, and I reach down and scoop up the dog with no problem, settling him into my lap easily. "What does that mean for your work today?"

"I was going to be here anyway, dealing with the load coming in from the other side of the mountain, so"—I shrug, trying to appear unaffected by the project even as that same icy coolness spreads across my skin thinking about it—"it doesn't really affect my day at all."

Willow grins at me. "Except you get to sit in here and play with a puppy, which is fun."

Leave it to her to see the bright side of everything.

After all she's suffered, her endearing spirit and refusal to allow what my father did to her dictate her future is enough to give anyone hope.

And that's what I've clung to for months.

The fact that *she* could find happiness and some sort of peace.

Which meant it had to happen for me, too.

Eventually.

Right?

Time sure hasn't proven that to be true.

But I still force myself to return her grin. "True."

She waggles her eyebrows. "Speaking of fun..."

The tone in her voice makes my shoulders stiffen. "What?"

"Well, I was hoping you could help me with some shelves, and maybe some seating for the candle shop."

My gaze cuts over to Killian, who gives me the *please do it* look.

Considering everything Willow has been through at the hands of my father, there isn't any way in Hell I would be denying this woman anything—even if Killian wasn't asking me to help.

I nod. "I can help you out with that. I'll stop by so you can show me exactly what you're thinking."

"Oh, great!" Niall releases a tiny little strangled wail, and she pushes up from the desk chair. "I'm going to head home with him. It's the witching hour, and he definitely needs a nap in his own crib."

Killian crosses over to her and takes her face in his palms, kissing her long and deep and whispering something I'm glad I can't hear.

I'm happy for them.

That they finally found...this.

That they finally have each other and their family.

But it's impossible to see them together with the baby and not think about everything they went through. Everything that Willow suffered at the hands of the man who gave me half of my DNA.

That icy shiver rolls through my spine and floods through my veins, chilling any warm feelings that playing with Gizmo has brought to my morning.

Willow offers me a smile and says goodbye as she slips out, and I feel Killian's eyes on me, even before he says anything.

"Are you all right?"

I grit my teeth. "I'm good."

He releases a sigh as he runs a hand back through his long, blond hair. "Well, you didn't *seem* good at the festival yesterday.

And I saw that look that just crossed over your eyes as you looked at Willow."

"What look?"

"The same one you've been giving her and me for months, like you somehow feel that everything that happened was your fault."

I shake my head. "No. I don't think that."

But I'm not about to tell Killian that my thoughts have been haunted by what having *that* man's blood running through my veins really means.

Killian's jaw hardens, and he watches me for a moment before he sighs. "You didn't even *know* the man. The fact that you are biologically related to him in no way makes you responsible for what he did to her."

I shove up behind my desk. "You think I don't know that?"

He throws his hands out. "I don't know *what* you know, Liam, because you won't talk to me! You won't talk to Connor, you won't talk to Willow, you're just completely shut off from the world, and I don't know what the fuck to do about it!"

Fucking hell.

I knew this confrontation was coming.

It's been building for months.

As they've settled into their lives together, mine has grown more and more out of control, twisting into darker and darker places as I think about all of the horrible things that man did to my mother, to Willow, and to who knows who else over the years.

It doesn't matter that I didn't know him, that I was raised by Constance McBride, the most wonderful woman on the planet, or that Killian and Connor are my brothers in every way *but* blood.

I can't help the way I feel inside, like knowing who I am and where I came from is some sort of rot that's working its way through every organ of my body and eating me alive from the inside out.

"I'm not talking to you about this, Kill."

He crosses his arms over his chest. "No shit!"

"No"—I shake my head—"I mean *ever*. It's none of your business."

"It's not?" His brows fly up. "Because I'm pretty sure I promised Mom that I'd take care of you when she was on her fucking death bed. This is part of taking care of you."

Putting me under the fucking inquisition again.

"Well, I don't want your help, and I don't need it."

Even as I say the words, they feel wrong.

We've always been close. We've always been there for each other and talked through all the tough moments in life. I've always been the one pushing everyone else to say the hard things they don't want to and to face those demons they're running from. But when it's my own, I can't seem to do it.

"Yeah." Killian releases an incredulous snort. "Seems like you're handling it pretty well yourself."

The sarcasm drips from his words, and it's enough to make me scoop up Gizmo and stalk toward the door.

His gaze follows me. "Where are you going?"

"Anywhere but here. *You* handle the fucking shipment."

LUCKY

I can see it coming from a mile away...

Like a train barreling down the track at you and being unable to leap out of the way before it crashes into you full force...

It's going down.

The tray rocks unsteadily in my hand, and the drinks

tumble from it, spilling all over the table and the two men sitting at the booth in front of me.

They both yelp and lean backward to try to avoid the deluge, but it's far too late to save themselves—sticky soda and ice soak them.

Shit.

Not again.

I cringe, squeezing my eyes closed in the hope that when I open them again, this will all have been a bad dream instead of a reality I know all too well. The sounds of the busy diner float around me—laughter and chatter, clanking silverware against plates, Elaine calling for orders from the kitchen—and I know I can't stand like an ostrich with my head in the sand any longer.

No matter how much easier that would be...

So. Much. Fucking. Easier.

I open my eyes to disgruntled faces as they try to use their napkins to mop up their clothes. "I am *so* sorry. I tripped and... I'm so, so sorry. Let me go get something to clean this up."

Or find somewhere to hide for real.

If that were actually an option, to hole myself up in the storage room or one of the bathroom stalls for the rest of my shift and pretend I was never here, or somehow sneak out the door without anyone seeing me, I would do it in a heartbeat.

But I'm not sneaking anywhere with this hair.

Definitely a bad call.

And I am paying for it now with nowhere to hide.

This day has been nothing short of a shit-show. Anyone who has come in and seen me working must have thought I've never held a damn tray or worked as a waitress before—and that I'm the clumsiest person on the planet.

They wouldn't be wrong about the last part.

My feet keep tripping over nothing.

My hands won't seem to grip anything securely.

And I can't concentrate on my actual job because I'm

worrying about the *one* thing I have no control over—when my past is going to catch up with me.

It's a mystery why Elaine hasn't fired me already.

I'm certainly more of a hindrance than a help at this point.

I grab the empty glasses off the table, put them back on the tray, and hustle to the kitchen, my face heating as my cheeks burn bright red.

"Shit, shit, shit." I open several cabinets, looking in every single one of them for more clean rags to use to sop up my mess. "Where are they?"

Probably all gone since this seems to happen every other table I deliver something to.

"What do you need, dear?"

Elaine's voice cuts through my panic, soft and welcoming, and for a moment, I want to luxuriate in the sound. It's precisely what I always imagined grandmothers sounded like for those kids who had them—warm, welcoming, comforting in a way almost nothing else is.

Yet it makes me cringe.

Again.

Because I don't want to face her and have to admit what I did.

But just as there isn't any hiding from my mess out in the diner, there isn't any hiding from Elaine, either.

I glance over my shoulder at her. "Oh, um, I spilled some soda. I need to clean it up, and I already used all the rags that were out under the counter."

To clean up my other half-dozen messes.

Yet, those were easy compared to the mess my *life* has become.

Not that it was ever exactly clean and orderly.

As early as I can remember, it was always chaotic. Nothing stable. Nothing real or true. Nothing I could rely on except myself.

Learning that truth young served me well, until I forgot it for *one* brief moment. When I gave in to that need to lower my guard and let someone else carry the weight. When I *trusted* for the first time in a *long* time...

And got burned.

Now that's what I've done to Elaine.

She trusted me, without any reason to, and I've burned her. I've made a mess of her diner and customers—and it's only my first day.

Maybe staying was a bad idea.

Maybe I should have just grabbed Gizmo and kept walking out the other end of Main Street and toward wherever the road led me—

Elaine pats me on the shoulder, halting my downward spiral before it reaches the point of no return. "I've got it, dear. Just refill the drinks."

I release a shaky breath, trying to regain my composure, but my hands won't stop trembling no matter how tightly I grip the edges of the counter.

I'm fucking this up left and right.

Of all the odd jobs I've done since I was fifteen, waitressing has always been the worst. Not in terms of the work itself—*that* I actually like—but in terms of my performance. What just occurred is not an isolated incident, and the longer I stay here, the worse it will become. Not because I can't do the job but because every time that bell jingles, my heart stops and I peer over my shoulder, praying I won't recognize the face that walks in.

It's hard to stay cool, calm, and collected and balance a tray when you live like that—jumpy and always on-guard.

And Elaine was right when she told me they needed help.

They're busy here. As one of the only restaurants in town, there's no such thing as a rush at lunch or dinner. It's a steady stream all day—apparently especially when the festival is happening and immediately before and after—which I've learned the hard way.

My feet ache.

So does my lower back.

But that could also be from all the walking I did before I got to McBride Mountain and sleeping in a place that certainly isn't meant for it.

I know my body will get used to this job, but I don't plan on being here long enough for that to happen.

All I need is to get enough cash to get me farther north.

A few days—*tops.*

You can tough it out until then, Lucky.

I close the cabinet and refill the sodas, then carefully carry them in both hands instead of balancing them on the tray as I make my way out to the table.

Elaine is chatting with the two gentlemen there, all of them laughing as if nothing happened, and they each offer me a kind smile.

"Just the first-day jitters, hon." Elaine pats me on the shoulder again as I set down the drinks. "You're doing fine."

I wish that were true...

One of the two men I soaked earlier motions to his jacket that's now covered in Coca-Cola and draped over the empty seat beside him. "Don't worry about it, hon. I never liked this jacket anyway."

He winks, offering me a reassuring smile after.

Kill me now...

Sticking my head back into the sand again sounds amazing, but with my cheeks heating and my boss standing next to me, all I can do is apologize. *Profusely.* "I'm so sorry!"

He waves me off with a grin. "Don't apologize again. Elaine said you're just starting today, so we'll cut you some slack."

I open my mouth to thank them for being so understanding, but the bells above the door jingle and I whirl toward it with my heart in my throat, my back stiffening immediately.

Liam walks in carrying Gizmo, and my heart starts beating again—

At seeing Gizmo's tiny little face.

Definitely *not* at seeing Liam's...

The way butterflies taking flight in my stomach aren't because of the grin that pulls at his lips as he approaches with my dog. It's merely residual nerves from spending the day here, constantly looking over my shoulder.

I force myself to move away from the table, leaving Elaine to deal with the customers as I approach. "Hi."

God, that sounded stupid.

Yet, even though I must look a complete mess, my hair falling from the messy bun I threw it into earlier, my clothes stained with the various items I've spilled all over myself, that grin of his widens. "Hi. I see you're still working, so I'll just hang out until you're done."

"Oh, are you sure?" I glance at the clock hanging above the window to the kitchen behind the counter. We'll be closing in fifteen minutes, but Liam has already done enough. Making him sit and wait for me to finish doesn't feel right. "Don't you have somewhere to be?"

He shakes his head and wanders over to settle in the same booth he was in this morning. "One thing you'll learn about McBride Mountain is no one's ever in a rush to go anywhere."

I can't help the smile that tugs at my lips. "That sounds nice, actually."

My entire life has been spent moving from one place to another, never staying anywhere long enough to form any real connections, rushing to find somewhere better, somewhere safer.

The ease with which Liam said those words proves he means them, and somehow, the thought of there being somewhere like McBride Mountain sounds like a fantasy. A wonderful one that can't possibly be true.

Because there's *always* a catch.

Liam sets Gizmo down next to him on the bench seat of the booth, and he curls up, pressing his back against the thigh of the man he met less than twenty-four hours ago but has somehow bonded with already.

Little traitor...

He's never taken to *anyone* like this before, and certainly not to a man.

"Was he any trouble?"

Liam chuckles and rubs Giz's back absently. "Not at all, though you were right about him not liking men."

"Was I?"

Oh, God...

Liam just grins again, chuckling softly to himself. "He wasn't too fond of my older brother."

Acid crawls up my throat, and I choke it back along with the rising panic. "What did he do?"

If he bit someone, that is going to get local law enforcement involved...

My stomach churns violently, and I glance toward the front of the diner, watching the door before Liam's chuckle draws my attention back to him.

"Don't worry." He waves me off dismissively. "Just a little growl of warning. Killian was smart enough to get his hand away before he bit."

"I don't know what it is." I shake my head, watching how serenely he naps next to this stranger when he's typically a snarling, growling little menace around almost men. Though, he likely feeds off my energy, and he knows what I need from him when I need it. "He's just always kind of been my protector..."

Liam's gaze softens as it zeroes in on me, but something else lies in the evergreen depths. Something that looks an awful lot like resolve. "What do you need protecting from, Lucky?"

You.

I said too much.

And he *sees* too much.

This is why I shouldn't have stayed. *This* is why Liam McBride and McBride Mountain are dangerous, maybe even more so than the reason I'm in this town in the first place.

I plaster on a smile I've perfected over the years—one that has convinced countless foster parents, social workers, police officers, and anyone else I needed it to that everything was fine. "Nothing. Everything's great. Do you want anything while you wait?"

He eyes me speculatively, as if he can see through my fake response as easily as a fish moves through clear water. But he eventually shakes his head. "I'm good waiting. It's almost closing time, anyway."

The breath of relief I release at the end to his questioning rushes out of me before I can pull it back. "Yeah, okay."

"Do you...have somewhere to stay tonight?"

He looks as uncomfortable asking the question as I am hearing it, and I shift on my feet, glancing around the diner at anything but him.

"Uh, yeah, actually." I force myself to meet his gaze again. "Elaine says that she has an empty apartment above her garage."

Liam's eyebrows rise. "She's going to let you stay there?"

I nod, chewing on my bottom lip, an old habit I haven't been able to break no matter how hard I try. "Yeah, just until I move on. You know, it's only a handful of blocks away so I can walk there and back." I shrug. "It's convenient, and she isn't going to charge me."

He glances down at Gizmo, continuing to smooth his hand

over his short fur. "I'm glad you're going to be staying long enough to need somewhere *to* stay."

Warmth floods my chest with his words, and I have to clear my throat to remove the emotion suddenly lodged there.

But I can't bring myself to respond, even when Liam finally looks up at me again and I see the heat in his gaze and how genuine his words were. Before I can say or do something stupid, like actually consider staying longer, the bells above the door ring, reminding me of my reality.

I spin toward it, and my breath catches at the familiar star on the uniform of the man who walks in, chatting with someone on his cell phone. He waves at Elaine behind the counter, his attention focused that direction rather than our corner of the diner.

Swallowing thickly, forcing myself to breathe, I casually make my way back to the kitchen, hoping he doesn't get a good look at me.

4

ONE WEEK LATER

LUCKY

*S*he lied.

Staring at the shattered dishes and food splattered on the diner tile floor, those words keep repeating in my head.

She lied. She lied. She lied.

Elaine *lied* when she said it would get easier over the last week. Whether it was intentional or simply her nature to keep reassuring me and saying those words, they definitely weren't true. And that sweet woman's insistence that I'm getting better and she couldn't possibly do it without me—along with the really good tips I keep getting despite my ineptitude—is the main reason I stayed longer in McBride Mountain than I had originally intended.

Far longer.

But the extra time in the diner hasn't done anything to improve my skills.

I still keep fucking everything up—getting orders wrong, dropping trays, spilling on customers.

For the life of me, I don't know why the old woman keeps me around anymore. She must be a glutton for punishment.

And so am I, apparently.

Or maybe I've just gotten so used to things being fucked up in my life that everything that's happened the past week here has barely even been a blip on the radar.

A very messy blip...

I lower myself to my knees and start scooping up the pieces of ceramic that were once a bowl and plate, cringing at the chili scattered across the tile floor that I'll have to clean up, too.

The chatter in the diner has already returned to a normal level after my epic performance momentarily shattered the mood, but over it, the now far too familiar bells above the door ring.

My spine stiffens, and I peek back to check who entered and cringe.

Why does it have to be him?

Of all the people that could've walked in right now, it just *had* to be Liam McBride.

While there are certainly other faces I would like to see *less* —ones whose presence would end this little stopover in McBride Mountain the moment they walked through that door —Liam arriving to see me like *this*, yet again, feels like a slap in the face from karma trying to pay me back for the things that brought me here in the first place.

He's been in here every day since I arrived, and every time he steps through that door, I lose a little bit of my ability to remain unaffected by his easy smile, calm demeanor, quick laugh, and genuine friendliness.

It gets a little harder to pretend he isn't the type of white knight hero from the fairytales because he's the closest to it that I've ever met, and I'm Cinderella, on my hands and knees scrubbing the floors. Only, unlike in the children's stories, I'm cleaning up after *myself* instead of some wicked step-sisters.

At least this time, Liam didn't witness the actual event, only the messy aftermath, but instead of making his way to his usual table, he beelines for me and drops to his knees, reaching out for a rather sharp-looking piece of the bowl.

"You don't have to do that."

The corner of his lips curls slightly as he leans closer, and his pine and spice scent reaches me over all the smells of the diner. "I know, but I want to. Are you okay?"

I don't know if he's talking about the fact that I just destroyed more dishes, or that at this point, I've probably broken enough that I should be paying Elaine rather than her paying me. Or maybe he's asking in the broader sense, because he's been watching me so closely every day when he comes in here and can obviously tell that my life is a hot fucking mess.

Whatever his reason, tears well in my eyes at the fact that he's asking at all, that he's noticed and recognizes how hard *all* of this has been for me even when he doesn't have the slightest clue what's really going on behind the scenes. But just like I always do, I blink them away before they can fall and draw in a deep breath.

"I'm fine."

You are *fine.*

I keep telling myself that every day, but the longer I stay in McBride Mountain, the more frequently I'm looking over my shoulder, watching every car that passes, jumping every time those damn bells jingle above the door, spending sleepless nights staring at the street in case I need to grab my bag and Gizmo to run.

The longer I stay, the more I realize I *have* to go.

Because of these people.

Because they've welcomed me and offered me so much I don't deserve, and bringing this down on them would be the ultimate betrayal of that trust they've given me when they don't even know me.

Liam continues to gather the larger pieces while I pile up the smaller shards on the tray. We both reach for the same fragment, and his fingers brush against mine. Just like that first night, when our hands met, a strange warmth spreads through me with the slightly fleeting touch.

I jerk away, terrified of the heat becoming a flame I won't be able to put out.

He doesn't comment on my abrupt reaction. We simply work in silence, neither of us in any particular rush but both of us casting furtive glances, as if we each expect the other to say something at any moment.

But we don't.

We just work slowly and meticulously.

He was right.

Pretty much everything moves slowly here, and that isn't a bad thing.

Slow is exactly what I need right now.

A chance to take a *full* breath.

Which is yet another reason I haven't left yet.

I may be looking over my shoulder every minute, but at least I can breathe here. The clean, clear summer mountain air, coupled with the fact that I'm actually standing still in one place for longer than a few seconds at a time, has given me a chance to do something I haven't in years—enjoy the illusion of peace and safety.

Even though I know it won't last.

It can't.

Nothing is this perfect.

I steal glances at Liam as we work, searching for any signs of flaws, of red flags I've somehow missed with others, but all I ever see when this man comes to the diner is good manners, quick smiles, and those grins that seem to melt away the tension from my body for a brief moment.

As soon as all the pieces are safely on the tray, I push to my feet. "I'm going to go get the mop."

There's so much chili on the floor that it is a *major* hazard—as much as my waitressing skills.

Elaine looks our way from behind the counter and follows me into the back storage room, where I plan to grab the mop and bucket. "You okay, sweetie?"

I turn to her and force a smile. "Yep. And I know you don't want me to keep saying it, but I'm sorry."

She reaches out and grabs my hands, squeezing them gently. "Honey, we were all like that when we started. It'll be okay." Her gaze darts out in the direction of Liam where he stands guard over the spill, ensuring no one accidentally steps in it while I'm gathering supplies. "Nice of Liam to offer to help you."

"Yeah." I pull out of her hold and grab the mop and bucket to keep her from feeling the way my hands are trembling just thinking about the way it felt when we touched. "It was."

He's always nice.

Always helpful.

Always asking if he can take Gizmo with him to the office while I work on the days he will be there and not up on the mountain where it wouldn't be safe for the little guy.

"He's been here every day..."

I nod, filling the bucket with hot water and cleaner. "Yep."

The tiniest of grins pulls at her lips. "That's pretty unusual for him."

My back stiffens, and I try to remain casual as a now familiar warmth spreads through my body. I clear my throat, refusing to believe her words. "What do you mean?"

"Oh, he and his brothers come in maybe once a week, usually, but every day? I don't think he's coming for the food."

She slips out of the back room with that little weighted comment, and I hold my breath, considering her words.

Has he really been coming in just to see me? The shittiest wait-ress in McBride Mountain?

I hope not.

I would much rather believe it's because he likes Giz and the food here.

It can't be because he feels the same spark of attraction I do. Because I won't be here very long. Certainly not long enough to strike up a friendship, and definitely not long enough for some-thing more—if that were even possible.

Something more.

Those words make the tears burn in my eyes again, but I don't let them fall. I left tears behind me a long time ago, refusing to let them back into my life. No matter how frus-trated, how lonely, how upset I get, I promised I was done with them. Yet this job, this place, and that man are rattling me in ways I never could have anticipated.

I stand for a few moments while the water fills, trying to regain my composure enough to go back, and when I do, Liam has already brought the tray of broken dishes into the kitchen area and is still standing sentinel over the mess.

He moves to grab the mop from me, but I point to his table.

"No. Please go sit."

One of his brows rises. "Are you sure?"

I nod.

This is *my* job, not his.

My mistake.

And one thing I promised myself in addition to the no tears was that I would own my mistakes and live with the conse-quences of them, no matter what they might be, not push them off on others. Not even if they are willing.

I mop, feeling his eyes on me every moment until the floor is completely clean, then I dump out the dirty water in the storage room sink, wash my hands, and return to the main diner area.

A few more tables have filled since I've been gone, and I quickly make my way over to them and get their drink and food orders before I head to Liam, giving myself more time to appear unaffected by his presence. "What can I get for you tonight?"

"I'll have the chicken soup and a Coke."

"You got it." I start to leave the table, but despite how uncomfortable it might be, I can't walk away without acknowledging what he did for me. "And thank you. For your help."

He grins at me, relaxing back into the faux leather booth. "No need to thank me. I don't mind. Really."

And that's exactly the problem.

Nice men don't exist, at least not in my world. Men like Liam McBride are fairy tale heroes relegated to the pages of childhood books, not flesh and blood and sitting right in front of me, giving me a sexy grin that is downright dangerous.

The only thing that draws my attention away from it is the diner door opening and that sound tinkling out through the space.

I drag my gaze from Liam in time to see two men walk in— one incredibly tall and muscular with a scruffy beard and long, sandy blond hair that hangs past his shoulders who would look like he stepped off the cover of *GQ Magazine* if he weren't in the flannel shirt and ripped jeans, and the other with dark hair and even darker eyes but the same imposing build and commanding presence.

They both scan the diner and wave to a few people as they beeline directly for Liam and me, offering him a nod.

Some of the tension in my shoulders relaxes.

They aren't strangers.

He knows them.

And for some reason, that makes me feel better. A little less like I have to watch their every move. But I still keep an eye on them as I put in his and the other tables' orders and grab those ready to be brought out.

Liam's eyes follow me the entire time, heating my skin, and I do my best not to peek over at him. But that's impossible when I know he's watching me. It's like my body can feel his gaze like a fluid caress, and each time I move, that touch moves with me.

Somehow, I manage to serve both tables without spilling anything, and when Matt hits the tiny little bell on the top of the window that goes into the kitchen to let me know that Liam's order is ready, I snag it and hustle over to his table.

"Here you go." I slide his plate in front of him and set down his drink. "Is there anything else I can get for you?"

He glances down at it, then smiles at me. "Nope. This looks great."

I turn to the other men who have joined him at the table. "Anything for you two?"

They watch me curiously.

The one with dark hair raises a brow.

The blond's mouth tilts in a half smirk, and he shakes his head. "We're good. I think we have everything we need."

The way he says it makes my skin tingle, and I step back and disappear into the kitchen as quickly as I can, anxious to find somewhere to cool off.

LIAM

Killian drags his gaze away from Lucky once she finally disappears into the back and focuses on my plate, and I know, before he even opens his damn mouth, what he's about to say. "I know, for a fact, you did not order meatloaf, Liam. You fucking *hate* meatloaf."

Jesus fucking Christ...

For a brief millisecond, I had hope that when he and Connor walked in, I might not have the confrontation I now know is coming. But the moment Lucky set down a *plate* instead of a bowl and I saw what was in my glass, that hope vanished as quickly as she did into the back.

I scowl at him and pick up my fork and knife and begin to cut into the slab of minced meat smashed together on my plate. "Maybe I've developed a taste for it."

Even saying those words makes me almost gag.

Killian snorts, then reaches out and snags the glass in front of me that's clearly filled with something that's not Coca-Cola. He takes a sip of it. "And a Sprite! My, oh my, your tastes sure have changed significantly since we last sat at this diner only a week or so ago."

I stab a piece of meatloaf, my stomach already regretting the fact that I'm about to actually attempt to ingest it. But I refuse to give Killian—or Connor, who watches with a smirk— the satisfaction of admitting Lucky gave me the wrong order and I didn't tell her.

"You know what else has changed around here?" Killian leans forward, placing his elbows on the table with a grin. "The new waitress with the pretty blue hair."

He inclines his head in the direction that Lucky just disappeared, and Connor snort-laughs, drumming his fingers on the tabletop. "You've got it bad for her, don't you, bro?"

I kick Connor under the table, and he winces.

"What was that for?"

"For being you."

For being an asshole goes without saying since they both know exactly what they're doing right now.

It is very intentional—their way of giving me brotherly love.

I shove the bite in my mouth and force myself to chew and swallow despite how badly I want to spit it back out.

God, I've always hated meatloaf.

Killian isn't wrong about that.

I would much rather have the bowl of chicken soup I actually ordered, but after the day I can see Lucky is having, I wasn't about to tell her she messed up my order—again—when I can scarf this down quickly—and hopefully without really having to taste it—and make things easier on her.

At least, a little bit.

It won't help her keep food and drinks on the trays or stop mixing up orders, but it could get her through the end of this shift without more almost tears.

I didn't miss the way she tried to rapidly blink them away before they fell earlier. Despite her attempts to keep her head down and hide her distress from me, it rolled off her in waves I couldn't help but feel.

So, if eating this can make her day easier in *any* way, I'll do it.

Killian laughs at Connor's pain and my response. "Is this why we haven't seen you at home for dinner all week?" He raises a brow. "Willow was actually starting to get worried. She thinks you've been avoiding us."

Well, she isn't wrong.

I *have* been after our conversation at the yard last week, but the way he's watching me, I know he's not only talking about the past several days.

Is it better to let him think I've been avoiding his wife and the memories that seeing her bring up, or is it better to just admit that there's something about Lucky that keeps bringing me back to the diner every night, even if I don't have Giz to return to her?

It's a Catch-22 really.

Either way, I'm going to face the often relentless assault of the McBride brothers and their opinions.

"She's new in town. She doesn't know anyone, and she's struggling a bit, so I'm trying to support her."

Killian snorts and leans back, crossing his arms over his chest. "Uh huh. As a *friend*, right?"

I shove another bite in my mouth and chew a little more violently than necessary. "Of course, just as a friend."

I'm in no place mentally to be anything more than a friend to anyone, nor do I really have any experience in that regard. The only girlfriends I've ever had were in middle school and high school.

Casual.

A few dates here and there.

Never anything serious.

I wouldn't know what to do with a woman like Lucky. Because something tells me she has far more experience in this world than I could ever have, and not the pleasant kind.

The way she's always looking over her shoulder. How her eyes darken when someone she doesn't know comes into the diner. Her shoulders stiffening when anyone asks her literally *anything* about herself. All of it points in one direction—not a good one.

And I'm not about to let Killian or Connor make her uncomfortable by sitting here and giving her shit when she comes back.

"Are you two just going to sit there to harass me, or is there a reason you came in?"

I was stuck on the far side of the mountain today dealing with the new logging plan, in the one place I never wanted to return to again.

And it's left me...unsettled.

Maybe more so than I want to admit.

The turnoff to the homestead was far closer than driving into town. I could have been home an hour ago, eating dinner at Killian and Willow's and spending time with everyone. Yet the only thing I wanted after today was to drive *here*. To see *her*.

Walking in and finding Lucky on her hands and knees,

cleaning up another mess, felt like seeing myself today at that site.

Though the debris from the cabin has been long cleared and the trees are already being felled, I can still picture it all exactly as it was that day we hiked through the gorge.

I can still hear the gunshots and feel them whizzing past me. I can still hear Willow's sobs as the memories returned. I can feel the plea in her voice for my father to tell her where Niall was.

All that pain won't leave me.

And seeing Lucky in pain was enough to almost break me.

I am not in the mood for my brothers' bullshit tonight. Not by a longshot.

Killian offers an apologetic grin. "I came because my wife wants me to bring her home a piece of apple pie for dessert."

He elbows Connor.

Connor scowls at me, still reaching down to rub at his leg where I kicked him. "I just came for the wonderful company."

The meaning behind the comment isn't lost on me. People used to enjoy my company. Hell, I used to enjoy my own. But now, everything seems different.

Even this town feels different.

Almost like I don't know it though I've been here my entire life.

Maybe it's because I'm looking at it a different way, seeing it through different eyes. The eyes of someone who now knows that something so awful could have been going on with none of us even realizing it for an entire year. Or the fact that my mother could have been murdered and her body never found while my father went about living his life on and around McBride Mountain as if nothing had happened.

Any appetite I had is suddenly gone, and I push the plate away.

Connor chuckles. "I knew you weren't going to eat that."

"Shut up, asshole."

Killian climbs from the bench, makes his way to the counter, and leans over it to place his order for pie with Elaine.

Connor scooches around to climb out as well, but pauses next to the table. "Can I offer you a piece of advice?"

"If I say no, are you going to do it anyway?"

He smirks, then leans closer, peeking to the kitchen area where a glimpse of blue hair flashes occasionally. "If you like her, *do* something about it."

"That's it?" I raise a brow at him. "That's your sage wisdom?"

A low chuckle slips from his lips. "Believe me when I tell you, I wish I could take it."

"What the hell is that supposed to mean?"

"Nothing." He releases a heavy sigh and shoves his hand through his hair before he stalks toward the front door. "Later."

Killian holds up the plastic to-go container in my direction and inclines his head. "See you later."

I nod at him, and they both step out to the parking lot as Lucky reappears from the back, carrying a tray to one of the tables in the far corner. Each movement she takes is measured, careful. Her hips sway slightly in jeans that hug her magnificent curves, and she stops to unload everything with a smile at having successfully made it there in one piece.

When she's done delivering their meal, she starts wiping down the empty tables and getting ready to close for the night.

I should go home, head up the mountain, spend some time with the family who apparently think I'm avoiding them, or out in my workshop on one of the many unfinished projects waiting for me there.

Yet I find myself sitting here every night.

Watching her...

The way that long, blue hair slides down her back and over her shoulder when it's down. Or how adorable she looks when she wraps it up in a messy bun at the back of her head to keep it out of her way like tonight.

I never thought blue hair could be so sexy, but my fingers itch to know what it feels like. How soft it is. What it smells like.

Shit.

Killian was right.

I *do* have it bad for her.

And I don't know what the fuck to do about it.

When she finishes cleaning, she scans the diner and heads for my table. She glances at my plate and the two small bites I took from it. "You didn't like the meatloaf?"

I force a smile. "Just wasn't as hungry as I thought I was."

Suddenly her eyes widen. "Oh, God." She presses her hand over her mouth. "You ordered soup and a Coke." Her eyes dart to the glass, and she buries her face in her palms, shaking her head. "I'm such an idiot. I am so sorry. I don't know why I thought I didn't need to write that down, but—"

"Hey." I probably shouldn't do it. In fact, I *know* I shouldn't, but her distress calls to me in a way that won't let me not try to help. I reach out and gently brush her elbow until she looks at me. "It's okay, really. I didn't have much of an appetite anyway."

She lowers her hands. "I can go get you a bowl of soup. Get you your right order. I—"

"Lucky, really, I'm fine, but..." Maybe it would be wise to just let it go, but I can't help but push. "You seem a little rattled today."

She releases a long sigh and squeezes her eyes closed. "That obvious, huh?"

I don't know if telling her how obvious it is would help in this situation or not, so I simply offer her an understanding smile she sees when her blue eyes finally meet mine again. "I've been there. A lot, lately, if I'm being honest. Just take it one day at a time."

That's all I've been doing—struggling through every day

with the memories, the nightmares, the unanswered questions, just hoping that they'll eventually stop.

The only thing that has managed to distract me from my own demons has been the woman standing in front of me, who clearly has ones of her own.

5

LIAM

Leaning against my truck, I watch the diner as the lights slowly go off around inside it, plunging it into the same darkness that has descended outside. A few widely spaced streetlights along Main Street and a couple exterior bulbs outside closed businesses provide the only reprieve.

McBride Mountain decided a long time ago that too many harsh lights would impede the ability of citizens to see the stars at night, and the ones placed judiciously around town are just enough to allow a low, warm glow but not enough to block out the beauty of the twinkling dots spread out above us.

I glance up at them, watching them disappear then reappear from behind the few light clouds that also float over the moon.

It's a peaceful night, like all of them are in McBride Mountain. But Elaine has her quilting bee tonight, and always leaves early. That meant Lucky had to close up the diner alone.

And despite knowing that crime is virtually non-existent around here—save for my own father's actions last year—the thought that Lucky would be walking home alone in the dark weighed heavy on my chest. Precisely where her eucalyptus scent still lingers from when I worked beside her cleaning up early.

I sat in my truck for almost an hour while Lucky finished her end of the evening tasks required to close the place, but I couldn't bring myself to leave.

Not without her.

Lucky steps out the front door, drawing my attention back to the diner. She turns and twists the key in the lock to secure the building without ever glancing my direction.

I push off my truck. "Hey..."

She startles, dropping her bag and the keys, pressing a hand to her chest. "Jesus, you scared the hell out of me."

"Shit. I'm sorry." I hold up my hands, approaching her cautiously as she struggles to regain her breath. "I waited because I didn't want you walking home alone."

But I can see now that maybe that was a bad idea.

Lucky's reaction to finding me waiting makes guilt eat away at me for scaring her.

She releases a long, shaky exhale, then bends down and picks up her things, sticking her hand into her bag to ensure they're all there. By the time I get over to her, she's re-secured her bag on her shoulder with everything inside of it and looks up at me with trepidation in her gaze.

If I wasn't so concerned about her heading home alone in the dark, I might forget the whole thing, but I can't ignore this feeling in my chest that this woman needs someone to watch out for her, to have her back. That maybe she's never had that before.

I swallow through my uncertainty. "Do you...mind if I walk with you?"

It's only a few blocks to Elaine's house, but that doesn't

relieve the tension that permeates my body as I wait for her response.

She chews on her bottom lip, scanning Main Street, which is quiet tonight. Only a few people meander on the sidewalks. A single car drives down the pavement away from us—someone finally heading home.

Which is what I should be doing, too.

And I will, as soon as I get Lucky to her temporary one.

Eventually, her gaze returns to mine and some of the ice there has melted away. "Okay..."

"You don't sound so sure about that."

She forces a smile. "I'm just used to being on my own."

The way she says that makes an ache bloom behind my ribcage, and I shove my hands into my pockets to keep myself from rubbing at it and drawing attention to my strange reaction.

I've never really been alone. Since the day Mom brought me into the McBride cabin, I was one of them. I always had her, Killian, and Connor around me. There was always someone watching over me, taking care of me, offering companionship and whatever else I might need.

Yet, I've felt nothing *but* alone since I learned the truth about who I am.

Like I'm standing at the peak of the mountain in pitch blackness with no way to descend and nowhere else to go.

Maybe that's why I stayed tonight.

For *me* more than for *her*.

Because Lucky and her dog are the only ones who have made me truly smile or laugh in months.

Because thinking about *her* means I'm not thinking about *me*.

I clear my throat, trying to work out the tension there, as I fall in beside her and we start walking toward Elaine's house.

"So, what do you think about McBride Mountain now that you've been here for a week?"

A grin plays at her lips and her eyes warm in the few lights coming from the shops we pass on Main Street. "It's beautiful here. Quiet. Peaceful."

All those things are true.

Mostly.

The mountain wasn't so peaceful when we found out what happened to Willow. When we found out what my father had done to her. When Killian almost killed him right in front of me. But her observations about McBride Mountain are exactly the reasons everyone loves it.

"We're a small town." I scan the nearly empty street. "Everybody knows each other. It can be annoying, people constantly being in your business, but it's home."

And I've never left it.

I never even considered it, until the last several months. But somehow, getting away from the stares and the history here has sounded more and more appealing the longer the nightmares have plagued me.

Lucky watches me out of the corner of her eye. "I can't help but notice the name of the town…"

Her initial reaction when I introduced myself that first night flashes through my head, and I try to figure out how to explain the family history to her without discussing all the things I have been running from for months.

"The McBrides have been here for 250 years…"

"Wow. I can't imagine having those kind of roots anywhere."

Which means I was right—Lucky doesn't have anywhere to really call home.

I wave a hand out toward the town square. "They founded the town."

"Wow"—she offers a playful grin—"so you're like, *royalty* or something."

A chuckle slips out of my mouth, but there's no real humor in it. "Some people might say we are, but I'm actually adopted, not a McBride by birth, so I guess I can't inherit the throne, anyway."

She raises a brow. "Really?"

Fuck.

I hadn't meant to tell her that.

But now that the cat's out of the bag, there isn't really a way to put it back.

"Uh huh..."

I kick a pebble and watch it bounce along the sidewalk in front of us, holding my breath and hoping she doesn't try to delve any deeper into what I just inadvertently revealed. Tonight, after spending the day out on the far side of the mountain, I don't think I could handle discussing the realities of where I came from.

A moment of silence hangs between us before she glances at me again. "Were those your brothers earlier tonight?"

"Yeah." I offer her an apologetic smile. "Sorry if they were being assholes. That's just kind of their usual state."

She chuckles. "I know what that's like."

"You have brothers and sisters?"

A wistful look overtakes her face. "Like you, not by blood. But yeah. A lot of them."

I raise a brow at her. "How many is a lot?"

"Thirty or forty?"

"What?"

Those perfect lips of hers curve up, but even in the relative darkness of Main Street in downtown McBride Mountain this time of night, I can still see the pain flash across her eyes. "I was a foster kid. Moved around to a bunch of different houses when I was younger, so..."

"Ahh."

For some reason, knowing that one thing about her past explains so much about her.

The way she keeps to herself.

Not wanting to accept help.

Not wanting to open up.

I can understand why she'd be like that, growing up without a family and getting bounced around a lot. Making connections would only have led to pain when she had to leave.

The McBrides might not be blood, but one thing we always were was a family. We looked out for each other, cared for each other, and Connie loved Connor and me as if we were her own and never treated us any differently than she did Killian. And now that she's gone, Killian has held us together and ensured we didn't drift apart.

Until my blood drove a wedge between us.

And learning something so important about Lucky only makes me need to know more. I need to know *everything* about this mysterious woman who showed up with the adorable dog and the wild blue hair and has somehow broken through the shroud of fog I've been lost in.

The more I know, the easier it will be to figure out how to get her to let down her walls.

What she just told me cracked a door I plan on pushing open. "So, where did you grow up?"

She fiddles with the strap on her purse and continues to stare straight ahead while we walk down the sidewalk toward Elaine's. A car passes by, and her back stiffens as she watches it until it turns and heads off to the west. "Kind of all over. Mostly in Savannah, but a few other places."

"Always the city, though?"

Her head bobs, the messy bun she has her hair pulled back in shifting as if it desperately wants to be freed. "Yeah, the way people are around here is...different."

That's one way to put it.

And I don't think she means it as a bad thing.

I grin. "It can make a small town like this feel a little strange."

Her laugh fills the night air, settling over me like a warm blanket. "A *lot* strange."

"That's fair." I can't help but smile at her because seeing her like this—relaxed, almost carefree, *happy*—is so different from how I've seen her over the past week. "You feel like you're doing okay, though, staying at Elaine's and working at the diner?"

She considers my question for a minute, long enough that I know she actually *needs* the time to determine her answer. "I like it here. It seems like the type of place where you can catch your breath."

Why does she need to catch her breath?

That choice of words seems very deliberate. Something tells me Lucky isn't a woman who says anything without considering it very carefully first.

So, what's she running from?

Whatever it is...I don't like the fact that she ever felt like she couldn't breathe. That's a feeling I know all too well and wouldn't wish on my worst enemy.

Her saying McBride Mountain helps with that gives me hope. "Do you think you'll stay?"

Because though I want it for *her,* I also want it selfishly for *me.*

I'm drawn to her like a moth to a flame, and even though she's the type of woman who will probably burn me in the end, I just keep circling the light, hoping to feel the heat.

She shrugs. "I don't know. I don't stay anywhere very long, and I've already stayed far more than the few days I had planned."

The sadness in her voice when she says those words makes my chest tighten even more. If she's constantly moving, it doesn't sound like that's by her own choice, or if it is, it isn't necessarily because she *wants* to, but more like she feels like she *needs* to.

"I'm the opposite. I've spent my whole life here." I pull my hand out of my pocket and spread it out as we reach the end of Main Street. Pausing, I turn and look back at downtown McBride Mountain. "It's always been home, this town and the mountain itself, but sometimes, I can't help but wonder what's beyond it."

She glances back and looks at everything, the dark mountain towering up behind the quaint street lined with small shops. "I don't know why you'd want to leave when you have a place like this."

Because she doesn't know who I really am or what really happened here.

To anyone else, this place probably feels ethereal. It exists in a bubble of sorts, where the outside world rarely enters and everything is predictable and understood. That bubble burst for me, though, and I don't know how to get it back.

I shrug as we return to walking toward Elaine's. "I don't know that I *want* to leave. I'm just curious, I guess."

If going somewhere else would end these nightmares and visions...

If leaving McBride Mountain might quash the agony I've lived with wondering what I'll become because of this poisoned blood flowing through my veins...

Lucky peeks at me again. "So, why don't you go somewhere?"

I chuckle. "Well, my brothers and I own a lumber company here. We have a lot of really big contracts, and we're the largest employer in the area."

"And they couldn't handle it without you?"

I think about that for a moment, but I don't really need to. The answer is yes, they could. When Killian took so much time off to try to figure out what happened to Willow, then to be with her and their son, Connor and I held everything down just fine.

"They might be able to, but I'd feel guilty about leaving them, abandoning the business and everything my mom built for us."

"Your mom?"

"Yeah." I smile thinking about the woman who did so much for so many people, especially me. "Killian's father died when he was really young, and Connie raised him by herself as well as took over his family's business. Then she took in Connor when he was two. And I was left on her doorstep as a baby."

"Left on the doorstep?"

There I go again, dropping information I never had any intention of giving her because around Lucky I'm just more open, more relaxed. I feel more like the person I was before I knew about Earl Byers.

"It's a long story..."

One I definitely don't plan on telling her, but thankfully, she seems to sense that I don't want to talk about it and doesn't push.

Elaine's house comes into view, and we slowly make our way toward it in a comfortable silence, nothing but the chirping crickets and the occasional call of a night bird filling the air.

It is peaceful.

It's home.

I never really *could* leave McBride Mountain.

I love this too much.

Even if it does hold the darker realities that haunt me at night.

LUCKY

Walking up the stairs to the small apartment above Elaine's garage, I can't help but feel every step Liam takes behind me as strongly as I hear them. Heavy boots thud on each tread, matching the rhythm of my heart beating in my chest.

Somehow, completely in tune with him.

Because I understand him so much better now after a five-minute walk than I think I have most people I knew for years.

The way he talks about his family, about how much love there is between people who aren't even related, makes so much sense to me because that's how I always felt about my foster brothers and sisters in the various homes I spent time in.

We had to stick together.

We had to protect each other from all those things children shouldn't have to worry about, but we did.

We had each other's backs, but then, I'd get moved again without warning and I'd lose all of them.

I would lose that sense of safety and family and start all over in a new place with new people who didn't always have my back or my best interests at heart—if they even had one. The good homes, the ones with truly caring and loving families who wanted to help us, were few and far between back then, and when I did find one, it was always fleeting. Almost like a dream dangled in front of me and snatched away quickly.

And that's the way it went for years and years, until I was finally forced to break the cycle. Until I finally made that decision that I was better off on my own than being caught up in a system that didn't seem to care about what happened to me as much as I did.

No child should ever feel that, should ever wonder if their actions will bring violence, or starvation, or physical or mental abuse, yet that was my life for so long. Never truly having a home or place to rest my head where I could close my eyes and not worry that the nightmares would come true when I did.

But Liam didn't have to suffer that.

Liam had *this*.

This place. These people.

He was so fucking lucky that whoever put him on the McBride doorstep chose them. That someone loved him enough to ensure he was going somewhere warm, and safe, with people who would care for him as if he was their own.

It explains why he is the way he is.

Why he's so warm.

So kind.

So giving.

So willing to bend over backward for someone he doesn't even know.

It explains why I'm so drawn him—something so pure and unadulterated. Like this town is. Not tainted the way I am.

I pull my key out of my purse with a shaky hand and slip it into the lock. The moment I open the door, Gizmo shoots out, immediately bounding for Liam instead of me.

After all our years together, his loyalties sure changed quickly.

Liam squats on the small porch and pets Giz affectionately. "Hey, buddy."

"Well"—I release a little sigh that really isn't filled with any hostility, just more shock at how easily he took to Liam—"it is now one-hundred percent confirmed that he is a little traitor."

Though, who can blame him with this man?

It would be so easy to give into this attraction and the easy way my body and soul drift toward him.

Too easy.

Liam grins up at me, and my heart skips a beat, my blood heating at the way his eyes rake over me with so much appreciation. He holds my gaze for a moment, the silence between us drawing out as Gizmo excitedly accepts scratches on his belly.

I finally can't handle the tension anymore. It thickens the air so much that it almost hurts to breathe. "Um...thanks for walking me home."

"You're welcome—"

An engine revs on the street, and I whirl toward it, every muscle in my body priming as I reach into my purse. Liam simply glances that direction at the huge, lifted truck that rolls past slowly.

He waves at the driver, then returns his attention to me. "Manny Metzler. He's always been kind of a show-off. Just ignore him." He inclines his head behind us. "He lives down the street."

"Ahh."

I relax slightly, but Liam keeps watching me curiously, then pushes to his feet, tilting his head slightly. Gizmo finally comes over to me, and I squat to greet him, though I'm clearly old news compared to Liam.

"Lucky, are you sure you're all right?"

Liam's question draws my gaze back up to him, and I do my best to appear confused even if he clearly noticed my response to the neighbor's preening. "What do you mean?"

He leans against the railing, his gaze intense while he tries to appear nonchalant. "What I mean is...shit." Running his hands over his hair, he gives me a sheepish grin. Almost as if he's embarrassed to even be bringing it up, maybe because he can sense my unease. "I just wanted to make sure you know that if you need anything, you can come to me or one of my brothers."

Hell...

The incredibly sweet offer makes something unexpected ignite deep in my chest. My eyes burn, threatening to release something I refuse to let happen. I look down to Giz so Liam won't notice how easily something so simple as what he said can bring me to tears.

And for a split-second, the truth sits on the tip of my tongue.

The thought of coming clean and telling him everything crosses my mind long enough to consider what that would look like, how he would react to learning what happened, what I did...

But looking up into his green eyes so filled with compassion and worry, I absolutely cannot throw my baggage on anyone else's shoulders. Nor could I bear seeing the way his gaze would change. Knowing he would see me so differently would break me right now when I'm so close to that already.

I can't.

"I'm good. Really." I force a smile and push to my feet, keeping my focus on Giz instead of Liam, whose eyes remain locked on every movement I make. "Gizmo, go potty." He darts off down the steps and out into the yard, then comes shooting right back up after he's done doing his business. I can tell Liam is waiting for more. He's expecting me to address his concern head-on, and the simple brush off I have offered it's enough. "I have Gizmo here, and he's the best guard dog I've ever met."

He's also my only true friend.

The only one I can rely on.

Something I think Liam knows as he offers me a tight smile, like he sees right through my attempt to reject his offer with a cute, wrinkled face. "You know, everyone may be up in everyone else's business here"—he runs a hand through his coppery reddish hair—"but the flip side to that is that everyone has each other's backs. Nothing goes down in this town without everyone knowing about it, and if somebody needs something, every single person who lives here will step up to give it to them. That includes *you*."

"I don't live in McBride Mountain."

He gives me a grin that says far more than what he actually says. "You do now."

The hope in his voice shatters my ability to remain unaffected. I can't let Liam think *this* is anything or that I'll be around long enough for it to *become* anything.

"I'm not staying, Liam."

I try to say it with some sort of finality because I already feel like I've been here too long, like the net is closing in around me, strangling me and any chance I might have to put more distance between me and the mistakes of my past.

I'm looking over my shoulder more.

I'm jumpier.

And at some point, it's going to give.

It's going to break, or I am.

Sadness seeps into his evergreen gaze. "McBride Mountain's a good place to disappear, too, you know."

"You just told me everybody's in everybody else's business."

"True, but"—he motions toward the mountain towering behind us in the distance—"we live up there."

"You do?"

"My brother, Killian, lives in the old cabin on the property and Connor and I have each built one. We own the entire mountain."

I gape at him. "The whole thing?"

He nods. "I told you we've been here a long time."

They're apparently billionaires, too, which I guess I could have guessed based on the fact that the town is named after them. But Liam certainly doesn't come across as someone who was raised around that kind of wealth and privilege.

Unless this is all an act.

It wouldn't be the first time someone's played me like that. Pretended to be someone they were not. Got under my skin and used my trust and faith in them to burn me. But I promised that it would be the last.

Which means keeping Liam at arm's length even when, in this moment, all I want is to let him draw me into his.

Even though I know this isn't an act.

Even though I know he is genuine.

I can't risk it.

I can't risk him.

"I have to go in and shower and go to bed. I have an early shift at the diner again tomorrow."

He offers me a soft smile. "Make sure you're not working too hard. You should do something fun, too."

"Like what?"

"The falls are great. Have you been?"

I quickly avert my gaze.

He doesn't need to know that that's where I was camped out the night he found Gizmo on the road and that Giz probably ran off chasing a squirrel or something else while I slept on the dirt with my backpack as a pillow.

"No"—I shake my head, trying to keep my voice level—"I haven't been."

"I'll take you one day."

I should say no.

But right now, I just need to put some space between us so I can think and try to figure out what I'm going to do next.

"Okay. Well, good night." I pull open the door, and Gizmo darts in, anxious to eat after my long shift. I start to follow him in, then turn back to Liam. "Thank you for walking me home. I appreciate it."

"Any time."

Liam inclines his head toward me, then slowly makes his way down the steps and disappears into the calm summer night.

I stand at the door for a few moments, watching the street through the glass, looking for signs of anyone who might still be lingering in the heavy darkness the groups of trees every-where provide, but all is quiet.

That's the thing about McBride Mountain, it's almost *too* quiet.

Every little sound startles me because there isn't that constant buzz of energy and adrenaline like there is in the city. I can sleep through fire engines, airplanes taking off and landing overhead, screaming neighbors, crying babies, and barking dogs as if they don't exist, but chirping crickets and light breezes are enough to send me spiraling now.

I close the door, throw the deadbolt and secure the chain, then reach into my purse and pull out the .22 tucked there, setting it on the table next to the chair arranged so I can watch out the front window—the same place I've set up every night since I've been here.

Gizmo runs ahead and leaps up onto the bed that only he has slept on, and I follow him and rub his belly as he rolls onto his back.

"This would be a lot easier if you didn't like him."

His tongue lolls out to the side.

This dog isn't the least bit worried about Liam McBride, and that's more dangerous than if he saw him as a threat.

You can't stay.

I've told myself that so many times over the past week, whenever it starts to feel comfortable and safe.

Because I know it's just an illusion.

My gaze drifts to the window, and I move back to double check that the gun is loaded before I settle in for another long night.

6

LIAM

Terrified eyes stare up at me.

Tears stream down her temples.

Her voice cracks as she begs for me to stop, but I don't.

I can't.

My hands tighten around her throat as rage courses through me.

Heating my blood.

Tightening my skin.

Blurring my vision until I can barely see the woman beneath me.

Her fingernails claw at my hands and wrists, trying to get me to release my hold, but I'm lost to it now.

The darkness.

The need to end her, to pay her back for what she's done to me.

This bitch is as good as dead.

Only, I'm not looking down at her anymore.

I'm in her position.

Looking up.

At myself...

I bolt awake drenched in sweat, my chest heaving, my labored breaths the only sound in the dark loft of my cabin.

Holy.

Shit.

Fuck. Fuck. Fuck. Fuck. Fuck.

I scrub my hands over my face, trying to wipe away the last lingering vestiges of the nightmare, trying to clear my head of that horrific vision—my face on the man strangling the life from her.

But I know it will stay cemented there.

Just as it has for so many months.

Because it's the same every night.

My father morphs into me as he kills my mother.

Not the one who raised me; the one who sacrificed her life to give me one.

Roberta Byers...

Bobby...

I only recognize her in my dreams because after I learned the truth, I went to the library and searched for any information on her and found several old newspaper articles with her in them from before I was born.

Some where she's smiling next to my father.

Whatever happened between them, whatever went wrong, either she was very good at hiding it, or they hadn't reached that point yet because they look *happy.* And Earl looks *normal.*

Not like a deranged killer and kidnapper.

Not completely unhinged like he was up on that mountain when Killian finally confronted him.

But the problem is, he doesn't just look normal in those old photos, he looks like *me.*

How could no one have noticed it?

The Byers have been here for generations, and even though they lived around the far side of the mountain, well away from town, Earl spent enough time here that people knew him.

So how come no one saw how much I looked like him?

Maybe as I got older, someone put two and two together and figured out I was his missing son and never said anything. Maybe Connie always suspected and never said a word because she knew Bobby and that if she left me on that doorstep, there was a reason for it. Maybe everyone was "in" on keeping this giant secret about my identity from me my entire life...

Just more questions that never *will* have answers.

Just more agonizing unknowns that will plague me day and night.

I shake my head and throw back the covers, climbing from bed in nothing but my boxers and staggering down the stairs and over to the kitchen to get a glass of water. But as soon as I have the glass in my hand, I know it won't be enough and instead open the cabinet and pull down a bottle of bourbon, pour myself a shot, then double it.

My hand trembles as I bring the glass to my lips to gulp it down greedily. The burn in my stomach helps wake me up even more, but that feeling still lingers...

That *rage* that consumed me during the nightmare that wasn't mine—that was *his*—hovers like the mist that always covers the mountain.

How the fuck did I know how he felt?

Why do I keep seeing it?

I pour another shot and slam it back, hissing at the sting in my throat and that vision I want to burn from my memory.

It's just your imagination.

Deep down, I know that.

I *know* that it isn't real.

Everything I'm experiencing in these nightmares is really my own brain playing tricks on me, creating the scenario I've imagined so many times during waking hours. Turning them into these flashes that play endlessly like horror movies in my head.

But it's just my imagination.

It. Isn't. Real.

Because no one knows how he killed my mother, whether he strangled her or shot her or did something else unspeakable to her that snuffed the life from her before he tossed her in the river. And we will never know since her body was never discovered.

I'll never be able to give her a proper burial.

And I may never be able to get these images out of my head.

I pour myself another drink and down it.

My body vibrates.

My skin feels too tight.

The cabin feels too small.

I glance at the clock and see it's only three am.

There's no way I'll fall back asleep. I need to *do* something to work off all this coiling tension writhing inside me. There has to be some release before I explode.

For a moment, my gaze drifts back to the bottle of bourbon, but I shouldn't have any more.

Fuck.

I stalk back up the stairs, tug on a pair of jeans and a t-shirt, shove my feet into a pair of boots, and yank open the front door.

Crisp, clean mountain night air hits me, and I suck in a long breath, filling my lungs with it before I head out to the secondary barn that doubles as my workshop.

My footsteps crunch on gravel and grass, the noises familiar and soothing in a way I hadn't imagined they could be.

All these *real* things help ground me in the now, keep me from thinking about the past.

By the time I reach the barn and slide open the door, my heartrate has almost returned to normal, and the trembling in my hands seems to have somewhat abated.

With as much time as I spend out here, I should have

created thousands of pieces by now, but I'm too much of a perfectionist. I spend too much time picking out the perfect tree, cutting the perfect pieces from it, then carving them into whatever it tells me it wants to be.

Which means that each and every piece I make is unique, and each and every piece takes time. Like the one sitting in the middle of the workshop now.

This is the one that set everything with Willow in motion.

I'd been waiting to cut down that particular tree and build this rocking chair from it for over a year before the day Connor, Killian, and I went up there to chop it down and instead discovered Willow in the river. And now it sits only a quarter finished because working on it only reminds me of that day, and of the spiral it sent me down after.

Yet tonight, my hands itch to do something.

To mold something.

To build something instead of breaking it down the way *I'm* breaking down.

I snag my tools from the workbench and try to push the nightmare to the back of my head as I focus on the task at hand.

The scent of fresh wood fills the air, and the sound of my tools moving across it, slicing off pieces, sanding it down, becomes a soothing melody that finally starts to lull me away from that dark place I went.

By the time I hear footsteps approaching, sunlight is already starting to trickle in through the open barn door.

Killian steps in, then leans back against the wall, crossing his arms over his chest as he watches me work. "How long have you been out here?"

I shrug as casually as I can, knowing full well that if he knew how little sleep I'm really getting, he'd worry. "Not long."

He snorts and pushes himself off the wall, making his way toward me. "Given how much you've done on it since I came over here yesterday, that's a fucking lie."

Killian eyes me with an all-too-knowing look. I try to avoid meeting his gaze, but eventually, I do and he raises a brow.

"Have you been sleeping?"

Hell.

I must really look like shit for him to want to get into this so damn early in the morning. "We're not doing this, Kill."

After hours losing myself in this work, fighting against the nightmare, I'm not ready to confront it with him. I push up to my feet and stalk over to the workbench to grab a different pad of sandpaper, then return to my spot, trying to fine tune one edge.

Killian releases a long sigh. "I know you just want me to leave you alone, Liam, but I wouldn't be a very good brother if I did that, would I?"

"Right now? Yeah, you would."

He shoves a hand through his hair, clearly frustrated with my unwillingness to discuss anything with him. It's been an endless battle the past several months—him trying to push me to open up and me trying to push him away.

Please don't do it, Kill...

I squeeze my eyes closed, willing him to drop it.

A resigned sigh fills the barn, then he clears his throat. "So, what are you going to do with this when you're done?"

Relief courses through me, and I open my eyes and stare at the chair.

I hadn't really thought about it yet.

Selling it somehow doesn't seem right. Not with how it's tied to the mountain. To Willow and her rescue. To the family. There's too much history built into it. But it doesn't belong here either, on our land or in one of our homes. I don't know that I could live with that memory forever staring me in the face.

"I'll find somewhere for it."

"I'm sure you will. Willow is going to be working at the store today getting things ready. I'll bring down the shelves." He motions to the stack of black walnut shelves I built over the last several days for her shop. "Will you be able to swing by to hang them? I would do it, but I have that meeting with the city council today and she wants to keep moving forward on getting set up."

I nod. "Yeah, I can do it today. I might be tied up later this week up at the site."

Killian pauses for a second. "I can take care of that, if you're not up for it."

Hell...

Apparently I haven't done a very good job at hiding my unease about having to go beyond the gorge, but I won't open that can of worms. Nor am I going to concede defeat by refusing to face the remnants of the past.

"No. It's all right." I glance up at him and hope I'm offering a convincing smile. "Let me do my job. And I'm more than happy to help Willow."

It's the least I can do for her, and maybe, just maybe, it's a start to making amends for the sins of my father.

LUCKY

Careful.

Slow and steady.

I nudge open the door to the kitchen with the tray in my hands and make my way over to the table in the corner, trying my damnedest not to trip or spill as I have twice today.

At least nothing broke, but my shirt and pants are already stained with more food than I've managed to eat in the last twenty-four hours. My stomach rumbles, reminding me that I need to as soon as I take my break in a bit. Today has been busy as hell, and now that things have started to die down a bit, I can't wait to get off my feet for a few minutes.

I somehow manage to get their plates on the table and their drinks in front of them without another catastrophe.

I'm just returning to the kitchen with the empty tray when the bells jingle above the door and a beautiful blonde enters, followed by a stunning dark-haired woman with a baby strapped into a carrier on her front and a stack of papers in her hand.

They wave to Elaine and beeline straight for the booth Liam normally occupies whenever he's here, chatting excitedly about something. They each slide into one side of the booth, and the dark-haired woman sets the papers down, spreading them across the table.

I make my way over to them. "Hi."

The one with the baby strapped to her looks up with wide gray eyes and smiles broadly at me. "Oh, you must be Lucky."

My back immediately stiffens. "Um, yeah...and you are?"

The blonde snorts. "Sorry, she's a little direct. I'm Raven, this is Willow."

Willow smiles and points down to the sleeping baby. "This is Niall. I'm Killian's wife."

"Oh. Liam's brother..."

She nods, resting on hand on the back of the baby's head and rubbing it gently as he sleeps in her hold. "I met your dog the other day. He is *so* cute. Is he here?"

"No." I shake my head. "Health code and all that. Can't really have the dog running around in here all day while I work." I release a heavy sigh. "I'm having enough trouble not tripping on my own feet without having him under them."

A little laugh bubbles from her lips. "I'm sure you're not that bad."

I blow my hair from my face with a huff. "Oh, I am."

Her dark brows rise with interest. "You don't like wait-ressing?"

Shit.

There I went and opened my damn mouth again inadver-tently. I don't want Elaine thinking I'm not happy here or thankful for the opportunity she gave me with this job.

I shrug. "It's not bad; it's that I suck at it."

Willow exchanges a look with Raven, then surveys the diner. "Can you sit with us for a bit?"

"Umm..."

Raven scans the diner, checking out the three currently occupied tables, which are deep into their meals and don't look like they need anything right now. "Come on. Just for a minute."

"I don't think I should..."

Willow twists in her seat until she faces the kitchen. "Hey, Elaine!"

Elaine pops her head out the door. "What do you need, hon?"

"For Lucky to sit with us for a little while. Can she take a break?"

My boss waves her off. "Of course. Take all the time you need."

Willow grins at me. "There. It's settled. Now...sit."

Do I have a choice?

That all happened so fast that I barely followed it, but somehow, these two women wandered in and finagled getting me an unlimited break from my boss.

Raven slides over and pats the bench for me to sit next to her, and Willow points to the papers spread out between us on the table.

"So"—she waggles her eyebrows excitedly—"I'm opening a candle shop."

"Oh, that sounds cool."

I don't know the first thing about candles other than they provide light and sometimes smell pretty good.

Willow continues, shifting one of the pages over for me to see a sketch of a shop someone drew a design for. "I raise bees, and I make the candles from their wax and use only organic ingredients. I've been doing it for a long time. Killian finally got me a space, and I'm hoping to open in the next month or so."

"That's really awesome." She sounds so excited about the project, and her enthusiasm is contagious, drawing a grin from me, too. "Congratulations."

Raven clears her throat. "Why don't you get to the point, Willow? She doesn't have a lot of time."

Willow glowers at the woman. "Fine. As I was about to say..." She tosses Raven another dirty look before focusing on me and smiling again. "I haven't hired anyone to help me yet in the store. Because of this little one, I can't be there all the time. I'm setting up an area for him to sleep in the back office, but there are definitely days when I'm not going to be able to stay and he's going to want to be at home."

Where is she going with this?

I must be staring at her blankly because she sits and waits for me to respond.

"Oh. Did you mean *me*?"

She nods vigorously, her dark hair sliding over her shoulders. "It would be running the register, helping customers find anything, and I could even show you how to make the candles, too, if you want."

This woman is offering me a job?

The longer she and Raven examine me, the more I realize they aren't joking.

"You're serious."

Willow nods again and runs a hand across the baby's hair that looks incredibly soft. "I know it might be kind of stupid to be starting up a business when I just got married and I have a baby, but I didn't want to wait any longer. I also know I can't do it on my own. And I don't know anyone else looking for a job right now."

"I have a job."

I'm literally *at* my job now.

What is even happening?

Raven snorts. "A job that you just told us you suck at."

Willow gapes at her. "Did you really say that to her?"

The woman sitting at the counter. "What? She's the one who said it first."

"That doesn't mean you have to agree with her!"

"No, no." I hold up my hand and then tug at my shirt, showing them the stains. "I do suck. This is all from today. But I don't know that I'd be any better helping you."

Willow dismissively waves her hand at me. "Oh, it won't be hard. And you can start right away. I'm working on getting the place set up right now. You know, hanging shelves, getting the product that I already have displayed, figuring out where I want things. All that jazz. I could *really* use your help. Raven doesn't offer much of it."

"Hey!" Raven feigns offense —at least, I *think* it's fake. "I have a job!"

Willow glowers at her again. "You have a job you can do anywhere at any time. You could help me a little too instead of just sitting in the corner typing away every day."

I can't help but grin at the way these two bicker.

They're obviously best friends who are incredibly comfortable with each other to talk like this. "Have you two known each other long?"

They both look at me, then burst out laughing.

Raven casts a glance at Willow. "Sorry. I forgot you aren't up on all the McBride Mountain history yet. We've been best friends since elementary school."

"Ahh. Well that certainly explains it."

Willow's brow furrows slightly. "Explains what?"

"The way you two talk. It's just…" I laugh, my chest warming with an old memory of being in one of the foster homes where I stayed long enough to form those kinds of bonds with some of the other girls. "I miss hearing people talk like that."

"Like what?"

"Like family."

Raven gives me a sympathetic smile. "Oh, we definitely are. Everyone in McBride Mountain kind of is."

That's exactly what Liam told me last night when he walked me home, and, over the last several days, I've been learning that this town really is like one big family.

Whenever anyone comes into the diner, they always say hi to everyone else at the tables as if they've known each other their entire lives.

I've never heard a single argument—at least, not a real one. I've only heard familiar bickering between husbands and wives and friends like Raven and Willow. The type of arguments that show they know each other very well and actually love each other, not that they're mad.

This is the kind of place where strangers become friends, friends become family, and family becomes your life.

Willow raises her brows, watching me expectantly. "So, what do you think?"

I scan the restaurant where I've spent most of my time since I arrived in McBride Mountain. "I can't just abandon Elaine."

She gave me a job, a place to stay, and unwavering support when I've likely done more harm to her business than actually helped it. But she *is* busy enough that having an extra set of hands—clumsy or not—seems to free her up to work behind the counter, handle the register, and help Matt in the kitchen. Leaving her doesn't feel right.

Nor does taking *another* job when I still plan on leaving very soon.

I've made decent money here at the diner, and a few hundred dollars more will give me enough of a cushion to hopefully get me far enough away that my past won't ever find me.

Willow bites her bottom lip and nods. "True. Let me take care of that."

"What do you mean?"

"Just give me five minutes."

She pushes up from her seat, adjusting her hold on the baby in the carrier, then walks straight back into the kitchen as if she owns the place.

"Umm..." I glance at Raven, who looks unconcerned. "Should she be going back there?"

Raven laughs, shaking her head. "Willow kind of does whatever she wants. But to be fair, so do I. You should really take her up on her offer. I know Elaine, and she will definitely be able to find someone else to help her if she needs it. She'll want you to help Willow and do something that you might enjoy better."

The offer is enticing.

But the thought of working with Liam's sister-in-law also tightens my gut.

It means I might run into him more, and that's the last thing I need when I'm trying to get out of this town, not get sucked deeper into it.

7

LIAM

The new sign above the old McBride Mountain Newspaper office hangs proudly in the afternoon summer sun.

Mind Your Own Beeswax

A grin pulls at my lips, just as it does every time I've seen it since Killian had it hung a few days ago.

Only Willow would choose a name like *that* for her new business, but it couldn't be more perfect. Because I think she's as sick as I am of everyone giving her the pitying looks and asking about her ordeal. It's incessant—everyone in town buzzing around like...bees. Waiting for a chance to sneak in and sting with a question they seem to have no idea is only going to aggravate wounds she wants to let heal.

God knows she has them.

The trauma I suffered is all mental—a massive mindfuck that crumpled the world I was so comfortable living in—but hers was so much worse. On top of the horrific psychological torture she endured, she suffered physically, too, leaving very visible scars that rival the invisible ones.

It's taken a lot for her to claw her way back to some semblance of a normal life. Finally settling down with Killian and Niall helped—being a wife and mother—but once this place is open and operating, she'll finally have something that's *hers*.

All that joy she's always found out in her tiny workshop on the homestead making her candles can be spread to everyone in McBride Mountain on a level I don't think any of us would have anticipated before she disappeared almost two years ago.

And I'll do whatever I can to help make her dream come true.

So will Killian.

The majestic carving he did of a bee that now stands right outside the front door of the shop leaves no question about how much he worships the woman inside and how desperately he will work to ensure she gets whatever she wants or needs for the rest of their lives.

Even though I've seen it hundreds of times, my eyes still roam over it in appreciation as I tug open shop door. I glance up, expecting bells to jingle above it that would alert my arrival like they do in almost every shop along Main Street, but apparently, the newspaper office never had one.

Which I guess makes sense since either Old Man Murray or Raven were almost always here, seated at the desks that once occupied the space, typing away at whatever articles they were working on.

And right now, Willow doesn't need one since the windows are still covered with paper, making it clear the store isn't open yet.

From the looks of it right now, it's far from ready, too.

The place is kind of a disaster.

Shelves I built for Willow lean up against the walls in various places and half-unpacked boxes are strewn across the floor along with random packaging materials that appear to have been chaotically tossed to the side.

An old cash register sits on the vintage display case Killian found for her when they went on their trip down to Asheville searching for cool things for the store, and various other items lie haphazardly around the room, waiting for someone to organize them.

It definitely looks like she could use some help.

I let the door close behind me, and I move in deeper, starting to imagine what it will look like when it's finally completed.

I'd be the first to admit I didn't know how she could transform the newspaper office into a retail space, given I had only ever seen it used for *one* thing and set up in *one* way, but even in this state, I'm starting to see her vision.

The inherent charm of the historic building that's stood here proudly on Main Street for over a hundred years brings a warmth to the room that's been improved by a fresh coat of paint in a barely-there honey tone that was absolutely intentional on Willow's part.

But where is the woman behind it?

Willow should be here, waiting for me to come hang the shelves as we arranged earlier. I start to call out for her, but if Niall is here and sleeping in the back and I wake him up, neither he nor his mother will be very happy.

Best to find her quietly.

I move through the space toward the back room that I know she was setting up as an office, my boots thudding on the worn wooden floors, but just as I reach the door, Lucky steps out, clutching several glass candle jars in her hands, and almost slams into me.

"Oh, shit!" She jerks back, her eyes widening. "Christ, you scared me!"

"I seem to be doing a lot of that lately." I offer her an apologetic smile, retreating a step once I'm confident she isn't going to drop any of the candles. "Sorry about that. What are you doing here?"

She chews on her bottom lip, scanning the space with an unreadable expression that almost looks like *confusion*. "Um...I guess I work here now."

Works here now?

Clearly, something happened between me dropping her at her place last night and today that I have been left completely out of the loop on. Not that I expected Lucky to call and let me know wasn't waiting tables at the diner anymore, but *Willow* certainly could have offered me a heads-up before I walked in here.

I raise a brow. "You do?"

She nods, clearing her throat, almost as if she's not completely sure it's true or isn't on board with the job change. "Your sister-in-law and Raven came into the diner earlier."

That explains it.

I can already see where this is going before she even completes her story. When Willow and Raven are together and they set their minds on something, they're like bulldozers and it's almost impossible to get out of their way.

If they saw Lucky struggling at the diner the way she has been, both of them would have felt inclined to find a way to help her...by finding her another way to make some money.

"And let me guess, they somehow convinced you to quit the diner and come here?"

Lucky releases a little laugh. "It honestly wasn't all that hard. I'm a shitty waitress."

Her self-deprecation makes me wince, and I feel the need to defend her, even if she won't defend herself.

"No, you aren't."

She gives me an incredulous look, that perfect mouth of hers twisting. "I appreciate the morale boost, but we all know I *sucked* at that job."

"I wouldn't say *sucked*."

But I can't fight the grin that pulls at my lips as I say the word, nor can she mask her own.

"It's fine, Liam." She blows a lock of blue hair off her face with a huff. "I know where my strengths lie, and it isn't there."

Maybe it's here...

That makes me realize I'm still blocking her path into the store where she needs to set down the candles in her hands. I retreat a few steps, allowing her to move past me into the main sales floor and unload the jars on the top of the display counter.

"What did Elaine say?"

Another little laugh filled with disbelief slips from her lips as she arranges the various candles. "Well, I'm not entirely sure what Willow said to her, but Elaine came out from the kitchen and gave me a hug, told me that she wished me well, and that she didn't need me to finish my shift. She insisted I help Willow instead."

I lean against the edge of the counter as she slips behind it and starts peeling price tags off a piece of paper and slapping them on the bottoms of the jars. "And here you are."

She bobs her head, her loose hair falling to partially cover her face. "And here I am."

Alone, apparently.

"Where's Willow?"

"Oh"—she glances up—"she left about twenty minutes ago. Niall was really fussy and didn't want to take a nap in the Pack-n-Play she has set up in the back, so I told her to just go home and I would do what I could without her here."

"That was very kind of you."

Her cheeks pinken beneath the smattering of freckles, and

she tips her head down, continuing to work and hiding her face behind the long flow of blue that looks like the falls on a summer afternoon.

I force myself to look away from her and to examine everything in the space. "Well, I was supposed to help her get the shelves up today..."

"Oh." Lucky peeks up from behind the veil of azure. "She told me she laid them out where she wants them. So, I kind of have some idea, if you want to do them. I don't know how much help I'll be, but—"

"All I really need is a second set of eyes to check the placement because I'm definitely not an interior designer and have absolutely no idea what that woman wants."

Lucky laughs, shaking her head. "Well, I'm not either, but I'll do my best." She gets quiet suddenly, stilling and staring down blankly as if she's trying to gather her words. "I really appreciate everything everyone has done for me since I got here."

The ache in her words places one squarely in my chest. There's a lingering disbelief there that tells me everything about the type of people she's encountered in her life before coming here.

"I told you, that's just McBride Mountain."

"But people aren't like that." Her gaze shifts up to meet mine, and the pain in her eyes matches one I've felt since the day I looked into Earl's eyes and saw my own. "You know...out there." She waves her hand vaguely toward the street. "People don't do things just because it's the nice thing to do. They usually want something in return."

I shake my head. "Not here."

The only way a town like McBride Mountain survives is by people helping people. By being generous. By being selfless. By looking out for each other and knowing it will come back to you when you need it.

Her lips press into another tight smile, then she shifts away from the counter and moves over to the shelves leaned against the wall, effectively ending any additional conversation on that topic. "Willow told me she wants one here and one here." She motions vaguely toward the wall—one hand higher and one lower. "The higher one more for display and storage of stock. And then over here"—she moves down a few steps—"she wants them staggered, not at exactly the same height as the other two. That's the layout she wants repeated the whole way down. She thinks they'll look better that way."

I stand back and examine the wall, trying to picture what Willow was seeing when she described it to Lucky, then nod. "I see what she's going for. That's doable. Killian said he was also leaving my toolbox for me when he dropped off the shelves."

She nods, motioning toward the room she came out of when I arrived. "Yeah, it's in the back."

"Great. I'll go grab it."

And give myself a minute to snap my focus back to the task at hand instead of on that woman.

I make my way into the small office, where Willow has a desk, a Pack-n-Play, and more boxes stacked, and snag my toolbox and the ladder that's leaning against the wall, then step back out into the main room.

Lucky's on her knees, digging through one of the boxes, humming idly to herself. I don't recognize the tune, but I'm immediately immobilized by it. The soft, light melody floats through the air, and I watch her for a moment.

It's the calmest, most content, dare I say the happiest I've seen her since she got to the mountain.

The diner was too stressful for her. Too busy. Too many ways she could mess up. And she's right—she did suck at it. I never would have used those words, but Lucky certainly wasn't meant to be waiting tables. Already, she seems more at home here, and she couldn't have left the diner more than a few hours ago.

She glances up as if she can feel my eyes on her. "Is something wrong?"

Shit.

I shake my head. "No, not at all. Just...checking the place out."

Checking *her* out.

Because my eyes can't seem to stay off her.

Whenever we're in the same room, they magically move in that direction, and it isn't just the vibrancy of her hair that makes my gaze lock on the mysterious woman. It's the energy she puts out, like a scalding hot supernova in the vast, cold darkness my life has been lately.

But if I keep staring at her, I'm going to make her more uncomfortable than she already is here under the scrutiny anyone new gets in McBride Mountain.

I bring the ladder over to the wall, set it up, and then pull out what I need to place the anchors for the shelves.

Lucky pushes up from the floor and slowly walks over, then runs her hands across one of the shelves, a small smile pulling at her lips. "These are really beautiful."

"Thank you."

Her brows fly up. "Did you make these?"

I nod. "Yeah."

"Wow." She examines them more closely. "That's impressive."

Now *my* cheeks heat.

"Thanks, but not really. They're pretty easy to do; just slabs of wood."

"No." She runs her fingers over them lovingly, dipping them into each and every hole and divot natural to the black walnut I used. "Picking the right wood, cutting it perfectly so that it displays all of its natural beauty, making it shine like this; that takes talent."

I don't know why her compliment affects me so much, but my eyes start to burn and I have to look away.

The last thing I need is this woman thinking I'm so emotionally unstable that simple words like that will set me off. But I am apparently...when it comes to her.

LUCKY

I step back and survey the final shelf Liam just secured to the wall, trying to visualize how it will look when they're covered with products, filled with Willow's hard work, but instead of focusing on my new job, on the reason I'm here, my eyes keep drifting to him.

The way his muscled arms bunch and flex as he moves.

How good his ass looks in those jeans...

Hell...

Liam turns on the ladder and glances at me. "The level says it's perfect, but it looks good to the eye from back there too?"

I'm not sure I'm the best person to be assisting with this, since I have absolutely no expertise whatsoever when it comes to hanging shelves. Plus, I've probably spent more time watching him out of the corner of my eye than I have assisting with anything, but I still search for anything amiss.

The only thing uneven is my heartbeat as I watch him work.

"I think it's perfect."

The *shelf.*

I definitely can't be thinking about how perfect the man hanging it seems to be—ruggedly handsome, strong, loyal, intelligent, intuitive, and downright *hot.*

Those are dangerous thoughts. The kind that have gotten

me into trouble before. The kind that brought me here in the first place.

He pulls back slightly, trying to see more of the wall. "I'm not sure about the placement, though. Should we move it higher or lower?"

I chew on my bottom lip and tilt my head, forcing myself to remain focused on the shelf—not the man hanging it. "I don't know. It's kind of hard to envision it without anything *on* them."

This would be so much easier if Willow were here.

It's her store.

Her vision.

I shouldn't be the one making these decisions. Frankly, I shouldn't be making *any* decisions since mine always seem to lead down roads no one wants to be on. But Willow was so worried about leaving because she wanted these up and entrusted me with whatever needed to happen today.

A warning Liam was the one coming to do it would have been nice, though...

My heart hasn't stopped thudding against my ribs since the moment I walked out of the office and almost ran directly into him—and it isn't due to the fact that I've been jumpy as hell the entire time I've been in this tiny town, nor is it the surprise of finding him here.

This seems to be my natural state when Liam McBride is around.

Off-kilter. Hyper aware. Desperately, hopeless drawn to him even when I know I shouldn't be.

He steps down off the ladder and moves back to stand at my side, tilting his head, too, to examine the wall of shelves. "Agreed."

"Why don't we put some of the candles up and see how they look?"

It will give us a much better idea of the proper spacing for these shelves if we can see how they'll actually appear when filled like they will be once the shop opens.

Some are meant as for purely display—higher up to hold extra stock and decorative pieces with them. Others will be used for actual sales, right at the proper height for customers to snag items from them.

But it's so hard to visualize.

Liam nods. "Good idea."

I walk over, snag two candles from one of the boxes, then move over to the ladder, climb up the couple rungs, and set them on the polished dark wood. "How do those look?"

From up here, at least, they look amazing. Liam somehow selected the perfect wood for this so Willow's candles are showcased on something as beautiful and natural as what she produces.

In the vintage recycled jars with handmade labels, they look like they were created with care. These are the types of products that would make a fortune in some of the bigger cities I've lived, but they look right at *home* here.

I glance back at him, and a slow grin spreads across his face.

"Great, actually. Those are the largest size?"

"I think so."

"Then we should be good." His gaze sweeps across the wall. "If we moved the shelf any higher, I think they'd look too cramped in under the ceiling, and any lower would be too much space above them."

I grin at him. "Agreed."

Maybe we can do this without Willow.

Of course, she can just move things when she comes in tomorrow if she doesn't like what we've done, but I would love to get these all up for her so when she opens that door in the morning, these candles are already displayed and she can really *see* things starting to come together.

Even though I only met her a few hours ago, her sweet,

caring nature has lured me in and her genuine excitement about this new business venture is contagious.

I slide my foot down to the next rung on the ladder to get down, but it slips right off the metal and I start to tumble backward. Strong arms wrap around me, catching me before I can fall to the hard wooden floor.

Liam's grip tightens around me, and he turns me in his arms, scanning my face. "Are you all right?"

My heart thunders against my chest even harder than it already was, but it isn't because I almost broke my neck. It's the feel of Liam's arms around me. It's how close his lips are to mine. It's how damn good he smells—like fresh pine and spicy bourbon, like something forbidden that I have no right to want but do all the same.

I try to find the words, but they get stuck somewhere in my throat along with my objection to him continuing to hold onto me like this.

His green eyes stay locked on mine, searching them for something, and the heat blazing there ignites a fire deep in my core that spreads out through my body and sears right between my legs.

Pure, unadulterated want shines in his gaze.

I recognize it because I feel it, too.

He tips his head closer. Slowly. As if he isn't sure what he's doing or if he should be doing it, and I can't muster up any words to stop him when I want to feel his lips on mine. I want to know what he tastes like. I want to know if he kisses with the same intensity that he looks at me.

When his lips meet mine, my eyes drift closed and the world around us evaporates in an instant.

Liam's hold tightens, and he drags me more fully against him, his hard body and strong arms supporting me completely with my toes barely even touching the floor. His mouth moves over mine hungrily, like he's been starving, dying to do this forever and now that he finally has the chance, if he stops, it might actually kill him.

And God, can he kiss.

It's all-consuming. A complete consumption of my mouth, my breath, my will.

I collapse into him, allowing him to hold me up.

To sustain me.

With this strength.

His passion.

Every flick of his tongue across my lips and along my own coils me tighter and makes that blazing heat sear through me hotter. The longer we kiss, the harder it becomes to even process what's happening.

I'm *lost* in Liam McBride, and I don't want to be found.

The sound of the front door opening and heavy boots on the wooden floor finally breaks us apart and shatters the spell, and I glance behind me to see Sheriff Briggs walking in, scanning the place.

Shit.

I quickly turn my head, hiding behind my hair, and kneel down to busy myself in one of the nearby boxes.

Shit. Shit. Shit. Shit.

Somehow, I've managed to avoid a direct conversation with the man since I arrived here on the mountain, keeping to the back room or kitchen and busying myself at tables when he's stopped into the diner over the past week.

What the hell is he doing here now?

Every muscle in my body primes to *move* in case I have to quickly.

"Liam, I thought I saw you come in here..." Footsteps thump in our direction, but I keep trying to look busy rather than peeking to see how close the sheriff has come to where I kneel and Liam stands beside me. "The place is looking good."

Liam clears his throat. "Hey, Tony. Yeah, things are really starting to come together."

"Is Willow around?"

"No, she took Niall home. It's just me and Lucky."

Fuck...

"Oh, hello, there."

I peek over my shoulder, trying to keep most of my face concealed behind my hair, and offer him a smile that I hope looks genuine to a man whose literal career it is to find criminals and see through people's shit. "Hi."

"Well, I was popping in to say hello to Willow, and I wanted to talk to you about something, Liam, if you have a minute."

Liam hesitates for a moment before responding. "Uh, sure."

And I can feel his eyes on me.

He wants to discuss what just happened, but I've been gifted the perfect opportunity to get out of here while the sheriff is occupied with the man whose kiss has left my head spinning.

I push up and move toward the register where I left my purse, keeping my head tipped down so my hair falls to cover most of my face. "I actually have to get going. I will leave the key, if you don't mind giving it back to Willow?"

Liam shifts in my peripheral vision, clearly distressed with being interrupted and by my abrupt attempt to leave. "Okay..."

Glancing up, I see the confusion marring his handsome face. The way his hooded eyes watch me, the lips I just kissed turned down slightly, he's searching for a reason.

Please let me go...

I gather my things, throw my purse over my shoulder, and set the key on the counter, turning toward the door while the sheriff examines the shelves we hung. If he stays occupied, I might make it out of the shop without an issue.

And I almost make it to the door when Liam takes a step

toward me, hand out like he wants to try to physically stop me. "Lucky, please, don't run off. I'm—"

Shit.

My gaze darts to the sheriff, and Liam's follows.

His head snaps back to me, his brow furrowed and eyes narrowed on me now like he just saw the answer to the question he was about to ask.

As much as I hate the idea of him thinking I'm so desperate to get out of here because of our kiss, the thought that he figured out I don't want the sheriff to really see me is even worse.

Because Liam isn't stupid.

He's far, far too observant.

Plus, he isn't the type of man to just let things go.

I turn and slip out before he can say anything else, before he sees the fear in my eyes. The fear of what that kiss meant. The fear of the man in the uniform in there. The fear of what staying this long may bring down on him and everyone else here.

When the door closes behind me, I don't look back.

I can't.

Because even though there's paper blocking the windows, I can still feel Liam watching me. I can feel his pain and his confusion. And I know I'm not going to be able to resolve it for him. I'm not going to be able to make it better.

All I'm going to do is cause him more of it if I don't leave.

8

LIAM

She's going to run.

I don't know *how* I know that, but I do, deep in my gut. The moment she saw Sheriff Tony Briggs walk in, Lucky shut down and hid behind that wall of blue hair like it was a waterfall concealing her. But then I saw it in her eyes when she reached the door.

Lucky wasn't just leaving the shop.

She is going to flee from McBride Mountain—today.

Whatever brought her here, whatever she's running from, seeing the sheriff has set her in motion now.

She won't stay.

She's been threatening to leave since the moment she walked into the diner, and that gave her the reason to do it.

The thought of her disappearing, especially after that kiss, when every breath I take still smells like eucalyptus was enough to make me rush through my conversation with Tony as quickly as possible. To get out of the shop. To *stop* her before she bolts.

My hands tighten on the wheel as I barrel down Main Street, away from Willow's shop and toward Elaine's house.

The few short blocks feel like thousands of miles, though. Each second that ticks by might as well be hours as far as my anxiety is concerned. It's all time Lucky has to gather her things and find a ride out of town.

By the time Elaine's finally comes into view, I'm vibrating. Every muscle in my body is tensed, ready for the argument I can see coming—if I get there in time.

Please, God, let me catch her...

I pull into the driveway, throw the truck into park, turn off the ignition, and launch myself out of the cab, racing toward the steps that lead up to her apartment.

My boots thud heavily as I take them two at a time, and the door opens as I reach the top. Lucky steps out with Gizmo in her arms, a backpack on her shoulders, and her purse strapped across her.

Ready to leave.

"I knew it."

Her gaze meets mine, filled with so much fear it makes my heart clench.

I grip the banisters on either side of the stairs, channeling my frustration into the wood instead of directing it at her. "You're *running.*"

Lucky's mouth opens and closes a few times, as if she isn't sure what to say. She swallows thickly and locks the door behind her. "What are you doing here?"

"I came to stop you."

She turns to face me fully. "Stop me from what?"

I release my death grip and throw my hands out. "From *this*! From *leaving*!"

Fuck.

That came out all wrong.

I hadn't meant to yell, to sound so...unhinged like that did.

But she can't seriously be asking me that after what just happened in the candle shop—both the kiss and the very *obvious* way she avoided the sheriff.

Lucky gulps in air, as if she's gathering up the nerve to say whatever she's about to. "I told you the day we met that I wasn't going to stay, Liam."

She did.

I didn't like it then, and I certainly don't like it now.

"Yeah, that was then, and things are *different* now, Lucky."

"Are they?"

Her attempt at deflection stings, but it isn't going to work on me. I am not going to turn around, march down these steps, and walk away from her after everything that has happened.

I am not going to walk away from how this woman makes me feel simply because she's afraid of it.

"You *know* they are." I level my gaze on her and watch her shift in her worn Chucks as if she can physically feel it. "Open the door, Lucky."

"Why?"

"So we can go in there and talk."

She shakes her head. "There's nothing to talk about."

"Like hell there isn't."

I reach out and grab the key from where it's still clutched in her hand.

Her eyes flare wide. "Hey!"

There isn't any time to worry about her incredulity over my actions. I simply unlock the door and throw it open, then motion for her to head inside.

She glares at me, and I don't miss the way she has inched toward the steps in the time it took me to get the door open. Gizmo watches me, too, his ears perked up as if he can sense the tension permeating the air between us—which he probably can.

"Please, Lucky..."

I don't have it in me to fight with this woman.

It feels like I've been fighting with myself, the rest of the McBrides, and the entire town endlessly for months.

All I want is a conversation with her—to plead my case.

Lucky considers me for a minute, glancing down the street toward downtown, then back at me.

Without her even saying it, I inherently know what she's searching that pavement for. "The sheriff isn't looking for you."

She does a really shitty job of hiding her surprise, her lips falling open and eyes widening slightly. "What do you mean?"

Instead of answering and potentially getting into this while standing out here on the porch, I close the distance between us, slide my hand on her lower back beneath the backpack, and usher her into the small apartment.

She doesn't fight me, but her entire body vibrates with tension.

Anger?

Fear?

Both?

Lucky sets Gizmo on the floor, and he excitedly jumps at my legs until I pet him as I toe the door closed behind us.

When I turn to face her, she hasn't relaxed at all. "Take off your backpack and set it down."

"Why?"

"Because I want to have a conversation without being worried that you're going to run out that door with everything you own on your back."

She stiffens before she slowly lets it slide off her shoulders and onto the floor. But just because she gave me *that* doesn't mean Lucky intends to make this easy on me.

Her glacial gaze locks on me, and she crosses her arms over her chest, wrapping them tightly around herself as if she needs that protective layer for what's about to come.

Maybe she does.

A lot of things I've let go since meeting her aren't so easily brushed aside now that I've seen her fear when the sheriff appeared. This doesn't seem like a woman who just wanted to get away from a stale or boring existence. She isn't here because she wanted to try out small town life. She was actually *afraid*.

"I saw the way you reacted to Sheriff Briggs coming into the shop. You know..."—I rub at the back of my neck, trying to release some of the tension building there along with my frustration—"when you first showed up, I suspected you might be running, that something brought you here to McBride Mountain that wasn't just the Memorial Day Festival or your desire to experience the Blue Ridge Mountains in all their majesty. And you've said a few things that had me wondering if you were running from something in your past, if you had something you wanted to put behind you, which, shit, I, of all people, can understand, but what just happened with the sheriff is more than that. You're terrified."

She flinches at my choice of words, confirming precisely what I feared.

Lucky has been hurt. Badly. By someone. By something. Enough that she's living in actual terror every day.

"This isn't just you wanting to leave something in the past. This is you actively being afraid of it. What are you running from, Lucky?"

Please trust me.

I'm terrified to say those words, to ask that from a woman who clearly doesn't trust anyone and who doesn't know me at all. She has no reason to open up to me except that I'm asking her to. And that might not be enough.

She watches me with her big blue eyes, her whole body trembling the longer we hold each other's gazes.

I risk taking a few steps toward her, and when she doesn't retreat, I close the last of the distance and take her arms in my hands. "Please. What I said about wanting to help you, about everyone here being willing to help you, is true. But I can't help you if you don't tell me what's going on."

Her bottom lip quivers, and she bites it to try to stop it and prevent me from noticing, but I reach up and brush my thumb over it until she releases it.

"Don't do that. Talk to me."

"Why?" Her question comes out breathy and filled with her distress. "Why do you want to help me?"

"Why do you think?"

I don't want to have to say the words because, honestly, I never have before.

I don't know how to tell a woman that I'm basically obsessed with her. That since the moment she waltzed into the diner and accused me of stealing Gizmo, I haven't been able to stop thinking about her—day and night. That the only time she doesn't occupy my thoughts is when I actually fall asleep and the nightmares come. That she's been the only thing that's kept my mind from drifting there when I'm awake, too.

I don't know how to tell her that without making her want to run even more because it makes me sound fucking irrational.

We barely know each other.

We don't really at all.

And yet the thought of her leaving makes me want to get in my truck and follow her wherever she goes.

That plump bottom lip that still bears the indentation from her teeth quivers. "You don't know me, Liam."

"I want to, if you would let me."

She shakes her head, and her eyes start to fill with tears that she tries to blink away. "It's better if you don't. Safer for you."

"Safer?" Her choice of words stiffens my spine, and I tighten my grip on her arms. Not enough to hurt her, just enough that she understands how serious I am about this. "If you're in trouble, Lucky, tell me. I can protect you. *We* can protect you here. You don't have to keep running."

"You only say that because you don't know."

"Then *tell* me."

She shakes her head again. "I can't."

Frustrated, I release her and take a step back, running my hands through my hair and focusing on Gizmo where he waits at our feet, watching our conversation as if he understands it and somehow comprehends how important it is.

"Let me ask you something." I peer back up at her. "If you left, where would you go?"

She glances toward the door. "I had been making my way toward Charlotte."

"What's in Charlotte? Family?"

Why did I bother asking when I already know the answer?

She shakes her head no.

"Friends?"

Another small shake.

"Do you know *anyone* there?"

One more.

"And would you stay in Charlotte?"

She doesn't have to respond at all this time because she knows *I* know.

Lucky has nowhere to go. No one to take her in. Nowhere she can settle and have any sort of support system at all.

"How long have you been moving like this?"

"Since I was fifteen."

"What?"

A tiny sob slips from her throat, but she tries to swallow it back. "I mean, basically my whole life. Moving constantly in foster care, and then I left when I was fifteen. I've been on my own ever since. Almost seven years."

Despite feeling like my heart is being ripped out of my chest at the possible reasons why, I have to ask. I *have* to know. "Why did you leave?"

Her only response is a flinch.

And I can't stay away anymore.

I eat up the space between us again with a few determined steps and capture her face between my palms. "You know what? You don't have to tell me that if you don't want to. I just...I need you to understand that there's nothing you could say to me, nothing you could admit or tell me, that would change what I'm asking you right now, which is for you to stay."

LUCKY

I have *never* wanted to say "yes" so badly in my life as I do at this moment. As I stare into his green eyes filled with so much hope and longing, so much compassion, so much determination, I know that if I did, he would do everything in his power to try to save me.

Liam would try to make everything right, no matter the cost.

And that's why I can't tell him.

I have to protect this incredible man from what I've done. Keeping him in the dark means keeping him safe.

It means keeping *everyone* safe.

I shake my head, the feeling of his calloused palms rubbing against my cheeks almost too much to bear. "I-I can't."

My voice cracks, giving away just how fucking hard this is when I never expected it to be. This was only supposed to be a few days, a few hundred dollars in my pocket, and then I would have been on my way, leaving this small town behind me the same way I have dozens of others.

It should have been *easy* to leave. It was *supposed* to be.

"Why not, Lucky?" Liam prevents me from dipping my head and looking away like I so badly want to. He holds me firm, forcing me to stare into those mossy green eyes that so closely match the color of the trees on McBride Mountain that it almost feels like I can see the leaves and boughs blowing in the wind when I stare into them. "*Tell* me."

Those eyes *plead*. For me to talk. For me to open up. For me to *trust* him.

Good God...I want to...

Every fiber of my being says that I *can* trust him. That he might be the only person on this planet who potentially could help me.

It might have been enough if I didn't already care about what happens to him. If I didn't already feel that horrific sense of dread tightening my gut when I think about what could happen if my past catches up with me *here*.

"It's just...safer if I go, Liam."

"There's that word again." His voice deepens, his eyes hardening with his determination and frustration. "*Safer*. And the more you mention it, the more I understand that whatever it is you're running from isn't something you should be facing alone, so here's the deal." His coppery brows rise. "You listening?"

I nod.

I'm listening because he's making me.

He's holding me in place with his strong grip and the intensity of his gaze and words.

Even though I know I should pull away and run right out that door to save this man from my mistakes, I can't bring myself to do it. Not when he focuses on me so intently, holds me so tightly, and seems so determined to make me listen, as if what he's about to say could change everything.

"You're going to *stay* in McBride Mountain." His hands tremble against my face. "And when you're ready, you're going to tell me exactly what's going on. But I'm not going to force you to do it right now because I've been in your shoes—hell, I still am—and I know what it's like to not want to talk about something that's traumatic. So, I'm not going to pressure you." He shakes his head. "I'm just going to pray that eventually you'll understand that this place is safe. That *I'm* safe. That you can *trust* me. That we can protect you here, and whatever the problem is, we can face it together."

My heart lodges in my throat, and I struggle to swallow through it while his piney, spicy scent invades my breath. "Why would you want to do that for me?"

It's the second time I've asked that question, but it's the one that won't stop running through my head endlessly.

No one in my life has ever done anything even remotely so kind for me.

No one has ever seemed so intent on helping me when it doesn't benefit them in any way.

No one has ever cared.

Just like before, the look he gives me answers it before he opens his mouth.

"Because *I* need you to stay. Selfishly." He grins. "Because I'm in love with your fuckin' dog."

Gizmo barks as if he heard what was said about him and not only completely understood it but agrees with the sentiment. Given the way he smothers the man, I'm sure he appreciates the declaration as much as I do.

Giz tries to climb up Liam's leg, but his hands stay locked on my face.

I fight the quiver in my lip that matches the unsteady beat of my heart right now. "My dog, huh?"

Liam nods, trailing his fingertips across my cheek reverently. "Yep." His gaze dips to my mouth before coming back up again. "And I really like you, too."

Hell...

If I hadn't already started falling for Liam McBride, I would have taken that dive just now. At this exact moment. Because staring into his eyes after he said those words feels like I'm cartwheeling down the mountain all the way from its highest peak. Spinning out of control but in an exhilarating way, not a scary one.

But I should be scared.

I should be terrified.

Everything in me, all those learned behaviors and self-protective instincts, scream at me to move, to grab my bag and keep running, to do what I've always done and keep going, to find a new place and people I won't care about. Somewhere I can disappear and live quietly with Gi without handsome mountain men complicating things.

It would be the easier decision. It would be the one I would have made had I met Liam under any other circumstances. I would have chosen to run.

But I can't force myself to move away from him.

I can't make my legs go.

And I can't back away as he leans in and presses his lips to mine again.

This kiss is softer, sweeter, more reserved than the one we shared at the shop. More like a promise that everything he just told me is absolutely true. Not that I didn't believe it then, but the way he kisses me ensures it. It seals his resolve and my inability to walk away.

I'm safe with Liam McBride.

I'm safe wrapped in his arms and in his town.

As long as the past doesn't catch up with me.

Right now, that's all I can hope for—that these nightmares I have when I manage to doze off sitting in that chair at night don't come true. That my mistakes don't come back to hurt this man or anyone else in this town I've come to care about.

He deepens the kiss, his mouth moving over mine with an insistence and urgency I feel all the way to my core.

I groan and press my body to his, needing to feel his hard strength, needing to know that he's right here and he's not going anywhere; exactly what he just promised me. When he pulls away and presses his forehead to mine, both of our breaths labored, a little rumble of appreciation floats from his chest to mine.

"It'll be okay, Lucky. Whatever it is, I promise you, we'll figure it out."

God, I wish it were as simple as he's making it sound.

I wish my mistakes were minor ones that could be washed away as easily as what I spill on the floor at the diner, but my life has never been easy.

Absolutely nothing about it has been.

And what brought me to McBride Mountain, what sent me walking down that highway that night, will eventually find me.

It's only a matter of time.

Some things can't be outrun. Some mistakes follow you forever. Some decisions haunt you for the rest of your life.

This is one of them.

But I'm so tired.

Of running. Of hiding. Of constantly looking over my shoulder. Of being alone...

He brushes his thumb across my cheek, wiping away the single tear I've let escape. "You're going to stay."

I nod.

"As long as I can" goes unspoken because if I said those words to him right now, it would break the spell.

He would say it's not enough.

He would make me promise to never leave.

And that's something I *can't* promise because if it comes down to it, if it comes to him, or Willow, or Raven, or Elaine, or anyone else being put into danger because of me, I will hightail it out of McBride Mountain so fast they will wonder if I was ever here.

But for a moment, in this tiny, quiet North Carolina mountain town, I'm going to take a moment to just breathe. To breathe in his pine and spice scent, the fresh air, and the ease with which people have accepted me here.

Because after so many years walking, so much time searching for something, anything, to ground me, somehow the man in front of me managed to do it in the span of a week with his easy smiles, his gentle nature, his kind words, and the way I saw him interact with everyone that came into the diner.

Liam McBride is the real deal.

Nothing about him is an act.

That makes everything about this even more terrifying.

I collapse in his arms, burying my face in his neck, and he pulls me against him, holding me steady. Keeping me from completely coming apart like I want to right now.

Seeing the sheriff up close and personal shook me far worse than I imagined it could, and relishing in the warmth and comfort this man provides for a few moments will be my new guilty pleasure.

One I could definitely get used to.

I don't know how long we stand like this, wrapped around each other, silently saying so many things we never could verbally, but eventually, Gizmo clambers up and starts pawing at my legs. His insistence makes me drag my head back and glance down at him.

Liam releases me, then bends down and scoops up the dog, scratching behind his ears. "I think he's happy that you're staying."

"I'm sure he is." I watch Giz lick Liam's face. "You've become his new favorite person."

He raises a reddish brow at me. "Just his?"

I can't help the smile that pulls at my lips because apparently I've been doing a shitty job of hiding my reaction to the man standing in front of me.

Liam McBride is going to be a problem for me.

But maybe, for the first time in my life, it'll be a good one.

9

LUCKY

It seems that agreeing to stay in McBride Mountain—at least temporarily—means Gizmo and I are moving up in the world—*literally*.

With my backpack containing everything I own in the back seat of Liam's truck and Gizmo on my lap, we set out to head up to his place. As in...*up* McBride Mountain itself.

Despite trying to remain calm about the change of scenery and what this all means, my knee keeps bouncing, the nerves getting the best of me as we pass all the way through town, pause at the one stop sign that still seems absolutely unnecessary, and move out onto the road that loops around the mountain.

We drive past McBride Timber to our left and the falls where I spent that night camped out on the ground and finally to a turnoff that leads up the mountain that I barely even noticed when I walked past it over a week ago.

In the pitch-black, it's hard to see much of anything, but it doesn't seem to faze Liam. He turns onto it easily, casting a quick glance my way, then slides his right hand on top of my knee, stopping it from bouncing.

He squeezes gently. "You'll be safe at my place. I told you, this mountain belongs to us, and nobody fucks with the McBrides."

I wish I could believe that were true, that simply being somewhere with someone with a certain last name was enough to protect me from what might be coming down on us, on *him* now that he's done something stupid like gone and attached himself to me—or that I've gone and done something stupid like let him.

But his large, warm palm pressed against my knee, the heat of his body seeping into the exposed skin through the rips in my jeans, is enough to at least stop my leg from shaking momentarily.

There's no telling what will happen as soon as he releases it, but he keeps it there as we move up a dark gravel drive, almost like he knows I need the physical contact to keep myself from spiraling again.

Massive trees loom on either side of the truck, cocooning us in an almost-gothic archway that offers no view of where we're headed or what lies beyond this very narrow strip up the otherwise wild mountain.

"How can you see anything?"

The headlights of his truck illuminate only a few feet in front of us before the darkness and the trees swallow it up.

He quickly tosses me another grin. "I could probably drive this with my eyes closed."

My grip on the handle of the door tightens. "Please don't try."

His deep chuckle rolls through the truck cab the same way thunder does the sky, but it has the opposite effect most storms do. While billowing dark clouds and sinister skies usually mean I'll be miserable and cold on the road, Liam's laughter warms me like lying in the sun on a hot summer day.

"I told you, Lucky, I've lived here my whole life. Driven this road more times than I can count. I know every bump, every turn, every tree."

"That's reassuring..."

But I won't release my death grip until we're out of the trees and squarely on the flat-ish ground where I hope his home stands.

This mountain is intimidating. The way it towers over the town, like an evergreen sentinel standing watch. Seeing how deep the darkness is out here, I can't believe I slept outside that night beside the falls.

Even with my gun within reach and my flashlight lit all night to attempt to keep away the worst of what mother nature could bring, it was still hard to see anything beyond a few feet around me. And thinking about what is lurking out there— then and now—makes me shiver.

I glance down at Gizmo asleep in my lap, apparently completely unbothered by our sudden change of location.

It could be because he's tired, but I think part of how relaxed and serene he's been instead of his usual crazed self has to do with the man beside me.

Since the moment I met Liam, his calm, reassuring energy seemed to radiate from him effortlessly, and Giz feels it, too.

I guess it's true what they say about dogs being a good judge of character.

If I had only listened to him before...

Things would be so different.

I close my eyes and try to fight off the memory, but it still comes, like it always does, especially at night when I'm sitting by that door. When I'm waiting. When I'm watching. When I'm wondering how much longer I'll have before this bubble bursts.

Anger. Fear. Panic.

All those old feelings rush back through me.

Liam's hand tightens on my knee. "You all right?"

I open my eyes and nod, trying to shake off the chill in my blood. "Yep. Just excited to see your place."

He releases a tiny sigh. "Well, don't get your hopes up too much. It's a homestead, not the Four Seasons. We work it, and it's very rugged."

"I hope this doesn't make me sound dumb, but I have no idea what that really means."

Another light chuckle fills the cab, relieving a little of the tension. "I guess I wouldn't expect you to. It means we live off the land, for the most part. We have two cows, horses, chickens, goats—"

"Wow, a whole farm."

He grins. "Not quite, but close. We only raise the animals that have some usefulness to us and that we have room for. When my mom was still alive, we were a hundred percent dependent on everything coming from our own land."

"Not anymore?"

Even with his focus on the drive, I can see the wistful look overtake his eyes. "Things have changed a lot, even though I always say McBride Mountain never changes. As it's gotten easier to get supplies, and as the lumber business has expanded and we've had to be at the yard more and out at the logging sites, I hate to say that we've become a little more reliant on things we can buy at the general store. But we still like to do as much of it on our own as we can."

"Seems like a fun way to grow up."

And having that kind of environment explains how he can be like *this*.

So content.

So happy.

"It was." He grins at me briefly. "I don't have any complaints."

"Can I ask you something?"

"Of course." Liam takes the truck around another bend, and all the air freezes in my lungs at how narrow the road gets here. He tightens his grip on my knee again. "Don't worry, it will fit."

"Okay..." I release a shaky breath, not entirely sure I believe him, but the truck somehow manages to squeeze between the massive trees overarching it. "You said you were left on the doorstep..."

His body tenses slightly, and he swallows. "Yeah..."

"Up here?"

He nods.

"So, someone drove up this"—I motion to the road—"and left you."

"Yeah." His brow furrows. "I mean, I assume so. It would've taken hours to walk, and carrying a baby..."

Exactly what I was thinking.

When he briefly mentioned that tidbit of family history to me, it was apparent the entire situation weighed on him in some way.

"So...someone must have really cared about you to have gone to all that trouble, right?"

He nods again, swallowing thickly.

"Do you know who your biological mother is?"

Liam glances at me out of the corner of his eye. "I do, but that's a very long, very sordid ordeal that I definitely don't want to get into tonight." His hand slides higher on my leg. "Some other time."

"Okay..."

But I'm not so sure he meant that.

For all the promises he made and reassurances he gave me standing in that tiny apartment above Elaine's garage, he seems to have secrets of his own. Ones he doesn't want to discuss when this *thing* between us has shifted.

That warm palm squeezes my thigh. "We're here."

No sooner does he say the words than the road opens up into a vast field sitting under a stunning night sky with more twinkling stars than I've ever seen in my life.

"Oh, my God."

I stare up at the breathtaking God-created canopy instead of looking where I probably should—at the cabin that lies in the clearing just ahead, the single porch light above it the only thing that illuminates the area aside from the large moon.

Wow.

Liam doesn't stop beside the home. "That's Killian and Willow's place. It isn't the original cabin, but one built a little later in the original location."

"That's amazing..."

The history this place holds is mind-boggling. I've never been anywhere that has been in the same family for two hundred and fifty years, where people put down roots and spent the time nurturing them and making them grow strong.

I can *feel* the weight of the past here.

We leave the small, one-story cabin behind us, and I hold my breath as we drive deeper onto the homestead—both because the darkness encroaches on us again but also because I have no idea what I'm about to see around each bend on the gravel drive.

"Up that way is Connor's place." Liam motions to a gravel path that cuts up to the right a few hundred yards behind Killian's place. "Mine is this way." He points to the left toward a massive barn. "This is the main barn. Most of the animals are housed there, and Killian also uses it for his wood-working."

"He does woodworking, too?"

"Carvings mostly."

Flashes of the various animals that stand sentinel in front of most of the businesses in town race through my memory, including the bear holding the picnic basket at the diner that I walk past on my way in every day. "You mean the ones that were all along Main Street?"

He nods. "Yep."

"I had no idea."

His broad shoulders rise and fall. "I guess when you're chopping down trees and cutting lumber for a living, the most natural thing in the world is to continue to work with it in some other way in your free time."

It does make sense, but I've never been good enough at anything to do what Killian and Liam can.

A Jill of all trades but a master of none—that's how I've always seen myself. Part of moving around all the time and working whatever jobs I could find, even if they were only temporary, meant I didn't have the opportunity to get truly *skilled* at any one thing.

I never thought I'd be sad about that, but after seeing what Liam did with the shelves and knowing Killian created the carvings I've admired up and down the street in town, I can't help but feel like I've been missing out on something big.

There are so many big things I never had, though.

So, I'll just add it to the list.

We turn behind the barn and head up a small slope a few hundred yards until another cabin comes into view.

This one stands tucked back well from the road with a stone and cobble path leading up to it, and it is *magical*.

"This is my place."

Liam says it almost hesitantly, as if he's afraid of how I might react to finally seeing it, and it takes me a moment to respond. Not because I'm trying to think of something to say but because it's left me completely speechless.

"It's *beautiful*." Nestled in the middle of a grove of towering trees I can't identify, the two-story cabin looks as if it grew there naturally, part of the landscape with the massive logs that make up its structure. "It looks like something out of a fairy tale."

For a brief second, my heart skips a beat and the heat of his hand on my leg promises one of those swoony stories I always loved as a kid.

You don't get to have a fairy tale.

I have to keep reminding myself of that.

That I don't get the white knight who rides in on his steed and saves me.

I don't get to have a happy ending.

Not with what I've done.

I might get a few days, or maybe if I'm *actually* lucky for once in my life, a week or two here with this man, and then I'm either going to have to leave, or the shit's going to hit the fan, dragging him into it with me.

He parks the truck on the side of the cabin, turns it off, then slides out and comes around to open my door, offering me his hand. I accept it and slide out with a still waking Giz tucked under my other arm, scanning the wilderness around us that seems to suck me into it the moment I close the door behind me.

The faint light provided by a single bulb over the front porch can't block out the vast number of stars overhead or the inky blackness that surrounds us.

"It really is remote up here, huh?"

He squeezes my hand and grins. "We're the only people who live on the mountain itself."

"Really?"

His head bobs, and he swings his free hand outward toward the forest. "As far as you can see, as far as either of us could yell, it's just us." He offers a half grin as he tugs me up against him. "And my brothers."

I set Gizmo on the ground, and he groggily starts sniffing around, exploring his new environment.

Liam's hand shifts up into my hair, holding my head in

place firmly, forcing me to meet his gaze. "Nothing can get to you up here, Bluebell. I promise."

"Bluebell?"

Those sinfully tempting lips of his curve. "That's what your hair reminds me of—the bluebells that grow here on the mountain. They've always been my favorite."

He crashes his mouth to mine and just like before, at my place, I sink into him, wrapping my arms around his neck to cling to him. We kiss for so long that I lose all sense of time and space, forgetting why he had to bring me up here in the first place.

Liam groans into my mouth, then pulls away reluctantly, dropping another quick kiss on my lips before he takes my hand in his and leads me toward the cabin.

"Let me show you the inside."

LIAM

I don't know why what she thinks matters so much to me, but I hold my breath as I close the door behind us and Lucky takes in the interior of my cabin.

So much hard work went into this place—designing it, finding the right trees to fell for the main structure and interior beams, milling them for the flooring, cabinets, and everything else required to make this place a true home.

And no one but *us* has ever seen it.

Killian, Connor, Willow are the only ones who have ever set foot here, besides me. There hasn't ever been anyone I wanted to bring home. Never any reason to allow someone into my inner sanctum.

This has always been *my* space. Where I come after a long, hard day of work or simply to get away from Killian and

Connor when I need a break from...all that comes with older brothers.

It's always been quiet. Peaceful. The kind of space where the rest of the world can disappear for however long I let it, but now, a realization suddenly clicks into place.

I love this cabin, but something has always been missing from it.

Something *important.*

Someone to share it with...

Having Lucky and Giz here fills that void I hadn't even noticed was there.

She looks *good* walking around my cabin, like she was always meant to be in this space. Even the blue of her hair blends in with the soft greens and blues of the curtains and pillows on the couch.

That's why it's so scary—waiting to see her reaction, wondering what she's thinking about something I worked so hard on.

If she doesn't like it, doesn't feel the same way I do when I'm in here, it should shatter me more than I would ever admit to anyone.

Blood rushes in my ears, my heart beating far too fast under my ribs as I wait for her response.

Lucky's eyes move over all the hand-hewn logs and the massive beams cut from trees that grew on this very mountain. Her wide gaze sweeps up the hand-carved railing of the stairs that lead to the loft above us, then down the stone fireplace that rises two stories in the living room and to the small kitchen at the back of the cabin.

Her jaw falls open. "You did this?"

I nod, rubbing my neck awkwardly and shifting restlessly where I still stand at the door. "With my brothers, yeah."

"Liam, it's..." She gapes, turning to face me with awe overtaking her beautiful face. "It's absolutely *stunning*. You're incredibly talented."

My cheeks heat, and I tip my head slightly, overwhelmed by the compliment even when it was exactly what I needed to hear. I take the opportunity to toe off my boots and set them beside the door. "Thank you."

I peek up at her again as I right myself, and she spins in place, her head tipped back, examining the high beams over us that come together in a triangle peak.

"I'm not just saying that, Liam. Really." She takes it all in again, as if she can't believe what she's seeing. "I've never seen anything like it."

A second passes, and suddenly, that far-away look she seems to get anytime we talk about family or the past returns to her eyes.

The tight smile she offers doesn't reach her eyes. "All the houses I grew up in were very plain. To be honest, I think most of the families I lived with were worried about doing anything too fancy, that all the foster kids would destroy the place."

My heart clenches with her confession. Pain for the little girl she was replacing any personal concerns about her liking everything.

She trails her fingers over the bear carved into the newel post. They dip across the carefully crafted features of its face, its fur, its paws.

"Killian did that."

Her lips curve as she examines it. "I assume there are bears up here on the mountain?"

I nod, leaning against the wall to let her survey everything without my interference. "Coyotes, bears, an occasional mountain lion."

She cringes and glances at Gizmo, who's sniffing every inch of the place, his little tail going a mile a minute during his exploration. "He's lucky he didn't get snatched up that night."

"I agree."

The fact that they were out near that road, alone, at almost midnight has bothered me since the moment she walked into that diner, but she never offered any sort of explanation for why. By now, I trust that she wasn't trying to break into McBride Timber or doing anything else nefarious, but I don't like that she put herself and Giz in that dangerous of a situation.

Not one fucking bit.

"Are you ever going to tell me what you were doin' out there?"

She pauses and turns back to me, and I can see the hesitation in her gaze.

Shit.

I've gone and ruined the moment by pushing her when I only told her an hour ago that I wasn't going to force her to reveal anything she wasn't ready to. But asking her these things just feels so natural because I want to know her.

I want to *understand* her.

I want her to let me in.

I don't want her to run.

"You don't have to—"

"No." She shakes her head, squeezing her eyes closed for a moment before she reopens them and meets my gaze. "I know I don't have to, but it's okay. I was...sleeping out near the falls."

My shoulders stiffen. "What?"

I had figured she'd been walking, maybe hitchhiking to get to McBride Mountain since she doesn't have any sort of vehicle, but sleeping alone outdoors in this area isn't merely unwise, it can be downright deadly if you aren't prepared with the proper equipment.

Which Lucky clearly was not.

All she has with her is a backpack and that little dog.

A shudder rolls through me imagining what might have stumbled upon her and Gizmo while she was out there alone without any form of protection. "You're incredibly lucky nothing found you out there."

She releases a heavy sigh, running her hands through her hair which falls back into place around her freckled face like water cascading over the side of the mountain. "You have no idea."

I'm smart enough to read between the lines there.

Lucky isn't just talking about the wildlife.

But I promised I wouldn't ask even though every part of me desperately wants to push for the truth.

I push off the wall beside the door and close the distance between us, tugging her up against me. "You don't have to worry anymore, Lucky. I know you may not want to tell me everything that's going on, and that's okay because I know when you're here, and when you're with me, you're safe. You are *safe* with me, Bluebell. That's enough right now."

She gives me a look that suggests she isn't so sure.

Getting Lucky to actually trust me, and trust in the things I tell her, isn't going to be easy, but I've never been afraid of hard work. It's what my entire life has been built upon, and something tells me that putting it in with this woman will be both the easiest and hardest job I ever do.

Leaning in, I feather my lips across hers. "Come on, let me show you the rest of the place."

She kicks off her old Chucks, tossing them next to my boots by the door, and I take her hand and tug her up the stairs into the loft.

My bed occupies almost the entire space, save for one corner with a dresser and a large reading chair, small end table, and lamp where I sometimes sit before bed when I don't feel like lounging by the fire downstairs.

"Wow." She gapes at my California king. "That's a *big* bed."

Laughing, I step in behind her and wrap my arms around her waist, burying my face in her hair, which inexplicably smells like the eucalyptus that grows on the mountain—with the slightest tinge of bacon from having worked at the diner this morning. "After a long day, I want to be able to spread out."

Hopefully now with her...

"And you need room for whoever's with you, right?"

She doesn't say it in a callous way, or like she's jealous, but it makes me stiffen in all the wrong places.

I turn her in my arms to face me and take her cheeks in my palms. "I need to tell you something."

Her brow furrows, and the tiniest bit of trepidation I hate seeing seeps into her eyes. "What?"

Hell.

I didn't think this would be so difficult, but I honestly didn't really spend much time considering this moment until Lucky walked into my life—and accused me of theft.

"This is kind of embarrassing..."

Swallowing thickly, I glance away, but Lucky raises her hand and nudges my face back toward her, completely stealing my move.

Her fingers graze across my cheek. "*What* is?"

"I haven't..."

Fucking hell.

"You haven't what?"

Just say it.

Rip it off like a Band-Aid.

Fast is less painful.

"I haven't...*been* with anyone like that."

She raises a brow. "In a long time?"

"No." I shake my head. "Ever."

Her brow furrows. "But"—her eyes rake over me—"how is that possible?"

There have been times I've asked myself that very question, but more often, it's the furthest thing from my mind.

I work.

I build.

I help take care of the family and this town.

The fact that I haven't had *actual* sex with anyone wasn't top on my list of concerns or priorities.

But with Lucky, my cheeks heat under her assessment. "I dated some girls in high school but was never really in love with any of them. Opportunities presented themselves, and stuff certainly happened. I can't say I wasn't tempted a few times, but it just never felt right because I didn't love any of them."

She pulls that bottom lip of hers between her teeth and considers me for far too long, and I can't tell *what* she's thinking. By the time she releases that plump lip, I'm practically vibrating with anxiety I didn't think I would feel about this. "I can sleep on the couch—"

"No." I shake my head and lean in, ghosting a kiss over her lips. "You'll sleep with me. In my bed. Where I can keep my arms around you all night."

"Liam, I don't want you to feel like—"

I silence her protest with another kiss and press my body against hers, letting her feel my barely restrained desire for her that's been growing since the moment she stepped through my door. Letting her know that she wouldn't be forcing me into anything or putting me in a position in which I don't very willingly want to be placed.

God...

I don't think it's possible to love someone you barely know.

It's impossible when we met less than two weeks ago, but if it *were* possible, I would've said the words already because I haven't felt like this with anyone I've ever known.

I want Lucky.

I want this.

I want *everything* with her, if she'd only give it to me.

I'm not sure if she'll ever open up, if she'll ever be able to give me what I really want from her. Her past, her future, all the things she keeps hidden because she's afraid they're going to scare me. But after what I learned about my past, about who I am, there's nothing that can scare me anymore.

I pull my head back and see unshed tears shimmering in her eyes. "I want you, Lucky. Your past doesn't scare me. What does is the thought that you're going to run off without me ever getting to know you, without ever having this with you."

"Are you...sure?"

I nod and a tiny grin pulls at her lips.

She wraps her arms around my neck and drags me down for another kiss as Gizmo jumps up onto the bed and lays on it, tipping his head to the side.

I close my eyes as we deepen the kiss, ignoring the dog and the fact that there's still this darkness looming over us.

There's still some sort of threat that she won't tell me about that we will have to face.

Later.

In this moment, here at the homestead, she's safe.

When she's like this in my arms, nothing can touch us.

10

LIAM

Lucky trails her fingers along the hem of my t-shirt with the lightest of touches.

Soft.

Fleeting.

A tease.

A tentative experiment from someone who doesn't want to scare me off or push me too far, too fast.

But nothing scares me about this.

Quite the opposite.

She slowly lifts the fabric until her teasing fingertips brush my skin directly. The barely-there touch ignites a fire deep inside me that rages to be released, and I suck in a breath, my entire body seizing in response to the light trace of her skin over mine.

Lucky grins against my mouth, then spreads her hands up and under the shirt, across my chest, allowing her short nails to bite into the flesh there.

Fuck.

I growl lowly and tug her hips firmly to mine, grinding my hard cock against her body, ensuring she knows I am one hundred percent on board with where this is going.

She issues a needy little sound in the back of her throat that only acts like gasoline being thrown on the inferno already raging inside me.

Please God, don't let me fuck this up.

I already forewarned her to set her expectations low considering I haven't done *that*, but it doesn't mean I don't want it to be fucking perfect with her.

And not just because it's my first time, but because it's Lucky.

No matter how irrational it might be, I've wanted this since the first time I saw that blue blaze of hair and the flash of feisty fire dancing across her matching eyes.

My Bluebell...

I'll never be able to look at those flowers the same without seeing her like this, without feeling her lips and body pressed to mine, without hearing that little needy moan she made when she felt the press of my cock.

She tugs at my shirt, working it up until I'm forced to drag my mouth away from hers long enough to allow her to pull it over my head. Her eyes briefly drop to the tattoo on my chest as she tosses it onto the floor, then she glances at Giz watching us on the bed and waves him off it and toward the chair.

Offering an annoyed look, he jumps up onto the soft leather, does a few circles, then settles, letting out a little harrumphing sound before his eyes drift closed, finally giving us the privacy we need.

I slam my mouth against hers again, walking her backward until her knees hit the bed and she sinks down onto it. Her hands fumble at my waist to get the button of my jeans free and the zipper down, but I capture her wrist before she can slide her hand into the denim.

"Why am I the only one getting naked?"

Lucky's luscious curves have been a constant source of my fantasies since I saw those thick hips swaying their way across the diner toward me, and my hands itch to touch them, to run all over every inch of her.

The corners of her lips twitch, her eyes blazing with promise, and I release her wrist slowly. She reaches down and grabs the hem of her own shirt, then drags it up over her head and tosses it behind her.

"I wanted to do that..."

And now that her breasts are heaving in a bra that matches her hair color, all I want to do is tear it off and see them fully.

She laughs and grabs my jeans, tugging them down. "You'll have to wait."

I run my fingers through her hair, tilting her face up to me. "Why's that, Blubell?"

Instead of answering me, she dips her head and glides her tongue across the throbbing head of my cock before she sucks it into her mouth.

Jesus fucking Christ.

My body tenses as my eyes roll up into my head. It drops back on my neck, my muscles trembling as Lucky glides her tongue along the entire underside of my shaft. My hand tightens in her hair, seeking something to cling to as I spiral off into bliss with her attentions.

"Lucky..."

It's a warning that I'm not going to last. There's no way I could with her hot, wet mouth wrapped around me. But it doesn't seem to deter her. In fact, my groan of barely restrained control when she draws back slightly and reaches the head only seems to urge her on further.

She sucks and then swallows, drawing me even deeper again. I hit the spongy softness of the back of her throat in a way that makes my entire body bow up in warning.

"Fuck!"

I tug on her hair, urging her off, but as she pulls back, she glides her tongue across that spot right under the head of my cock and I twitch, which only drives me into her mouth.

She moans her approval and wraps her hand around my shaft, stroking it as she sucks me down almost greedily, like she can't wait for it when I'm the one who's barely hanging on by a thread.

It doesn't take long for that heated tingle to start at the base of my spine, and my balls to draw up impossibly tight.

It's been way too fucking long since I've felt a woman's touch, since anything has gotten me off beside my own hand. And even *that* hasn't happened in almost a year, since any inclination for that type of release disappeared as the nightmares came.

I groan, my hips wanting to thrust, to drive into her, to *move,* and she reaches out with her free hand and clutches my ass, urging me forward, encouraging me to do precisely what my body craves.

Fucking hell, this woman.

And I can't stop it.

I start to move in time with her motions. The twisting of her palm on my slick shaft. The licking and intense suction. It crescendos into a symphony of pleasure and agony that I can't take anymore.

Sweet torture.

"Lucky, I'm gonna come."

I feel, rather than see, her smile around my cock, and she somehow manages to suck me even deeper before she draws back on my shaft with a suction so tight my feet lift up onto my toes and I'm coming straight down her throat.

Wave after wave of pleasure surges through me as I unleash hot spurts that she swallows down greedily. Each one feels like releasing something that's been pent up for far too long—all that tension, worry, and fear melting away as she brings me pure ecstasy.

By the time I'm done and she finally pulls free from my cock, I can barely open my eyes to gaze down at her. I brush my thumb across her swollen bottom lip, hovering only an inch from where she still clutches my shaft. "Fucking hell. That was..."

Raising a pleased brow, she waits for me to come up with a word to describe it, but all I can do is shake my head and grin at her.

All my brain seems capable of doing right now is floating in this post-orgasmic haze.

Speaking isn't possible.

But I still need more. Of *her*.

She releases me and returns my smile, and I bend down to drag my jeans the rest of the way off before I seize her mouth with mine. Her tongue glides along my own, the taste of my release still lingering there, and all I want to do is taste her, to feast on her, to give her what she just gave me ten-fold.

I reach behind her and unhook her bra, and she slides the straps down her arms and lets it fall to the floor as she shifts back on the bed.

My bed.

Lucky.

In.

My.

Bed.

Part of me can't comprehend how the fuck this is happening even as I crawl onto it after her, not wanting to break the kiss, not wanting to allow any space between us.

When she finally reaches the pillows at the headboard, I run my hand along the waistband of her jeans until I find a zipper. My hand trembles as I tug it down before I quickly remove them and toss them unceremoniously off the bed, leaving her in only a small thong that matches her bra and hair.

I grin at it. "I love that you color coordinated."

She releases a laugh that fills the cabin with something it hasn't had—*ever.*

Christ, I love that sound.

I want it to stay.

I want to hear it every day and every fucking night, just like this.

Only a tiny slip of fabric now separates us, and I trail my fingers along the edge, relishing how silky soft her skin is below it and the way she squirms under the featherlight touch.

But I don't have it in me to tease.

Not tonight.

Not now.

I tug down the fabric and pull it from her legs, fully exposing her core.

She squirms under my assessment, but she has no reason to.

In the moonlight streaming in through the window, all I see is Heaven, the only place I want to be right now. I lower myself onto my elbows between her legs, spreading her wider as I graze my fingertips across her already wet flesh.

Her hips buck at the contact, her hands digging into the comforter as she tips her head back to the headboard. A little groan tumbles from her lips, and I've barely touched her.

She's just as worked up as I am.

"Did sucking my cock get you wet like this?"

Her eyes flash open and meet mine, her lips parting on a heavy exhale. "Yes."

"Good."

I dip my head and drag my tongue through her slit. The flavor of her arousal fills my mouth, and sweet mother of God, it's better than anything I've ever tasted in my life.

I could drown in it.

I could stay in this spot and die happy.

Her hips buck again, and I brace my left forearm across her pelvis to keep her down, pinned in place as I explore her. Figuring out what she likes. Learning her needs. Dragging the flat expanse of my tongue over her, then flicking the tip of it across her clit. Probing deep inside her until she's squirming and bucking.

Exploring every inch of this woman's body has become my ultimate goal. Memorizing every dip, every curve, every dimple, every scar; I want to know all of them.

I glide my hand up her inner thigh and slip a finger inside her, and her hips attempt to bow, but I press her down, keeping her prone as I curl up and find that soft spot deep inside her.

A mewl falls from her lips and her head tosses from side to side as I drag my finger along her inner wall and suck her clit between my lips the same way she just did my cock.

"Oh, God!"

Her hips begin to roll against my face, and it's all I can do not to come again instantly at the franticness in her motions. That same desperation I felt to drive my cock deep into her hot, wet throat is what she feels now as my mouth and tongue move over her.

She wants more.

Of everything.

Of *me.*

And I want to be inside her more than anything, but I need her to come like this first.

I need to do that for her.

I need her to do that for *me.*

It doesn't take long before her hands tighten on the comforter again, wrenching it almost off the bed, her hips slamming up against my face as her pussy ripples around my fingers.

I suck on her clit, flicking my tongue across it until she finally detonates, her thighs clamping down around my head and twisting with a violence I crave, because it means she's lost control.

She's giving it over to me.

She's let go, even if only for a moment.

She's forgotten all the things she's afraid of.

She's given me that, more than I ever thought possible.

LUCKY

My mind floats in that ethereal space that only exists after an incredible orgasm, my limbs somehow heavy and boneless at the same time.

Liam crawls up my body and captures my mouth, utterly devouring me the same way he just did my cunt, with the taste of my release on his lips and his still coating my tongue.

The weight of his hard body on mine, pressing me into the bed, cocoons me in his strength and warmth as his kiss deepens...

My pussy clenches, the heady mix making me hungry for more.

Desperate for him.

But after what he just told me, I'm not going to push. I'm not going to make demands or have expectations from this man.

He's already given me so much in such a short time.

Offered me friendship. Provided me safety and support when I don't deserve it. Invited me into his life and his world when he doesn't understand what he's opened his door to.

I won't take anything more from him that he's not ready to give.

His kiss becomes more urgent, and despite my best efforts to control my reaction to the feel of his body flush to me, my hips roll along his cock.

So hot.

So hard.

So unyielding in the best way.

He groans into my mouth, then pulls back slightly, one hand tunneling into my hair as the other grips my chin. "You're sure you want this, Lucky? Because I don't know how good it will be. How good I'll be..."

His almost shy nervousness when he's usually so confident and the concern in his green gaze only makes me want him more. The fact that he cares so much, not about what it means for him, but how it'll be for me, only proves how much I don't deserve him.

God...

He really is an incredible man.

Kind.

Beyond generous.

And all I want is to be with him.

Completely.

To give myself over to him for whatever time we have together like this.

Because it could end tomorrow.

This may be the only night we have together. Life beyond the mountain may come crashing down on me when I least expect it, and that would mean Liam McBride will disappear, along with anything else that has ever been good in my life.

But not tonight.

I refuse to let *anything* come between us here, in this beautiful place he built with his bare hands.

Hands that have already brought me so much pleasure and hope.

I reach between us and grasp his hard cock, and a strangled

noise rumbles in his chest where it presses to mine, the rever-beration traveling all the way through me. He kisses me deeply again, his mouth slanting as his hips roll against me, pinning my hand between us as I stroke him gently, gliding my thumb across the slick head.

And I realize I never answered him.

Not with words anyway.

When I manage to tear my mouth away, I'm breathless. "I want you, Liam."

His eyes slowly drift open to meet mine, and the tiniest grin graces his lips as he dips his head and kisses me again. Harder this time. More demanding. Filled with beautiful promises I want to grab hold of and cling to as badly as I do him.

Liam draws his hips back, putting enough space between us that I can guide his cock to my slick core. He presses just the head in, a low hiss slipping from his lips, then slowly starts pushing inside me.

My pussy stretches to accommodate his size, burning in the best way at his thick length filling me. So cautiously. Every muscle in his body tense. Trembling against me. As if he's trying to restrain some inherent animal instinct to *fuck*.

He freezes, his hips stilling and eyes opening again. "Is this all right? I'm not hurting you, am I?"

I lift my palm to cup his stubbled cheek as I wrap my legs around him and press at his lower back, urging him to drive in the rest of the way. "It's fucking perfect."

"Fuck..."

That single word comes out more like a growl than spoken, and he finally pushes into me completely. I tip my head back, my breath caught in my throat at the sensation of being filled by Liam McBride, and he drops his head, burying his face in my neck.

"God, you feel so *fucking* good, Bluebell."

Bluebell...

Something about that name coming from his lips, the reverence with which he says it, almost like a prayer being whispered in a confessional, is enough to make me squeeze around his length, clamping down on him.

Another strangled noise vibrates against my neck. He kisses his way across my cheek as he draws his hips back and slowly plunges into me again, drawing a little mewl from me as he bottoms out again. "If you keep doing that, I know I'm not going to last long enough to make this good for you, Lucky."

For me.

That's all he cares about.

His sole focus.

But this needs to be incredible for *him*, too.

It should be something he remembers, that he can never forget. Because I already know *I* could never forget Liam or what he's already done for me.

I push on his shoulders, urging him away slightly. "Roll onto your back."

His eyes flare in surprise, but he does as I request, wrapping his arm around me to take me with him. I push up, pressing my hand across the massive, colorful tattoo of a tiger across his chest. Trailing my fingers over the bright colors, I roll my hips, grinding down.

"Fuck..." He hisses the single word as his hands tighten on my flesh, pinning me in place while every muscle in his neck strains. "Good God."

Good God is right...

In this position, he's even bigger, my body stretched and filled so completely that I want to just luxuriate in the feeling of being consumed by Liam.

I lean down and kiss my way up those tight corded muscles of his neck to his ear. "Was it worth the wait?"

"Fucking hell, Lucky." His hands flex at my waist possessively. "I wouldn't want this with anyone but you."

The sentiment makes my eyes burn, and I squeeze them closed so he won't see the tears about to form as I pull my head back and set to work, slowly pushing myself up and sinking down on his thick cock.

One of his hands squeezes my hip as he reaches up with the other to cup my breast. He drags his calloused thumb over the taut nipple, and a flash of pleasure shoots straight to my clit, making me twitch and clamp down on him.

He grins and does it again, then switches to the other side and gives it the same attention.

Each brush of his thumb might as well be directly at the apex of my thighs, my body so primed and sensitive that the nerve endings flare with each pass of that rough skin along mine.

If he keeps playing with my breasts like this, I'm going to come fast.

I lean forward slightly, finding the perfect angle to grind my clit against his pelvis as I work his shaft, gliding up and down, bracing myself on his rock-hard chest as I set a rhythm that makes his entire body tense.

The head of his cock catches inside me, and his eyes roll back. "God." I rock my hips and clench. "Fuck. Do that again."

Fuck, yes.

Seeing him like this—completely given over to reckless abandon and pleasure was my goal. To give him even the slightest bit of what he's given me.

I repeat the motion, rolling my hips up at the final second, and his bow off the bed, plunging him even deeper inside me. Then he surges up, bracing himself on one hand and tunneling his fingers into my hair with the other, angling my face so he can devour my mouth while I take him.

That slight change in angle is all I need for my movements to become more frantic, more desperate. My labored breaths mingle with his as he continues to kiss me like he's seeking something more. Like he's trying to get to the truth that I've been holding back.

And I want to give it to him.

I want to give him *everything*.

But I can't.

Not right now.

All I can give him is *this*.

Heat spreads out from where our bodies connect, sizzling across my skin, searing away the reality beyond this cabin. That's where I want to leave it, to pretend it doesn't exist. For now, I will.

I give myself completely to Liam.

To his lips moving over mine.

To the sweep of his greedy tongue.

To the possessive way he grasps my hair.

To the way his cock feels just fucking right, like it was built to fit inside me and complete a part of me I hadn't been aware was lacking.

My orgasm slams into me, and I clamp down on him, rolling my hips and bucking on his length. He presses his feet into the bed and drives up, thrusting one final time before he groans and empties himself inside me.

Pleasure explodes through me that same way the falls burst from the top of the mountain and cascade down to the massive pool below, the scalding hot ecstasy enough to make stars explode against my eyelids and my breath rush from my lungs.

I want to live in this moment forever, to cling to the man and feeling for as long as I possibly can.

But when it finally subsides, only the tingling aftershocks left, I sink down on him, and he drops onto the bed, wrapping his arms around me and burying his face in my hair, holding me tightly to him.

Exactly where I want to be.

Making me feel safe for the first time I can ever remember.

11

LUCKY

The sun hasn't even risen yet when I have to sneak out of Liam's bed. I reluctantly pull out of the comfort of his warm, strong arms wrapped around me and the steady rhythm of his breath against the back of my neck.

Cooler air hits my naked skin, and I shiver as I glance over to ensure I haven't woken him or Gizmo, but they're both sound asleep. Liam's thick eyelashes lie softly across his cheek, his lips slightly parted as his steady breathing makes his inked chest rise and fall gently.

I want to crawl right back into his arms and stay there forever, but first, I need a drink of water. Our activities last night have drained me, in more ways than one, and I snag Liam's t-shirt from the floor and slide it over my head before I tiptoe down the stairs and to the kitchen.

Wow...

Even though it's my second time seeing it, I'm still stunned by how incredible his cabin really is. Every piece of wood, every fixture, the stones laid in the two-story fireplace on the far wall, they all demonstrate how much time and attention he gave to creating this place. How much *love* went into it.

If Liam and his brothers decided they wanted to build luxury cabins for people up in these mountains, they could make a fortune. Although, I'm more confident now that they already have one, they just don't live like it. Considering how long the mountain and the lumber yard have been in their family, and a few other things people have said about the McBrides as I've heard bits and pieces of conversations at the diner over the last couple weeks, they aren't just powerful here.

They're rich and *very* powerful.

So, when Liam made that promise to me, that I was safe up here, and told me that no one fucks with the McBrides, he meant it.

That, as much as what happened between us, gave me the best night of sleep I've ever had.

But I am feeling the *not* sleeping this morning throughout my body. The thirst. The glorious aches. The lingering tingle across my skin everywhere he touched.

A smile playing on my lips, I open the cabinet in the kitchen, searching for a glass, and have to go through two more before I finally find what I'm looking for in the darkness of pre-dawn.

I twist the faucet, fill the glass, and drink it down greedily, the same way Liam poured himself into me last night.

My entire body heats at the memory.

Good God...

Liam McBride might not be experienced when it comes to sex, but he is a fast learner and dedicated to becoming a fucking expert.

My thighs clench, my body throbbing again and demanding I climb those stairs, get into bed, and tangle myself back up with the man who has changed my world so suddenly and so damn fast.

I set down my glass next to the sink and start to make my way back to the stairs when dark movement outside one of the front windows of the cabin catches my eye and freezes me on the spot.

What the hell was that?

With darkness still engulfing the cabin and the world beyond it, it's impossible to see what might be lurking outside, but none of the options are good.

My heart leaps into my throat.

My hands tremble.

A very human-looking shape moves past the window toward the front door, and I hold my breath as my blood runs cold, raising goosebumps across my skin.

Someone followed us up here.

Every nightmare I've had. All those worst-case-scenarios that have rattled around in my head. They're all coming true.

All because I didn't leave.

I've put Liam at risk. I've put *all* of them at risk—Killian, Willow, their baby.

The thought of anything happening to any of them makes my stomach pitch violently, and I inch forward on unsteady legs toward the end table beside the couch where I left my purse last night.

Terrified to release the air in my lungs or to draw in more, because even that sound seems loud in the utter stillness of the cabin, I dig into my bag, and my hand finally closes around the only thing that might save us right now.

Forcing myself to take another labored breath, I pull out the .22 revolver.

Its familiar heavy weight in my hand offers a modicum of comfort as I ease my way toward the window to try to peek out. Unfamiliar shapes loom in the darkness, and I strain to see through the morning mist.

Footsteps sound on the porch outside, and I hold my breath

again and check the revolver to ensure it's fully loaded and ready, no matter what comes through that door.

The knob turns, and my hand starts shaking, but I brace the weapon with the other one and level the barrel at whoever's about to walk through.

The door swings open, and heavy boots appear on the hardwood floor, then a tall, broad-shouldered man with dark hair steps in fully, and I cock the hammer, the gentle clicking sound almost echoing in the quiet stillness.

He freezes and turns toward me slowly, barely visible without any lights on inside the cabin or the sun up yet. "Liam?"

The unfamiliar voice calls out, his plea booming through the lofted second floor.

Gizmo barks and the sound of him racing down the stairs mixes with the slight creak of the mattress upstairs. Stopping at the intruder's feet, Giz snarls and gnashes his teeth in warning, his deep growl filling the room as hurried footsteps sound upstairs.

Out of the corner of my eye, I see Liam look down over the railing as the first hints of daylight start to seep in through the window and wide open door, revealing the man who walked in.

"Lucky, no!" Liam's voice carries through the cabin as my eyes adjust more and more, allowing me to see the man standing in front of me. "Don't!"

Frantic footsteps pound down the steps, setting Giz off again as he snaps at the man's feet.

The man's eyes drop down to Gizmo, then dart back up at me before sweeping toward Liam as he reaches the bottom of the stairs. "I didn't realize you had such friendly guests."

Liam reaches me and takes my trembling hands in his, pulling the gun from me. "Lucky, it's just Connor."

"Connor?"

The name registers, but not the face looking back at me with raised dark brows.

I only saw him once, that day in the diner. Barely long enough that I would have recognized him on the street in broad daylight. Certainly not enough that I could in the dark when I'm already jumpy and on edge, worried about bringing Liam into my mess.

"Oh, my God…"

What did I do?

I stumble backward, embarrassment and absolute mind-bending horror at what I almost did racing through me.

Oh, my God.

I could have shot him…

Liam wraps an arm around me, catching me, preventing me from falling to the floorboards. I try to pull out of his hold, but he keeps it on me and hands the gun off to Connor carefully. "Unload that."

Connor nods and empties all the bullets then releases the hammer.

"Oh, God." I bury my face in my shaking hands, my whole body shaking so badly that only Liam's arm around me keeps me upright. "I'm so sorry, I…I don't know what I was thinking. I…"

I scramble for an explanation, for a way to truly apologize for what could have been a crushing mistake that would have destroyed the McBrides.

Liam holds me tightly and nods at Connor. "Put it over there."

Connor sets the gun and bullets on the end table next to the couch and looks at us for a few minutes before he releases a long sigh. "I came to see why you weren't at breakfast yet, but now I know." He releases a little humorless laugh. "I'll let Willow know to expect you in a few minutes, once you get things settled."

Get me under control is what he's really saying.

I could have *killed* him.

One more step into the cabin and I would have fired. I would have ended the perceived threat without even realizing who he was because in my mind, all I saw was the threat I know is coming.

A different dark-haired, broad shouldered man...

Liam walks us over to the couch and drops down onto it, pulling me into his lap as Gizmo follows Connor to the door with a low growl. Once it's shut behind Liam's brother, Giz jumps up on the couch, nuzzling against me.

One of Liam's hands slides into my hair, cradling my head to his chest. "It's all right, Lucky. Everything's fine. Nobody got hurt."

"But...I-I could have shot him."

He shushes me, gently rubbing his other hand up and down my back in the quiet stillness of the emerging morning.

We sit with me wrapped up in him for several moments as sunlight continues to trickle in more and more through the front windows of the cabin, and Liam finally pulls his head back, taking my face in his hands, tilting it until I'm forced to look at him, even though I don't want to.

How can I after what I just did?

He searches my face, his gaze soft but laced with concern. "Why do you have a gun, Lucky?"

Those green eyes watch me carefully as I try to come up with a response, anything that could explain my reaction short of telling him the truth, but I can't think of anything. Nothing that would justify almost shooting his brother, who had every right to come into Liam's house, who has probably done it a thousand times without even thinking about it, who certainly didn't anticipate starting his morning staring down the barrel of a gun.

The longer I refuse to answer, the longer Liam stares at me

with so much compassion and worry, the more I want to come clean. I want him to understand *why* I just did that, that I was trying to protect myself and *him* from the ramifications of my actions. But each time I try to open my mouth to say the words, they get choked on the reality of what telling him would mean.

Danger.

Unlike anything he's ever faced here on McBride Mountain.

Time passes, the cabin lighting up until most of the pre-dawn shadows have been chased away, but that darkness still lingers in his gaze, and he eventually presses his lips together in a firm line. "I told you I wasn't going to push you, and I meant it when I said it. And I don't want to make this any harder for you than it already is, but you have a *gun*. You're scared enough to pull it on my brother. Lucky, you have to tell me what's going on."

Tears flow down my cheeks, and I don't even bother trying to stop them now that they've started. Now that he's opened Pandora's Box and the dam has cracked, I won't be able to push back the tidal wave of terror that has kept me running for what feels like forever.

But it isn't this man's responsibility to solve my problems or to dig me out from under the weight of what I've done.

I shake my head. "I can't, Liam. I can't put you in that position."

"What position?"

A sob slips from my lips. "I've already said too much."

The more I say, the more I talk about it, the harder it will be to keep the rest of it in. But I promised myself I wouldn't let anyone else pay for my bad decisions. And if I tell him, that's exactly what will end up happening.

"I just...can't."

He releases a heavy sigh, then tugs me up against him again, squeezing me tightly and pressing my face into his chest protectively. "You will. When you're ready."

LIAM

If I had to describe the feeling permeating Killian and Willow's kitchen this morning in one word, "tense" wouldn't even begin to cover it. I'm not sure anything would.

Connor exchanges a look with our older brother as Willow finishes laying out the breakfast spread she always makes for us before we head out for the morning. But something tells me that none of us are likely to be eating much this morning. Despite the fact that we're going to miss lunch because all three of us have to go up beyond the gorge to the far side of the mountain to deal with ongoing issues with the clearing operation over there, I don't think anyone has an appetite.

It's impossible to think about eating after what happened this morning, when I'm sitting here looking at her like this.

Lucky sits in her chair next to me at Killian's table with a cup of hot tea in front of her, grasped between her hands as tightly as she had clutched that gun this morning.

Christ.

I scrub my hands over my face and take a sip of my coffee, trying to shake off the last vestiges of that fear that soared through me when I heard Connor call out my name and got to the top of the steps and saw through the filtering morning light that Lucky had a weapon pointed at him.

The true terror I saw in her gaze, that I felt in her body when I took the gun from her and held her, was enough to convince me that maybe letting her come to me and talk when she's ready isn't an option.

Not if she's carrying a gun.

Not if it's that serious.

She doesn't seem like the type to have a weapon, let alone be willing to pull it, unless she believed there was a very real threat. And I can already tell Killian and Connor will have a million questions once they get me alone.

Rightfully so.

I have a million of my own for the woman beside me.

Willow takes her seat at the table, setting down the final plate of food, and smiles, completely in the dark about what went down this morning. Though, just because she wasn't given any details doesn't mean she's clueless. She knows us all well enough that she can sense something happened even though we didn't tell her about it.

Connor went straight to Killian before we came over, but there was no way he was about to throw the situation we faced this morning at her without more information.

None of us will.

There isn't any point in getting Willow worried or worked up when we don't know what brought on that reaction from Lucky.

Willow looks at all of us and at our empty plates. "Why isn't anyone eating?"

She raises her dark brows, and we all clear our throats awkwardly and reach forward to pile our plates with pancakes, bacon, eggs, and sausage.

Killian leans over and presses a kiss to her cheek with a smile. "Thanks, Honeybee, this looks great."

It does.

And any other morning, we would have already dug into it and half-cleaned our plates by now.

Which is exactly what Willow does because we all know Niall will be awake soon and she'll lose the opportunity to eat without a baby on her hip. She chews a few bites as the rest of us force ourselves to do the same—except Lucky, who continues to sit motionless, as if in a trance. Willow watches her for a moment. "So, are you coming into the shop again today?"

Lucky doesn't respond, just stares down into her cup of tea.

I clear my throat, sliding my hand onto her thigh and squeezing gently. "Lucky?"

She glances up at me, and I incline my head toward Willow.

Lucky's blue eyes widen, then move over to her. "Oh, sorry, what did you say?"

Willow offers her a confused look laced with concern. "Um, I asked if you were going to come in and help today."

Shit.

I hadn't even thought about today.

With us gone up the mountain, that would leave Lucky here alone at the cabin on the unfamiliar homestead, but she likely planned to go into town and help Willow today—which probably isn't a good idea given how she reacted to the sheriff yesterday and after what happened this morning.

Willow's gaze cuts over to me, as does Lucky's, but I honestly don't know how to respond to Willow's question.

Without knowing what's going on with Lucky, none of the options sound particularly appealing. I would much rather bring her with me up the mountain, to keep her near me, but that is the last place in the world I want her to ever set foot.

I don't want the evilness that permeates that whole area to taint anything about Lucky.

She'll be better off here, at my place, with Gizmo to keep her company until Willow or I can get back and be with her. "I don't think—"

Lucky holds up her hand to stop me before I can fully voice my objection. "Yes. If you want me there, I'd love to come help at the shop."

I bite back my instinct to intervene, to object on her behalf, but she gives me a pleading look not to say anything. She doesn't want Willow to know what happened any more than we do. Instead, I force myself to take a few bites, even though I'm not hungry, because Willow is watching and she already suspects something is going on that we aren't revealing to her.

Killian and Connor do the same while peeking at Lucky out of the corners of their eyes.

Lucky hasn't attempted to put any food on her plate, but forcing the issue isn't going to get me anywhere. After what she went through less than an hour ago, I can't blame her for not having any appetite, but worry for her gnaws at my empty gut.

"Are you hungry?" She looks over at me and shakes her head, and I push back my chair. "Then why don't I walk you around and show you the rest of the homestead before Willow is ready to leave?"

Willow's brow furrows, and she gives me a questioning look, but I return one that tells her not to ask. She lets it go— for now—returning to eating while keeping one eye on us.

I reach out for Lucky's hand, and she slides it into mine, rising from her seat. She's still trembling, though the worst of it has subsided. If it hadn't, I never would have brought her here with the family. But showing her that everything was fine, that Connor wasn't angry and that things were normal, seemed like a good idea at the time.

Now, I'm not so sure.

Lucky lets me lead her out of the cabin and onto the front porch. I usher her forward as I close the door behind us with a click.

Before I can say anything, she releases a long, shaky breath. With her back to me, I can't see her face, and she doesn't turn toward me. "I'm so sorry."

I step up behind her and wrap my arms around waist, pressing a kiss to the side of her neck. "Stop apologizing. I just want to make sure you're okay. Do you really want to go to the shop today? There's no reason you have to be there. You can stay at my place. I have to go up the far side of the mountain with Killian and Connor all day, otherwise I'd stay with you."

She doesn't say anything, just leans into me slightly, staring out at the sun rising over the mountain, sending long fingers of pinkish-orange light reaching across the clearing through the morning mist toward where the cabin stands.

It's one of those perfect mountain mornings, the ones that draw tourists up here and make people stay forever.

I peek at Lucky's face and see her chewing on her bottom lip again, her hands twisting in front of her nervously. Capturing them with mine, I press them against her stomach. "Lucky?"

She turns her head slightly toward me, peeking at me out of the corner of her eye. "I want to go. I need to do something, not sit around here. I'll be okay there. With the paper on the windows, it's closed off. There aren't customers coming in or anything like that." She offers a half-smile. "And being around Willow and Niall is nice."

I grin at her. "Yeah, it is." Something about seeing them, his innocence and her absolute joy around him is enough to make even the shittiest of days better. "Are you going to take Giz with you?"

She nods. "Willow said it was fine if I bring him."

This morning was the first glimpse I've gotten of the Gizmo she warned me about—snarling and snapping at Connor when he thought she was in trouble. That dog will defend her as fiercely as Willow will. Which makes a little of my concern over the coming day dissipate.

But she's already started the morning on an incredibly stressful note, and she needs time to fully come back down from that scare before I send her off to town again.

"Let me show you around the property."

She nods, and I take her hand in mine and lead her off the porch and across the clearing to the main barn. The weather-worn building has stood for at least a hundred years, its main wooden structure still almost as solid as the day it was built thanks to the incredible skills of the men who erected it.

Lucky examines each of the stalls and meets some of the

animals who aren't out in the pasture or the pens, then gawks at one of Killian's unfinished projects as we move into his workshop. "That's *incredible*."

I nod, staring at the half-carved mountain lion that appears to be climbing out of the massive log he's being formed from. "I know. Killian is far more of an artist than I am."

She shakes her head. "I don't believe that."

"Why? Because you saw a few shelves?"

Her shoulders rise and fall softly. "No. I can just tell. You have an artist's soul."

"I'm not exactly sure what that means, but I'll take it as a compliment."

A small smile graces her lips, lighting up her face for the first time today. "It is."

I take her hand in mine again, squeezing it gently as I push a stray strand of hair behind her ear. "Come on...I want to show you something."

We wander out of the barn and behind it, up the slope toward my cabin and the secondary, smaller barn there. I slide open the door and her breath catches. "Is this yours?"

I nod as she circles the partially finished rocking chair in the middle of my workshop.

"My God." Her gaze flicks up to meet mine. "It's *beautiful*."

"It's not finished yet."

Because I haven't been able to do it.

I made some progress the other day when I woke from the nightmare and needed to do something with my hands, but the intervening conversation with Killian had snuffed out my ability to focus on it without all those horrible visions returning.

"What are you going to do with it when it is?" She raises a brow. "Sell it?"

I shake my head. "I'm not sure yet. It's...complicated."

An understatement if there ever was one...

Her brow furrows as she trails her fingers over the partially sanded wood. "A chair is complicated?"

I lean back against my workbench. "That one is."

"Why?"

Crossing my arms over my chest, I watch her as she studies it. Willow's story isn't mine to tell, and I don't want to scare Lucky any more than she already is by telling her what happened here, or who perpetrated it.

"Lots of history in that wood."

It's all I say, but she seems to accept it with a nod.

"Well, whoever ends up with it will be very lucky."

"Come on." I push off the workbench and hold out my hand. "Let me show you the fire pit."

"Ooh, that sounds fun."

I lead her back down the slope toward the far side of the clearing, away from the buildings. "We spend a lot of time out there in the evenings, especially during the summer."

"Doing what?"

"Drinking, talking, staring up at the stars."

She glances up at the blue sky just starting to lighten with the coming of morning. "I've never seen as many as I did up here last night."

"I know. It's like you're at the center of the galaxy and it's spread out around you, completely enveloping you."

Lucky nods, keeping her head tipped back as if she can still see all of them even though they've almost all winked out until later tonight. "That's exactly what it's like."

"It makes you feel incredibly small."

She lowers her gaze to meet mine. "Is that a bad thing?"

I shake my head. "Not really. At times, I wish I could disappear into them."

Her footsteps falter, and she pulls me to a stop. "You don't mean that."

I hadn't meant to say it, but now that it's out there, I don't know how to take it back. "There are a lot of things you don't know, Lucky. About me. About my family."

She tilts her head slightly. "Does any of it change who you are?" Her hand rests directly over my heart. "In here?"

I want to say "no" so badly, but I just don't know anymore.

Because it's definitely changed me.

I offer a slight shrug and she leans in, feathering her lips across mine.

"I don't believe it could."

Her faith in me is completely unwarranted at this point, but I let it soak in, let it soothe some of my frayed edges as I lead her toward the fire pit.

Maybe one day I'll tell her everything.

Maybe one day she'll learn my deepest, darkest secrets.

But that day is definitely not today.

12

LUCKY

The constant clicking of Raven's fingers against the keyboard mixes with the music playing from Willow's phone to fill the space as we work. I glance over at Willow's best friend, who has her head dipped toward her computer screen where she sits at the display case counter beside the register. She's deeply engrossed in whatever she's working on and doesn't seem to be paying us any attention.

Neither is Giz, who has curled up on an old blanket Willow brought in for him from the truck when we came into the shop.

I lean in toward Willow so Raven doesn't hear me. "Doesn't that incessant clicking ever get on your nerves?"

Willow snorts and hands me another candle to slap a label on. "Yes. Which is why I don't normally sit with her while she works. Most of the time, she's at Claire's."

"The bakery?"

Nodding, she continues organizing the candles she pulls from the boxes brought down from the homestead. "She used to work here." She spreads her hand out. "But Old Man Murray wanted to retire, and he shut down the paper. She lives above the bakery so she kind of took up residence at the corner table there."

I glance again at Raven, whose brow is furrowed, blond hair falling over her shoulders as she leans into her computer, her lips pressed together in deep contemplation about something.

"Then why is she *here* now?"

Willow laughs. "That's a good question." She tips her head toward her friend. "Raven, why *are* you here since you're not helping?"

Raven drags her gaze off the computer screen and scowls at her. "I *will* help. I'm just busy at the moment."

"That's what you've been saying all day."

It's true.

She has been.

In the few hours since we came down the mountain and started digging into the boxes of product Willow had readied for the store, Raven has barely moved from her spot at that counter, and certainly hasn't helped with anything other than occasionally picking up the baby out of the playpen we moved out here while he was awake. Now that he's napping in the office, she's dived right back into her work as if we don't even exist in the same space.

"And what is it you *do*, exactly, Raven? I know this place used to be a newspaper..."

Raven nods, blowing hair off her forehead. "I was a reporter. The *only* reporter who worked with Murray. But when he shut down the paper, I became a freelancer."

"So, what does that mean?"

She shrugs. "I research and write news articles for papers and websites all around the world on a bunch of different topics. And I also have my own social media page where I post important news about McBride Mountain since we lost the only real source of information for everyone."

Willow elbows me. "What she means is, it's a gossip column."

Raven gapes at her. "It is not!"

"Tell that to the McBrides." Willow laughs, turning to me with an exasperated look. "My husband and his brothers aren't too keen on some of the things Raven posts."

My throat starts to tighten as some of what they've just told me starts to fall into place in my head. "What sort of things does she post?"

Raven sighs. "Only information everybody in town needs to know."

Willow rolls her eyes. "She has definitely posted some very unflattering articles about Killian and Connor over the years."

Well, that's better than what I was imagining...

For someone worried about staying under the radar and anonymous, hanging out with the small-town gossip columnist who is likely constantly looking for juicy, sordid details to post isn't the smartest idea.

Right now, any excuse to move the potential topic of conversation away from me is one I want to latch onto. Plus, being able to learn anything about the man I'm losing my heart to and his family is too good an opportunity to pass up.

"Really?" I haven't really spent much time with them other than pulling the gun on Connor and the awkward breakfast, but there wasn't anything that would have caused me any concern during our brief interactions. "They seem nice."

Raven barks out a laugh, her green eyes flashing with humor. "Yeah, you don't know the McBrides." Her gaze cuts to Willow. "Killian can be a real asshole...and a grump and a half." Annoyance hardens her gaze. "And don't even get me started on Connor..."

Willow grabs my wrist. "*Please* don't get her started on Connor, or we'll have to hear it for hours, literally an all-day dissertation, about what a dick he is."

I sit back on my haunches, considering them. "I...have a really hard time believing that."

Liam has been nothing but sweet and kind to me. I can't imagine his brothers are much different people. Plus, I gave Connor the ultimate reason to show the negative side of his nature this morning, but instead, he cracked a joke and appeared to be more concerned than angry, even with a gun pointed at him. Killian obviously knew what happened during breakfast, but he only seemed to be worried, not mad.

Willow grins at me. "That's only because you've been spending time with Liam, and the youngest McBride is a completely different story."

"How so?"

She keeps digging through boxes, arranging the candles in piles for me to price while we talk. "I've known the McBrides since I was a child, and Liam has always been the most level-headed, the calmest, and the one who pushes his brothers and everyone else to do the right thing and to think logically. He's always lifting everyone's spirits and in a good mood." Her smile falters. "Or, at least, he *was*..."

"Willow..." Raven issues the admonishment, giving her best friend a look that tells her to shut up. "Stop."

"What do you mean he *was*?"

Willow swallows thickly and pushes to her feet, walking over to the shelves, and toys with the candles already set there nervously. "Oh, forget I said anything."

"No, please."

Whatever it is seems serious—serious enough that Raven doesn't want Willow to say anything.

They seem to know the McBrides better than anyone on the mountain, and if there is something I need to know about Liam, these are the people to tell me.

Willow glances over her shoulder at me and then looks at

her best friend. Her lips twist slightly as she considers my request. "Are you and he...you know..."

Shit.

It shouldn't be awkward—discussing my *situation* with Liam McBride—since we're all adults here. But they both seem unnerved by whatever we're not talking about, and whether I'm involved with Liam may or may not be the dealbreaker in getting this information.

I clear my throat. "Umm, I don't really know what we are right now, but I guess, yeah?"

We are *something.*

Last night wasn't just about sex. Liam said things and made promises that lead me to believe that he wants something more. But I also know I can't give him that, which leaves me in a very precarious position, especially talking to his sister-in-law.

She returns to the boxes and kneels next to me. "The last year has been really hard on him."

"How come?"

"Well..."

Raven clears her throat. "Should you *really* be telling her this?"

I raise a brow, looking between the two of them. "If there's something I need to know, then please tell me. I don't like surprises, and I'm not sure I could handle a bad one right now."

They continue to stare each other down until Willow finally throws up her hands. "Oh, come on, Rave! She's going to find out eventually."

Raven glares at her. "Maybe she should find out from *him.*"

"I have every right to tell her. It's my story just as much as it is his."

My chest tightens, that dull ache that appears whenever a situation gets a little too real threatening to steal my breath. "What is?"

Willow glances toward the back office, listening to see if

Niall's awake. Only the sound of the music still playing from her phone fills the shop. Once she's confident he's solidly sleeping, she takes a deep inhale, like she's bracing herself for what she has to say. "So, about two years ago, I was kidnapped."

The hairs on the back of my neck stand up, goosebumps breaking out over my skin as my body reacts to her words the same way my mind does.

Disbelief.

"*What?*"

Raven's typing has stopped, but that damn music fills the silence as Willow gathers what she wants to say, averting her gaze to the stacks of jars on the floor beside her.

"A man who lived high up on the far side of the mountain, well away from town, who had some very serious mental problems, had kind of a break from reality. He found me on the road after my car broke down and thought I was his wife who had left him decades ago and took their son with her. He brought me back to his cabin and…" She shudders a little bit, her hand tightening on the box lid, like she needs something to ground her. "And some things happened. I was newly pregnant when he took me, and I gave birth to Niall while I was up there."

"Oh, my God…"

Acid crawls up my throat, my stomach churning violently.

"Killian had no idea." She inhales sharply, then releases it slowly. "We had an argument, and he thought I left town. Then he and his brothers found me in the river right after Memorial Day last year. I was almost dead, and I had no memory of where I'd been for the previous year."

My throat starts to tighten, tears and horror at what must have happened to her threatening to break my ability to keep myself together.

Willow shakes her head. "I didn't know what had happened to me and didn't even remember having a baby. It took a while for those memories to come back, and some I wish hadn't, but once we figured it all out, we went back up the mountain to where I'd been held and found the man who did it."

I hold my breath, waiting for her to continue the story. "What happened?"

She swallows thickly. "Well, Killian almost killed him."

That doesn't surprise me in the least.

The McBride brothers don't seem like the type to let anyone who hurt the people they love get away with it.

"And"—she glances at Raven before she finishes—"we discovered that the man who took me was Liam's biological father."

What the hell?

I stare at her with my mouth open, trying to process what she just told me. "Wh-how? I...I don't understand."

Willow locks her gray gaze with mine, sympathy swimming in it. "His birth mother, Bobbie, took him when he was a baby and fled from Earl, who was abusive to her. She left Liam—"

I complete the sentence for her as everything clicks into place. "On Connie McBride's doorstep."

She nods. "And then, eventually, Earl caught up with her. He killed her. Never knowing what happened to the baby."

Oh, my God.

"And Liam just learned all of this?"

She nods. "We all did. Earl always kept to himself. We would see him occasionally in town, maybe every couple months. No one ever put two and two together, and he never saw Liam, never suspected. None of us did. Until we saw them together that day, and there was no denying it once they were together in front of us."

Oh, my God.

Suddenly, the way Liam reacted every time we talked about his family and his history makes sense. What he said to me last night about there being things I didn't know, about there being secrets...

This is what he was referencing.

This is what he didn't want to tell me—because he was scared about how I would react.

"Holy shit."

Willow presses her lips together for a moment, thinking about something. "So, ever since then, things have been rough for him. He doesn't want to talk about it. With any of us. Not even me. I think he feels responsible for what his father did."

"What? But that doesn't make any sense. He didn't even know him."

"That's what we've all been telling him, but he's kind of shut down. Shut all of us out. No one knows what to do about it. Honestly..." She offers me a half smile. "You're the first person who seems to have made him laugh, or actually gotten through to him, in almost a year."

Raven nods. "It's been hard...watching him change like that. He's just not himself anymore."

"Wow...I...had no idea."

And now that I do know, it changes everything.

LIAM

The familiar weight of the axe in my hands as it flies through the air and the reverberation up the handle when I slam the head into the tree trunk do little to relieve the tension that's permeating my body.

If anything, my normal source of release—coming out onto the mountain and obliterating something with steel—seems to be ramping me up more. Making every muscle even tighter, especially those squeezing my chest, creating a permanent ache there.

Maybe because of where I'm doing it.

The darkest place on the mountain.

Where the worst of humanity destroyed so much—where my father did.

I work the axe head free of the wood, then throw it back and slam it in again, repeating the same movement I've been doing for the last thirty minutes, already onto my second massive red spruce.

Thankfully, there's an entire forest of them up here for me to work out my frustration on because God knows I'm going to need hours at this to have *any* hope of getting some of these emotions out.

And it still won't be enough.

There's too much uncertainty.

Too much to process.

So many conflicting feelings that war inside me hard enough to tear me apart...

Footsteps crunch over twigs and leaves behind me, making me tighten my grip on the axe.

That didn't last very long...

I knew they'd find me eventually. The sound of my afternoon activity echoes across the mountain, and it led them *right* to me. I would have preferred more time —to try to work through this—physically and mentally. To gather my thoughts the only way I know how to. But I can't hide from them forever. I never could.

"You know we have machines that can do that now." Connor's sarcastic comment floats between the trees, laced with humor as well as an older brother's concern. "A lot faster, too."

No shit.

I swing again, driving the axe head even deeper into the wood before I turn to face him, wiping sweat from my brow.

My hands, shoulders, and back ache from the exertion, but it's the good kind. The kind my body craves. The kind that reminds me I'm still alive despite everything that's been happening.

It brings me back to the basics—Mom showing me how to use an axe. Teaching me how to properly fell a tree. Working with her, Killian, and Connor on the mountain with her employees from the yard. Learning the business and how to protect the mountain while only taking what we absolutely need from it.

Those were simpler times.

I didn't question who I was or why I was here.

I didn't worry about anything but my school work and having fun with my brothers.

I didn't have nightmares about this place.

Connor leans against a tree a few yards away, Killian standing beside him with his arms crossed over his chest, looking every bit the big brother with something to say.

For as stoically quiet he often is, lately, he's been pushing harder for me to talk about the very things I don't want to. And that now includes Lucky and what happened this morning.

Killian assesses me, his blue eyes hard and narrowed. "We've been looking for you."

I wondered how long it would take them to realize I had walked away from the site, from the meeting with the foreman who had a laundry list of issues that needed our attention.

They were deep in discussions I thought would keep them distracted longer, but apparently, I was sorely mistaken.

The guilt at shirking my responsibilities to come out here to do *this* starts to eke its way in, but I just couldn't be up there anymore, couldn't stand being in the place where Willow was held and where I saw *him* for the first—and last—time.

Part of me thinks Killian can only tolerate it because it helps remind him that it's over for her, for them. Because they have each other. They have their family. They have the confidence of what their future holds to help them work through the pain of the past.

But for me, all I see is my father's face.

All I feel there are his crimes.

Those nightmares become *real* up here.

So does my fear.

I give Killian and Connor my back again and return to demolishing the tree.

Killian releases a heavy sigh loud enough for me to hear over my own labored breathing and the slam of metal into the wood. Only a few more shots and this one will come down, and then I'll start on another, and another, until I work all this out.

"Are we going to talk about this?"

I glare at Connor over my shoulder.

I've been avoiding this conversation about Lucky as much as I have been the ones about my father, and I only managed to this long today because I drove up here in my truck and they followed in Killian's. If we had all been riding together, it would have been hours to get up to this site of them peppering me with questions I don't have answers for.

There are no answers.

I haven't been able to stop thinking about it since I found Lucky standing there with that gun, but I don't know *why* she had it or what is going on with her. I'm in the dark about the woman I slept with last night. A woman I really barely know even though everything in me *wants* to know everything.

She took me into her body and gave me the best night of my life, but she's still keeping me locked out of what's most important.

That hurts.

And I don't want to admit to them that she's shut down all my attempts to get the truth from her.

But I also can't ignore them.

They're not going away until we talk.

Nor should they.

This situation has become untenable in only one night, and my plan to give her space and time evaporated the moment I saw that gun pointed at Connor.

I finally release a resigned sigh, give the tree a final swing, and watch as it topples away from us, exactly as I expertly directed it. It crashes into the forest floor, releasing a plume of debris, and I drape my axe over my shoulder and walk toward my brothers.

"I don't know why she has a gun. And I don't know why she pulled it."

Killian snorts. "Well, I wasn't there, but I think we can surmise she didn't know it was Connor coming in." He glances at him. "Unless you're such an asshole that your reputation preceded you."

"Ha. Ha. Very funny." Connor pushes off the tree. "What *do* you know?"

I sigh, set the axe down on the ground and wipe the sweat from my brow again.

Not enough.

It's the real answer—that I don't nearly enough about the woman I'm falling so fucking hard for.

"That she's running from something. Maybe someone. And it has her scared."

A sympathetic look crosses both of their gazes, but I see the worry there, too. The deep concern over what transpired even as Killian jokes about it in an attempt to lighten the dark mood hanging around me and the mountain.

"Lucky doesn't want to tell me." That frustration surges to the forefront again, tightening my fists at my sides and making my voice come out rough. Strained by my desire to help her. "She told me it was *safer* if I didn't know."

One of Killian's blond brows rises. "She used the word 'safer'?"

I nod, remembering the look in her eyes when she said it—both times.

Pure terror.

"Shit." He shoves a hand through his hair. "Well, that isn't good."

No, it isn't.

I clench my jaw, trying not to lash out with everything I've been thinking, all the horrible scenarios I've been imagining that might be threatening to her. "My thoughts exactly, but I don't know what to do about it. I can't force her to tell me."

Killian scowls. "Why the fuck not?"

I glower at him.

I would think by now that these two would understand that forcing someone to talk about something that they're not ready to only creates more problems instead of making the situation better.

If I push her on this, it might push her away.

I can't risk that.

"Look, I realize you like this girl." Killian locks his gaze with mine, doing his damnedest to use his "big brother" voice that used to put me in my place when we were younger. "But if there's something dangerous out there coming after her, we need to know about it. We need to understand why it might be coming to McBride Mountain and how to deal with it. I have a wife and a son at home who just went through something incredibly traumatic. I don't need any fucking surprises, Liam."

"You think I don't fucking know that?" I throw my hands up. "You think I don't understand every single fucking thing my father did to Willow? You think I don't picture it and see it in my head every minute of every day. You think I don't dream about it? Fuck, Killian, you don't have to remind me of the fucking obvious."

Shit.

The way they're looking at me, I know I've said too much.

Again.

But rather than going the icy, glacial blue it does when he's angry, Killian's gaze warms and softens, which is almost worse. "Is that why you won't talk to us? Is that why you've been avoiding me? And her?"

Fuck.

I pace away from them, into the forest, needing to move, needing to do something other than stand there under their scrutiny.

They follow, their footsteps slow and deliberate across the underbrush.

He gives me a moment to try to breathe and find my center before he speaks again. "I've said this before, but you know that nothing he did was your fault."

"Fuck." I whirl toward him. "Of course I know that, Killian, but it doesn't mean that I don't still feel guilty about it. That I don't still feel like...fuck"—I throw out my hands again—"like I don't know, like maybe part of whatever did that to him is inside me, too. That if he's capable of it, then maybe I am."

Connor narrows his dark gaze. "You can't be serious. You're about as different from Earl Byers as anyone on the planet. You don't hurt people, Liam. You protect them. You help them. That's who you've always been."

Killian nods. "That's what you did for me when we found Willow. You're the one who forced me to come clean with her and to face whatever happened head-on together. You made things possible for us. And finding out whose blood runs through your veins doesn't change that. You're a McBride."

Despite his best effort to reassure me, Killian's insistence doesn't help.

"That's what I keep trying to tell myself but..." I shake my head, trying to break free from the dark cloud that's encased it. "But it doesn't stop the nightmares."

Connor rubs the back of his neck, tilting his head as he considers me. "But *she* does?"

Shit.

Is it that obvious?

How much I've become attached to her?

That woman and that dog are the only things that have given me any semblance of peace in nine fucking months, and now that peace has been shattered by what I witnessed this morning. Whatever's going on with her, I can't allow her to keep it from me anymore because it isn't putting only me in danger, it's putting Willow, and Niall, and everyone else in the line of fire, too.

What if she had pulled that trigger when Connor walked in?

What if I hadn't been able to talk her down?

Fuck.

I bury my face in my hands.

"You have to talk to her." Connor's voice comes deep and level. "Now."

He isn't angry, even though he has every right to be.

He's just worried.

"I know. I know." I scrub my hands over my face. "I don't want to push her away. I don't want her to hate me for doing it and try to run."

Killian steps forward and claps me on the shoulder. "If she runs, you'll just have to go after her."

13

LIAM

The moment I walk through the cabin door, the stress and anxiety that had drowned me all day up on the mountain evaporates, freeing me to take a deep breath for the first time in hours. And it isn't just because I don't have my brothers up my ass anymore.

It's because walking into this cabin, it finally feels like a home, like somewhere I have a life and a future.

And it's all because of who is waiting here for me, the warmth and presence that permeates the space that's all Lucky. That light eucalyptus scent that clings to her fills the air, along with something else that makes my stomach rumble.

She's cooking.

Gizmo bolts from where he stands near her feet in the kitchen toward the front door, barking and jumping, trying to get up into my arms. Grinning, I nudge the door closed behind me and scoop him up, allowing him to excitedly lick at my face.

It's a great way to be greeted.

So much better than coming home to an empty cabin.

"Hey, buddy." I scratch between his ears. "Did you have a good day?"

"I did..."

I glance up at Lucky where she leans against one of the hand-hewn beams that supports the loft above the kitchen. Her gray t-shirt hangs off her shoulder, exposing her collarbone and the fact that she's not wearing a bra. Casual. Relaxed. She looks *happy*. "How was yours?"

A lot fucking better now...

Allowing my gaze to rake over her further, I imagine a million ways I would love to spend tonight with her—most of them involving my head between her legs or my cock buried inside her.

I want to keep that contented look on her face, allow her to stay so relaxed, but this reprieve is only temporary, knowing what I have to do.

Even before talking with Killian and Connor, I knew. I just didn't want to accept it because the fallout may be something I can't fix.

Lucky isn't a woman you push unless you want to get pushed back. And pushing her could make her grab her backpack and this little dog and hit the road again.

That isn't an option.

But neither is ignoring what happened this morning and pretending it didn't change everything.

I set Gizmo down and release a heavy sigh, reaching down to take off my boots and set them beside her shoes near the door. "Honestly?"

She raises a brow, concern suddenly darkening her eyes. "Of course."

A little humorless laugh falls from my lips. "It was kind of shitty."

"How come?"

I make my way past the couch, forcing myself not to glance

down to the end table where the gun sat until Connor came and took it away before we left to drive up the mountain, and stop in front of her, allowing my eyes to roam over her.

She appears calm, not at all the same woman who was holding a gun on Connor this morning or trembling uncontrollably in my arms on Killian's porch. So, apparently sending her off to work with Willow this morning was a good idea, despite my reservations about it.

"I'd really rather not talk about it."

None of that matters.

My fears, my struggles, my nightmares are mine to deal with.

What does matter is finding out why she's so scared so I can do everything in my power to make sure it never touches her.

She nods slowly, chewing on her bottom lip, almost as if she's trying to force herself not to ask more questions even though she clearly wants to.

"Something in here smells good."

Definitely her, but whatever she's cooking, too.

Lucky glances over her shoulder, and her cheeks redden slightly. "So, you don't know me well enough to know this yet, but I'm not any better at being in the kitchen than I am taking orders and delivering them."

I grin at her and how fucking adorable she is when she's shy and embarrassed. "I'm pretty hopeless myself, which is why we eat at Killian's most of the time. Willow's a pretty good cook."

She nods. "I figured that after breakfast."

"What are you making?"

"Grilled cheese and tomato soup."

I chuckle lightly. "Honestly, that sounds pretty incredible."

It was always one of my favorites when Mom made it. Comfort food. And I could really use the comfort tonight.

I close the distance between us and pull her away from the beam, pressing my lips against her cheek. "I missed you today."

She smiles into my neck, her warm breath fanning my skin and making heat flare over it. "Did you?"

I pull back and nod, taking her face in my hands and kissing her lightly. "I was worried all day."

Maybe I shouldn't have admitted that.

Lucky doesn't seem to *want* my concern. She wants to act like everything is fine, hoping that I'll move on from wanting to know more about the things she won't tell me.

But I don't want to hold back from this woman.

Not about anything.

Certainly not about the way I feel about her.

She swallows thickly, still looking up at me with something in her eyes I can't entirely place.

"Bluebell, why are you looking at me like that?"

Her brow furrows. "Like what?"

"Like you have something you want to say."

She chews on her lip again, and I reach up and tug it free with my thumb.

"You have to stop doing that."

"Why?"

A low rumbling growl vibrates in my chest. "Because every time you do, it makes me want to bend you over and fuck you. Hard."

"Jesus." Her cheeks redden even deeper, and she shakes her head. "You have a filthy mouth."

I chuckle. "I have two older brothers."

She laughs softly, nodding. "That's true." But her humor fades as her gaze dips down, then flicks back up. "The truth is, there *is* something I want to talk to you about."

My chest tightens uncomfortably, wondering if she is finally going to tell me the very thing I've been dreading asking since I walked in. Knowing it's likely to ruin this light, happy mood. "Okay, but let's eat first."

Just thirty minutes to enjoy her company and the meal she prepared and pretend nothing else exists.

She pulls out of my hold and slips back into the kitchen, walking over to the small counter and stove, where I see she's already prepared one sandwich and has a second one ready to go. She sets it down in the frying pan, and the butter on the bread immediately sizzles.

I pull the lid off the pot and inhale the steam from the soup. "God, I didn't realize how hungry I was."

"Did you eat after breakfast?"

Shaking my head, I return the lid and lean against the counter. "No."

"Why not?"

She eyes me, waiting for my response, and I am not about to tell her that I felt nauseated all day due to the combination of worrying about her and being up beyond the gorge.

"I kinda lost my appetite."

Her back stiffens. "Because of what happened this morning?"

I hear the hesitation in her voice, the twinge of guilt, and I shake my head immediately, unwilling to let her think she's the reason for my mood.

"No. Because of something you don't need to worry about."

That lip disappears beneath her teeth again, and I watch as she realizes she did it and releases it with a quick glance my direction. I can't help but grin at her, and she flips the sandwich, one side now golden brown and perfect, just like the woman in front of me is.

She glances down and swallows thickly. "Was it...because you were up on the far side of the mountain beyond the gorge?"

Hell.

The fact that she used that phrase immediately stiffens my spine. Because she's been talking to someone. "Why do you ask?"

She gives me a hesitant look. "Fuck. Okay, umm, so Willow told me some things today."

Shit.

I swallow through my heart lodged in my throat. "What did she tell you?"

Her nervous glance and the way she's trying to focus on the sandwich instead of look at me tells me exactly what she's going to say before she even opens her mouth again. "She told me about what happened last year. To her and Niall." She looks up at me. "And you."

People often talk about wishing they could disappear, that they want to crawl into a hole and never come out. I never really knew what they meant until the last several months. And standing here looking at her now has amplified it by a thousand.

I've never felt so exposed, so naked while completely clothed as I do knowing *she* knows who I am. What I am.

"Is that what you were alluding to last night that you didn't want to tell me?"

I nod slowly. "Yes."

She snags the sandwich out of the pan and slides it onto a plate, then turns off the burner and twists to face me, resting her hip against the counter. "But you don't want to talk about it."

Fuck no.

Not with her.

Not with anyone.

I shake my head. "No."

"Why not?"

"Why do you think?"

She glances down at her bare feet, then back up at me. "Because you think it's going to scare me."

I shake my head. "No, because it scares *me*."

LUCKY

I can hear how much he means it, in his words, how his voice wavers, and I step forward, closing the distance between us, and wrap my arms around him, burying my face in his chest.

"You have absolutely no reason to be scared, Liam."

He reaches up and cups the back of my head, running his fingers through my hair while the other hand settles around my waist, holding me to him tightly. A few moments pass as he presses his lips to the top of my hair, breathing me in, like somehow the scent of my shampoo calms him. "Why do you say that?"

"Because you're the kindest person I've ever met. That man was a sperm donor. Nothing more. What's in your blood doesn't make you who you are; the people around you do. And you've been surrounded by people who have loved you your entire life, who taught you right from wrong, who turned you into this incredible person."

He chuckles lightly, his chest vibrating beneath my ear. "You barely know me, Bluebell."

I lift my head and look up at him. The way his green eyes seem to twinkle with a combination of fear and affection squeezes my heart almost painfully. "I know enough."

"I'm glad you say that because I talked to my brothers today."

My back stiffens, my shoulders tensing in his hold. "About what?"

He twists a lock of my hair around his finger. "About what happened this morning. I know I told you I wouldn't push you to tell me what all of this is about—what happened to you and why you're here." His gaze holds mine immobile even when I want to look away from the intensity there. "But I can't protect you if I don't know, and I can't risk Willow and Niall's safety if something's going to come looking for you that could be dangerous for all of us." He drops my hair and grazes his finger-tips across my cheek. "I don't want to push you. I don't want to force you to talk about something you're not ready to. But I don't know how much more time I can give you."

I swallow through the burn in my throat that threatens tears.

Because I know he's right.

"I could just go."

His eyes darken, and I thought I knew what his reaction would be before I said the words. It surprises me when he dips his head and presses his lips to mine, inhaling all of my oxygen and becoming my sole focus for a few moments. Long enough that my breath is gone by the time he pulls away from the kiss that felt an awful lot like he was staking a claim.

"If you think I'm going to let you leave McBride Mountain, you're fucking crazy, woman."

Maybe I *am* crazy for ever getting involved with him. For ever thinking I could get away with having a few days, or hell, maybe even a week or two, with this man and then walk away later with my heart intact.

We've only spent one night together, and I'm already hope-lessly falling for him in a bad way. I'm in deep, and there is no hope of finding a way out of it.

All that's left is to open myself up, to completely come clean. To let him see *all* of me and all the reasons I didn't want to stay. "Can I tell you tomorrow?"

He trails his fingers over my cheek and nose like he's counting my freckles. "Why?"

"Because I just want one more night where you don't look at me differently."

His mossy gaze softens. "I already told you, Lucky, I'm not

afraid of anything in your past. It's not going to change anything between us."

"You say that now, but—"

"No buts." He shakes his head. "Will it make you feel better if we do it in the morning?"

I nod.

"Okay." He feathers his lips across my forehead. "Let's eat and go to bed, and in the morning, I'll fuck you...and then we can talk."

Despite the seriousness of the situation, a chuckle climbs up my throat. "That sounds like a good plan."

He grins at me. "I thought so." His stomach rumbles, and he laughs. "Now let's eat. It smells incredible." Dipping his head, he kisses the side of my neck, up to my ear. "And then, when I'm done with dinner, you'll be my dessert."

Fuck.

My knees wobble for a second, my pussy clenching at the promise in his words, and suddenly, it doesn't seem so important to have dinner. But I know he's been out all day and barely touched his breakfast, so the needs of my pulsing body will just have to wait.

I squeeze my thighs together to dull the ache there and try to pull away from him, but he holds me steady. "What is it?"

"You think I didn't feel that?"

"Feel what?"

"The way your body just twitched."

Shit.

Heat floods my cheeks.

He kisses my earlobe and gently pulls it between his teeth, grazing them along the edge, sending a shudder through me. One hand softly brushes across my chest, cupping my breast, and even through my bra, my hyper-sensitive nipples twinge as he flicks his thumb across them.

"Maybe I'll have an appetizer."

Fuck.

He slides his hands down, deftly unbuttons my jeans, and slips his palm inside until his fingers find my already slick pussy. I twitch as he brushes them there, and he groans in my ear.

"Fucking hell, woman. Have you been like this all day?"

I nod my head against his chest, shifting restlessly in his hold on me, seeking more friction, and his fingers easily glide through my slick core, spreading my arousal over my clit in a way that makes my entire body pulse.

"Tell me what you were thinking about."

Fuck, is he serious?

I release a little noise that I don't think I've ever heard from myself before as he slides a finger into me.

It's embarrassing how many times I thought about being with him today. How often my body heated and shuddered remembering his touch and how it felt to have his cock inside me. Like I am right now.

I clench around him, and he groans his approval and kisses his way across my cheek to my lips.

"Tell me, Lucky. What were you thinking about that got you this wet?"

A whimper slips from my lips as I shift again, and he pulls his finger out until just the tip stays inside, then plunges it in again.

"I was thinking about"—I shiver—"last night."

"Yeah?" His warm breath flutters over my face. "What part?"

"When I was riding you..."

He grins against my lips. "Did you like that?"

I nod, and my body pulses as the memory flares even brighter.

"Want me to let you do it again?"

He slides his thumb up across my clit and rolls it there as he plunges his finger slowly in and out of me. I groan and nod, dropping my face to his chest again.

"What else would you like me to do?"

Fuck.

"You have to tell me, Bluebell, because you know I don't have any fucking idea what I'm doing."

I chuckle at that and pull my head back to look up at him. "Oh, yes you do. You did just fine."

He raises a brow, his hand stilling, much to my dismay. "Fine? That definitely isn't the word a man wants to hear from a woman describing having sex with him."

Shit.

I laugh and shake my head. "That isn't what I meant. I meant..." I push up on my toes so I can kiss him again, and he continues moving his hand between my legs in a way that has heat spreading through the rest of my core and into my limbs, making my knees tremble, barely capable of holding me up. "What I meant was you don't have anything to worry about. Last night was incredible."

"Mmm." He kisses me gently. Nothing more than a tease. "So, tell me what you want me to do to you tonight."

A thousand carnal possibilities race through my head, making me more frantic. I move against his hand, practically fucking it as he slides another finger into me, stretching me.

I groan. "I want you to finish me off like this."

He grins. "Already on my to-do list."

"And then, after we eat"—he laughs slightly at my aside—"I want you to take me upstairs and bend me over the bed."

His eyes flare, and I feel his hard his cock twitch where my body is pressed to it. "That can definitely be arranged."

His thumb rolling over my clit moves faster and he presses down harder, the contact enough to finally make me detonate. My body convulses in his hold, but he clings to me, ensuring I stay upright through my orgasm.

I gasp, and he catches the sound with a deep kiss, sliding his tongue in along mine, groaning as my pussy clenches around his fingers and I come apart in his arms.

Fuck.

When I finally come back down, resting my forehead against his chest, he kisses the top of my head, then pulls his hand free and lifts it to his mouth, sliding his glistening fingers into it and licking them clean.

"The perfect appetizer."

14

LUCKY

W arm lips skate across the back of my neck, and the strong arm circling my waist tightens posses- sively. Liam tugs me flush to his body and groans, his chest vibrating against my back with that now familiar sound of his approval. His hard cock presses to my ass, the promise in the grind of his hips helping clear away the last cobwebs of sleep.

Hell...

This is the way to wake up.

Cocooned in this man's unyielding hold.

Drowning in his heat and inhaling his scent that seeps into my lungs with every breath.

Groaning, I arch back into him and let my eyes flutter open to find the first filtering morning sunlight streaming through the window. "Don't you have to get up and go help your brothers?"

He grumbles against my skin, shaking his head. "They can handle it on their own." His hand skates up and cups my bare breast, his calloused thumb slowly drifting across my nipple and sending a little zing of pleasure straight to my clit. "I'd much rather be here handling you."

Fuck.

When he says things like that to me, my entire body goes molten.

Especially when he's touching me like this...

The light brushes of his rough fingers over my breasts, his other hand sliding down between my legs, cupping me where I've already started to ache for him.

Again.

I dreaded waking up this morning and what it was going to mean—that I am going to have to come clean with him. The sun coming up means I am going to have to tell him *everything*. Every single sordid detail about my horrible mistake will see the light. But Liam found a way to ensure the morning wouldn't bring with it anxiety and fear. He ensured we could have one more precious moment together before everything changes.

His fingers find me slick and ready for him, and he nips at my ear playfully, slowly probing inside me. A needy hum tumbles from my lips as I roll back against him, the pleasure already spiking mingling with the memories of how he took me bent over the bed last night, exactly as I asked for.

How goddamn good it felt from that angle.

How untethered he became.

How fucking *hot* it was.

And I want it again.

Need *him* again.

Before everything goes to shit.

He grazes his teeth along the column of my neck, then trails his soft lips across the same skin, sending goosebumps spreading wildly in their wake. I rock my hips on his hand, and he grinds his palm around on my clit, sending me spiraling off into a breathless need that has me twitching in his hold.

"How do you want me, Lucky?"

His murmured words against my heated flesh take a second to register.

The answer is easy.

"*Every* way."

He chuckles low and darkly in that way that only seems to come out when we're tangled together like this, when he completely opens up to me and lets himself loose from all the silent things that constrain him. "I meant right now, Bluebell."

I slide my hand back between us and grasp his cock, gliding my thumb across the head and spreading the slick pre-cum. He trembles, and the feel of his body aligned with mine, the way he completely controls me in this position, makes me never want to move from it. "Just. Like. *This*."

His cock twitches in my hold, and I arch my hips, giving him better access. He pulls his hand from between my legs long enough to lift my thigh up and back, spreading me open for him so I can guide his length into me.

And he doesn't hesitate.

He drives in on a long, slow thrust that makes my breath catch.

"Fuck..." Liam murmurs the word along my shoulder before his teeth dig into the flesh there, and the sharp bite of pain makes me buck onto him, allowing him to slip that final half inch inside, until he's buried so deeply inside me that I'm not sure where I end and he begins. "So fucking good, Bluebell."

It is.

It sooo fucking is...

He kisses my neck and pulls his hips back to drive into me again, starting a slow, sensuous rhythm that has me bowing into him. His hand slides forward from my hip and his fingers find my clit again.

Ghosting over it.

A fleeting glance.

Playful teasing that has my pussy clenching.

I gasp at the featherlight touches, at the exquisite torture as he rolls his calloused fingertips across it expertly. Because even though he's new at this, he understands *me* and has almost since the moment we met.

What I want.

What I need.

Because he's taken the time the last few nights to learn. To ask. To find out exactly what will send me flying. And the long, slow thrust of his hips, his thick length spreading me open so completely like this, and the head of his cock hitting that perfect place deep inside me is sure to do just that this morning.

Unlike last night, this is a harried rush to find release.

This is a sensual assault designed to drive me to the brink and leave me dangling from the precipice only to reel me back in again. Release hangs in front of me, just out of reach as the tide of pleasure rushes over me, threatening to drag me under, but Liam keeps me buoyed, keeps me tethered to him in the here and now.

"Liam—" His name comes out on a harsh exhale, my breath catching as he hits exactly the right spot. "Fuck...I—"

My head spins, making it impossible to speak.

Impossible even to think...

"Tell me what you need." The low growled order against my ear makes me move on him more frantically. His grip tightens, fingers digging into my sweat-dampened flesh and twisting me even tighter. "Tell me, Bluebell."

"Harder." *Gasp.* "Faster."

He obliges, increasing his pace, taking it from the slow, sensuous glide that it was to a harsher rhythm, the slap of our flesh against each other now filling the loft. His fingers play over my clit faster, and he takes it between them and pinches, twisting it sharply.

I gasp and buck in his hold, but his hand there keeps me pressed on him, keeps his cock filling me.

Good. Fucking. God.

Clinging to the sheets and to him, I dig my nails into his forearm where his hand moves between my legs. Seeking for him to ground me so when my orgasm hits, I won't completely float away.

I clench around him on each retreat, allowing the head of his cock to drag inside me and catch, and his mouth moving over every inch of my skin he can reach is pure fucking torture when all I want is to kiss him. Twisting my head back, I seek his lips with mine, and he pushes up with his free arm enough to allow it.

His tongue tangles with mine, each of us warring for supremacy, even though we know he's in control.

Liam McBride is consuming me the way flames do the logs on the fire.

He has me pinned, has me prone, has me exactly where he wants me, but it's also exactly where I want to be.

In his arms.

In his bed like this.

Waking up every morning to his voice, his kiss, his breath fanning against my neck, and his strong arms wrapped around me.

My breath hitches, and he doesn't miss that.

He never misses anything.

He knows I'm getting close.

And given the frenetic way he's moving, so is he.

It doesn't take long before heat starts to spread out from where we're connected. Until his thrusts become harsher to match his labored breath.

Time seems to still in the split-second before I come, as I

feel all the places and ways we're connected deep in my soul. And when I finally give in to the release, he captures my scream, swallowing it down as he comes on a strangled groan, emptying himself inside me.

Our frenzied movements eventually slow, becoming a drowsy rocking of our bodies together until we both sag into the bed. His arm wrapped around me tightly. His still-hard cock twitching in my cunt. His entire being filling my heart.

It thuds wildly.

Struggling to find a normal beat when the rest of my body tingles and nerve-endings fire off randomly with spikes of pleasure.

Silence settles over the room, punctuated by the birds starting to wake outside the window.

And eventually, my racing heart starts to calm.

My lungs begin to feel like they're working properly.

Liam releases a long, shaky breath, then slowly withdraws from me and allows my leg to slide down onto the mattress, earning a little groan from both of us.

I immediately miss the heat of his body, the possessiveness of his hold. When he climbs from the bed, I roll toward him, reaching out. "Where are you going?"

His hooded gaze rakes over me, as if he's trying to memorize every single inch of me and how I look at this exact moment in time. Before I can say anything, he bends down and scoops me up in his arms, earning a little yelp from me as I loop mine around his neck.

"What are you doing?"

He nuzzles my sweat-slickened neck. "Taking you to shower."

Like he did last night after he thoroughly dirtied me up...

My skin tingles with the memories of how he washed me. Cleaned me. Worshipped me *again* and *again* under the continuous fall of steaming water.

And I know what he's doing.

He's drawing out these precious few moments we'll have together before everything changes.

I want to thank him for that, but I don't want to break the spell by even mentioning it. Instead, I kiss him as he reaches the top of the stairs and press my forehead to his. "Thank you."

"For what?"

"For being Liam McBride."

LIAM

By the time I'm done with Lucky in the shower, she can barely stand. Her legs are a quivering mess, and the taste of her release coats my tongue. Knowing I was the one who did this for her fills my chest with a warmth I never thought I'd feel again.

Pure fucking joy.

The kind I used to feel all the time—*before.*

Before my world went to shit.

Before what I thought I knew about myself vanished like the morning mist from the mountain.

But since this woman has walked into my life, all those feelings of being disconnected, of seeking answers and not being able to find them, seem to have shifted away from being my central focus to merely inconsequential threads in the bigger tapestry that has now placed Lucky front and center of the intricate, stunning design.

I hold her tightly to me as I turn off the water and snag a towel. Wrapping it around her, I ghost a kiss over her forehead, cling to her for one final moment. Breathe her in and enjoy the way she leans into me and stares up with half-lidded, sleepy eyes.

She offers me a tiny smile, but already I can see the darkness starting to creep into the edges of her vision, those sky-blue eyes of hers starting to shift to the stormy version with the reality of what's going to happen now.

I tried to distract her this morning, tried to cushion the fall that I know is coming for her by assuring her that it won't change anything between us, but the fear is still there.

On both our parts.

Whatever she's going to tell me must be bad.

Something that she's been dealing with on her own for a very long time.

Something she's never told anyone.

Opening up to me is going to be painful for her, even if she *wants* to, which I'm not entirely sure she does. I understand that all too well. I don't *want* to shut out Killian, Connor, Willow, and everyone else, but I've *had* to.

Self-preservation instinct to keep the pain at bay.

The only way I knew to keep the nightmares that haunted me from seeing the light of day, to wrangle those demons that wanted to control me.

And now I'm forcing her to face her own.

But she won't do it alone.

I wrap another towel around my waist, scoop her back up into my arms, and carry her out of the bathroom and up the stairs to the loft, setting her on her feet near the dresser so I can dry her thoroughly.

The sunlight flooding through the window now illuminates the rumpled bed, and she keeps her gaze locked on it, as if she can't bear to look at me right now and wants to focus on that spot and what we did there this morning.

I let her.

Taking my time rubbing the soft towel over her skin. Gently swiping away every last drop of water before I tug open the drawer where I put all of her clothes and grab a bra, underwear, a pair of stretchy pants, and a t-shirt to put on.

She doesn't have much, only a few sets of clothes that she could easily carry in her backpack, but that's going to change.

As soon as we have this conversation.

Once she realizes I'm not going anywhere and neither is she, we'll get her anything and everything she could ever want. I'll fill these drawers and this house with everything she's always dreamed of having when she was moving from foster home to foster home.

A place that's hers.

That's ours.

Gizmo lifts his head from where he lies on the chair and watches us as she slowly changes while I finish drying off. And her gaze immediately shifts back to the spot where we woke and then lost ourselves in each other.

I snag her brush from the top of the dresser and move behind her, slowly running it through her hair. She lets me take care of her silently, but the longer she goes without saying anything, the more worried I become about what's going on inside her head.

Where are you going in there, Lucky?

She's getting lost in the past, the same way I have so often lately.

That can be a very dangerous place.

Grabbing the towel, I gently dry her hair the best I can, letting the long blue locks dangle down her back. I drift my fingers through it. "Why blue?"

She startles slightly at my voice and glances over her shoulder at me. "What?"

"Why the blue hair?" I lean forward and kiss her cheek. "It suits you, I'm just curious."

Her eyes darken again, and she gives me a tight smile. "I had this stupid idea that the louder I was, the more people might actually *ignore* me. That they would pay more attention to my hair than my face."

"And you could be anonymous?"

She nods.

I clench my jaw, despising the fact that her beautiful hair is tied to something as awful as feeling like she needed to hide.

A woman like Lucky should never be in the shadows.

She deserves to live in the light that matches how brightly the rest of her glows.

I place a kiss on her temple. "Well, I love it. Don't change it unless you *want* to."

The smile she gives me now is a genuine one, but it doesn't quite reach her eyes. They follow me, filled with trepidation, as I tug on a clean pair of jeans and a t-shirt, then grab the towels to bring them back to the bathroom.

"Come on."

I snag her hand and lead her down the stairs into the kitchen to sit her at the small two-person table while I go to hang the towels in the bathroom. When I get back, she hasn't moved, frozen in place by her own fear of the truth.

It twists my stomach as I fill the teapot with water and turn on the stove to boil it. I grab the tea I got from Willow and a mug, occasionally glancing toward Lucky to gauge how she's doing.

But it's hard to tell when she's rebuilding that wall.

Brick by brick, it goes up as I work, moving in near silence, the only sounds the cabinets opening and closing and Gizmo's little snorts as he finally wanders down the steps after us to see what's happening.

He sits next to me, staring up expectantly.

"You hungry?"

His head tilts to the side, and I open the fridge and pull out the food I grabbed from Killian's for him last night—a mix of ground beef and vegetables Willow made until we can get some sort of dog food for him since Lucky ran out of what she was carrying with her.

I toss it into a bowl for him and set it in the corner, and he runs right to it and digs in as I pour the boiling water over the tea leaves in the infuser for her and let it steep while I snag the honey harvested from Willow's hives and add some.

By the time I bring it to Lucky, all the tension this morning's activities removed is back, and she's trembling again, her shoulders tight and hunched forward as if she wishes she could disappear.

I set the mug in front of her and snag the other chair, dragging it over next to her so that I can touch her, so there isn't any space between us when we talk. Because I don't want her to put even more there, and I feel like she's going to.

Or at least she'll *try*.

She stares into her cup of tea. "So, I guess we have to talk now."

I nod. "Yes. And I'm sorry I have to make you do this, but—"

"No." She glances up, offering me a tight smile. "You're right. It's why I wanted to leave in the first place, why I never should have stayed, because I never wanted to put you in danger. And it's not just you. It's Killian and Connor, and Willow and Niall. Even Raven and Elaine. I've come to care about all of you, and"—she sucks in a sharp breath—"that makes this so much harder."

Sliding my hand over her knee, I give it a gentle squeeze. "Just start at the beginning…"

She nods and slowly lifts her mug up to take a sip. When she sets it back down, I don't miss the way her knuckles are white, clutching the ceramic in a death grip. "You know I left foster care when I was fifteen."

"Yes…"

Though I try not to think about it too much because the thought of Lucky out there alone, at such a tender, important age, when she desperately needed someone to be there for her, is enough to bring me to tears.

"Well, I wandered around a lot. Moved from city to city, primarily big ones. Places I could disappear and didn't have to worry about some adult seeing me on my own on the street and calling the police or Child Protective Services. You can disappear in a city. You can blend in." She pulls at her hair, referencing our earlier conversation. "Though I didn't have this, I had other ways of concealing myself. Of staying under the radar. And it worked for a really long time. Because I never let anyone get close." She peeks up at me, chewing on her bottom lip for a moment. "I dated a few guys, but it was never anything serious. It was always just"—she shrugs—"a release."

The thought of her being with anyone else makes my chest tighten, but I resist the urge to rub at that spot where my heart aches and instead focus on her and what she's telling me.

"Six months ago, I met a guy…"

"Okay."

She takes another sip, like she's trying to buy some time before she has to continue. "He seemed nice. Paid me a lot of compliments and attention. He seemed to really care about me."

The way her voice cracks makes me squeeze her leg again. "Where was this?"

She looks like she isn't going to answer for a moment, like telling me will somehow reveal something she doesn't want me to know. "Columbia, South Carolina."

I nod slowly. "Okay…"

"I should have known." She clenches her eyes closed, shaking her head. "I should have known who he was—*what* he was—when Giz didn't like him."

My eyes automatically drift to the dog. He finishes off his bowl, licks it clean, then trots over and sits by my feet, leaning against my leg. I reach down and scratch behind his ears. "Dogs are pretty good judges of character."

She looks down at him and nods. "He never liked Brad. Barked at him, growled. He never wanted him anywhere near me. I thought he was just being jealous, being difficult because he's Giz, but he *knew*. He saw something I couldn't."

I swallow the lump in my throat. "Which was what? What did he do to you?"

Her fingers tighten on the mug. "It isn't so much what he did to me. It's what I did *for* him."

15

THREE WEEKS LATER

LUCKY

With the front door of the store propped open, the people of McBride Mountain wander in and out of the shop at will. Everyone wears a smile, excited to congratulate Willow on the grand opening and to have literally *any* reason to get together and celebrate.

And after everything she went through, she deserves this.

She stands in the middle of the shop, greeting everyone and beaming from ear to ear, excitedly talking about all the different offerings around the shop while people explore and buy the candles she crafted with so much care and precision.

Her product is the kind of stuff people pay a fortune for at the boutiques I've worked at in various larger cities—handmade, organic, one hundred percent natural. Plus they smell incredible, the scents she's created perfectly matching the mountain around us, as if she's bottled them straight from the source.

I hang back near the entrance to the office, watching it all unfold, trying to stay out of the way and remain as inconspicuous as possible while witnessing her future happening before my eyes.

Despite how uneasy I am being here with all these people, I can't stop myself from smiling seeing the way she interacts with everyone and how happy the entire town is for her today.

Liam finishes speaking with Killian on the other side of the room—for the umpteenth time since we arrived—and his gaze meets mine. The worry swimming in it mirrors what I've seen in his eyes since that morning he learned the truth.

A constant darker undercurrent floating beneath his usually evergreen gaze.

He approaches, weaving through the throngs of people, giving tight smiles and hellos on his way, and stops in front of me, pressing his large, warm palm against my stomach as he leans in. "Are you sure you want to be here, Bluebell? We can go back to the cabin."

It's a familiar question.

He's asked me so many times over the last several days if I really wanted to come, if I wanted to be here, somewhere *so* public, with all of McBride Mountain coming and going through that door.

Somewhere so *exposed.*

After revealing the truth to him, I can understand why he would think I wouldn't want to be here. Why I wouldn't want to put myself out somewhere so visible. Why staying up at the homestead like I have been would be the safest place for me and where I would *want* to be like I have been for weeks.

But I just *couldn't* do it.

Not to her.

I shake my head and turn it toward him, brushing a kiss over his lips gently as I rest my hands on his chest to feel the grounding, steady beat of his heart under my palm. "I'm positive. I want to be here for her. It's her big day."

One I could *not* miss.

Over the last several weeks, Willow has become the closest thing I've ever had to a best friend. When she learned the truth, when she understood what the McBrides would be facing if I stayed, she didn't hesitate for a moment to throw her arms around me and tell me how sorry she was. To assure me that they would do everything in their power to protect me and to solve the problem. To make sure that everything would be all right.

Even when she had no idea how we would get there, she never wavered in her belief that there is an end in sight that doesn't involve me returning to the road alone or worse.

I wish I had the kind of faith she does. That faith Liam seems to share that though we don't have the answer now, we'll *find* it.

But I don't.

Which is why I watch that door carefully.

Which is why Liam, Killian, and Connor are all here, spread out across the shop, looking more like security guards than members of the family celebrating with Willow.

Because even though they keep insisting we'll figure this out, they also know the danger I've brought here, to this place, to them, and they won't let down their guard.

Willow keeps admonishing them to stop scaring away prospective customers, but the people of McBride Mountain know the brothers well enough to understand who and what they are.

After reading the backlog of Raven's posts—on what is *absolutely* a gossip site, whether she admits it or not—*I* also understand them so much better now.

Weeks secluded on the McBride homestead have taught me even more.

The *important* things.

They're good people.

They're good men.

They're just…a little rough around the edges.

And Liam truly is different—like Willow said.

He's their conscience. The one who always seems to be arguing in the role of the calm one while Killian and Connor want to fly off the handle, their baser instincts taking over their rational thought.

They would've been standing here with shotguns and axes, waiting for any signs of trouble, but Liam insisted that we don't go that far. That there's no reason to worry people in town when we don't have any reason to believe anyone knows I'm here.

It's been a month now, and the only familiar faces are the ones I learned working at the diner. None from my past, despite constantly looking for them.

And the McBride brothers' presences don't seem to be deterring any sales.

Candles are flying off the shelves Liam so expertly hung, and the register keeps dinging open as money flows into it with Raven behind the counter—actually helping, for once.

The entire community is here to support Willow, to help her rebuild her life after what happened to her, and it makes the promises Liam has made to me seem like something tangible instead of only placating words.

Now they echo in my head as I look around.

Once he knew the truth, he understood why I wanted to leave McBride Mountain, but now, seeing these people, watching the way they came together for Willow, I can't imagine walking away. I can't imagine going beyond McBride Mountain and being able to find anything even a fraction as good as this.

Because it doesn't exist anywhere but here.

Liam dips his head to search my gaze. "If you're sure you want to stay…"

I nod. "I am."

The constant unease I've lived with for months still buzzes under the surface of my skin like an entire hive of bees, but having the McBrides here, watching my back, keeps them at bay, prevents them from bursting free and causing a violent sting.

Raven approaches holding Niall and hands him off to me hurriedly, her smile somewhat forced, her eyes darting toward the rear exit of the store. "I...have to go take care of something for a few minutes. Watch him and the register. I'll be back."

Liam tosses her a look as she bolts out the back door, but my focus is on the little one in my arms. Niall reaches up and pulls on a strand of my hair, clutching it in his tiny fist and tugging on it.

"Oh, there's my smart, inquisitive boy!" I bounce him gently, trying to keep him entertained while his mom is busy schmoozing with friends and potential customers. "Are you having a good time seeing everyone? It's soooo exciting, isn't it?"

He smiles and coos at me, more interested in the vibrant blue of my hair than what I'm saying to him.

Liam stalks to the other side of the shop and leans in to whisper something to Killian, whose gaze cuts over to me. He offers me a tight smile that I know I shouldn't take any offense to despite how cold he looks.

Killian's a protector—the type of man who was willing to kill Earl Byers when he found out what he did to Willow—and when he learned what happened to me, what I was facing, it kicked him back into that mode.

He doesn't like me being here any more than Liam does and would much rather have preferred I had stayed in the safety of the homestead.

But I can't abandon my only real friend on her big day.

And it's his *wife.*

He wants her to be happy.

Having me here makes her happy, so he wouldn't deny her

that, even if it means spending the day being constantly on guard.

I walk to the register with Niall to be prepared to check out any customers as he continues to play with my hair. People come and go, purchasing product and saying hello to me and the baby.

A few express surprise that I'm still in town since I've been hiding out in here with the windows covered, or up at the McBrides' without real contact from anyone else for the past several weeks—very intentionally.

The seclusion was as freeing as it was stifling.

I thought I would be good today, but after that much time, being in such a tight space packed with so many noisy and nosy people is enough to make me happy I have Niall in my arms to distract me from my rising anxiety.

Elaine approaches and offers me a one-armed hug around the baby. "I didn't know you'd be here."

I smile at her, genuinely happy to see the woman who truly made me stay in McBride Mountain and who made everything I have with Liam possible. "I didn't know you'd come, either. What about the diner?"

She waves a dismissive hand. "I closed for an hour so I could come over. I figured everyone would be here, anyway."

I glance around the packed space. "You're not wrong."

"And how are you doing? I miss having you around."

Laughing, I shake my head, which only makes Niall tighten his fists on my hair tighter and tug. "No, you don't."

She pats me on the arm. "Well, my new waitress is a little steadier on her feet, but I liked talking to you. Come by and have a cup of coffee with me soon. Please."

I nod. "I will."

And I hope that's true.

I hope I can.

I hope that this plan that Killian, Connor, and Liam have come up with will actually work and I'll get my life back.

But not my old life.

A new one here that Liam has promised me, that I so badly want, that I never thought would be possible.

So many things have to happen before we reach that point. Nothing moves quickly. The pace feels glacially slow at times. But there is that flicker of light at the end of the dark tunnel that once felt endless.

I just have to keep my focus *there,* not on what might linger in the shadows.

Elaine wanders off to say hello to someone else, and Willow approaches and takes Niall from me, carefully pulling his fingers from around my hair.

"You don't have to let him do that, you know..."

I smile at her and tickle him until he giggles. "I don't mind, really. He's my buddy."

Willow grins. "I know. Some days, I think he might like you more than me."

"That's just the hair."

She laughs, gives me a quick hug, then returns to whoever she was talking to who clearly wanted to see the baby. I scan the shop for Liam and find him near the far corner with Killian, eyes surveying every person who walks in that door for any unfamiliar faces.

One good thing about this small town—strangers stand out.

And if one shows up today, the McBrides will be on high alert to swoop me out of here if necessary.

At least, Killian and Liam will...I have no idea where Connor disappeared to.

Or Raven, for that matter.

I search for her, anxious to hang back in the rear of the shop instead of dead center of the hustle and bustle, when a familiar voice fills the store from behind me.

"Lucky! There you are!"

LIAM

The moment Sheriff Briggs walks in, Lucky freezes like a deer in headlights where she stands behind the register. Killian goes rigid beside me, and my own spine tightens as I struggle to keep my face neutral and not lunge across the store to her. Which is hard, when all I want to do is throw Lucky over my shoulder and *run*.

Tony approaches her, a smile on his face. "I've been trying to catch you. We never got a chance to formally meet, and it seems as though you might be staying in town."

He offers her his hand, and I watch as she swallows thickly and accepts it with a stiff motion that tells me she's trying not to let him feel her trembling.

Fear seeps into her gaze, and her eyes dart across the room to meet mine, begging for help. But if I charge over there and intervene, Tony will *know* something is wrong.

Right now, this is simply a friendly conversation between McBride Mountain's sheriff and one of its newest residents.

Don't turn it into something else.

I make my way toward them as casually as I can, sidling up beside her and sliding my arm around her shoulders. "How are you, Sheriff?"

He pulls off his hat and runs a hand through his hair as his head bobs. "Good. Good." His gaze travels over the store. "It looks like the opening is going well."

Better he focus on that *than Lucky.*

I nod. "It definitely is. Willow has worked hard for this."

Tony offers a knowing look and glances to where Willow stands, holding Niall and chatting with the town clerk, Eugenia, who gesticulates wildly with her hands, making the baby giggle.

Sheriff Briggs is a good man who is supremely dedicated to his job and to protecting the people of McBride Mountain. He put all his time and effort into helping Killian and Willow figure out what happened to her, and into ensuring my father and aunt were brought to justice for it.

He has always stood by the McBrides.

Which is why doing this hurts so much.

Lying to him.

Keeping something so essential to the safety of the residents here from him.

But I can't risk that he would do his job right now.

Not until there are protections in place for Willow.

He turns back to her. "Are you going to be working here at the shop?"

She tips her head down and tries not to look at him as she answers, pretending to fiddle with something on the counter. "Oh, I'm not sure yet."

I tighten my grip on her. "I keep her pretty busy up at the homestead."

Shit.

That came out all wrong.

I hadn't meant to make it sound sexual—not that it isn't also true—but was referring to the way she's stepping in to help with Niall, learning how to make candles with Willow, and even assists with caring for the animals and other chores on the land as if she was meant to always be a part of it.

"I'm sure you do, son." He winks and claps me on the shoulder, then leans his head down to look at Lucky's face until she tips it back up to him. "It was nice to formally meet you. I didn't get your last name."

Her back stiffens, the tension in her shoulders under my

arm so intense it feels like she might shatter, and her cheeks start to redden. "Oh. Marlowe."

He smiles. "Lucky Marlowe. Well, welcome to McBride Mountain." He tips his hat to her. "Formally."

With that, he steps away, heading toward Willow.

Lucky releases a long, shaky breath. "Oh, my God…"

Her body trembles, and I pull her into me, ducking my head to whisper in her ear. "I'm getting you out of here."

"He saw my face, Liam." She keeps it tipped down against my chest. "He looked *directly* at me."

Looking at Lucky is one of my favorite things on this planet, and any other time, I might have told her that. But not now. Not when the panic and risk are so very real.

"It'll be okay, Bluebell. Let's go."

I glance over my shoulder to where Killian stands watching, but there isn't any sign of Connor.

Where the hell did he go?

Killian inclines his head toward the back door, suggesting we leave, and I nod and urge Lucky in that direction, past the closed door to the office, and out into the alley behind the shop. Which is thankfully quiet and empty.

Lucky immediately turns and leans back against the brick, releasing another shaky breath. "Oh, my God." She presses her hands over her chest and looks up at me with tears pooling in her eyes. "I can't do this. What if he recognized me? What if—"

"Hey"—I step in front of her and take her face in my palms —"I told you we would protect you, and I meant that. That means from *everyone*. Including him."

"He's the *sheriff,* Liam. There's only so much you can do."

I offer her a tight smile, raising my eyebrows incredulously. "Did you forget I'm a McBride?"

She shakes her head. "No, but you aren't *God*. And that man has a job. One that involves taking *action* if he ever figures out who I am."

"He won't." I try to sound convincing, for my own sake as well as for hers, but she isn't wrong about Tony Briggs. "At least, not until all this is cleared up."

We just have to hope he doesn't recognize her until then...

"What if that never happens?"

I tug her up against me again, letting her take a few moments to gather herself and steady her breathing before I lead her down the alley toward where I parked my truck nearby, in case we needed to leave quickly.

"We're meeting with the lawyer in a few days, Bluebell, and once we've talked to him, when we have a firm grasp of what's happening and a plan in place, things will change. They'll look better."

"You're so confident this is going to work."

I squeeze her hand as I open the truck door and help her up into it. "It has to. There isn't any other option."

Because I *won't* lose her.

I can't.

Seeing her prepared to run that night broke something in me that has stayed jagged, that has drawn blood each time I've thought about how close I was to losing her.

That *will not* happen.

I close her door and walk around the truck, releasing my own heavy breath.

She should have stayed on the mountain today. No one would have thought anything about me not being here, and since only a few people know she's been working with Willow, no one would've questioned the fact that she was MIA, either. But now the one person in town we never wanted her to interact with has seen her face.

He looked directly in her eyes and spoke with her.

She easily gave him the fake last name we prepared, but the way her cheeks heated...if he was looking carefully enough, if he was watching for it, he would've noticed something was off.

I just have to hope he didn't.

Pray he didn't.

I tug open my door and slide in, starting up the truck and immediately reaching to place my hand on hers resting on her knee. Her lips twist as she looks out the window toward town square. When she glances back at me, that fear has returned. The one I thought we had wiped away over the last few weeks. The one I thought we had buried.

"What if I have to leave town?"

My stomach twists violently, bile rising up my throat. "You don't."

"But what if I *do*?"

I watch her for a moment, hold her gaze as she waits for me to respond.

She's been considering it.

The longer it takes for all of this to play out, the harder it becomes for her to sit still, for her to believe that enough time has passed that maybe, just maybe, no one is looking for her.

There's a good chance she will *never* believe it, that she will never truly relax and feel safe here.

And what she needs is a safe place.

"If it comes down to it, Bluebell, if you have to leave, if you have to run..."—I swallow thickly—"then I'm running with you."

A little hiccup-sob slips from her lips. "You don't mean that." She shakes her head, her hair floating around her face. "You can't leave McBride Mountain."

"Why not?"

Tears stream down her face now. "Because this is your *home*. Because your family is here. Everything you love is here."

Fuck.

I hadn't wanted to do this, here, in my truck, when she's in the middle of a fucking panic attack—maybe rightfully so—but she needs to hear it.

"Not everything I love is in McBride Mountain. Not if you're not here."

Her breath catches, her bottom lip quivering. "Liam…"

I reach up and grasp her chin in my fingers, dragging her across the center console toward me. "I love you, Lucky. I have since the moment you walked into the diner and accused me of stealing Giz. You've done more for me in the past month than anyone I've known in my entire life was able to over the previous nine. I need *you*." Shaking my head, I hold her gaze, refuse to let her look away. "I don't need to be in McBride Mountain. Not anymore. I was already considering leaving before you showed up. Thinking about putting space between me and this place and the memories and nightmares. But now the nightmares are gone. Now that I have you beside me in bed every night."

"But your family—"

"Will still be here. They're not going anywhere. But I can. We can have a new life somewhere else. We can start over. Is that what you want?"

She shakes her head. "No. I want to be here. This place, it's…"

Watching Lucky struggle to find the right words makes my lips curl. "I know. It's kind of magical, isn't it?"

She nods.

"So just trust that we're going to figure it out. Trust me. Trust in the magic of the mountain and in the McBrides."

Her gaze softens. "I *do* trust you."

Those are the only words I needed to hear, and I lean in and press a kiss to her lips, silencing her tears and making her the same promise I have been for weeks.

That I'm not going to leave her to face this alone.

She'll never be alone again.

16

LUCKY

My knee bounces rapidly, all the nervous energy overwhelming my body seeking an outlet. I attempt to hide it underneath Liam's desk so he doesn't see it and worry, but the way his eyes are narrowed on me tells me I'm doing a shitty job of concealing my building distress.

Either because I've been trying to for so long that it's written all over my face, too, or simply because Liam can read me so easily.

He *sees* me so completely and knows exactly what's going on in my head, even when I try to protect him from the dark places it often takes me.

In moments like this.

This is our only chance.

One shot to potentially find a way to dig me out from under the shit I've found myself buried in.

If this doesn't go well...

My stomach roils, and I press my hands to it, trying to settle it before I dry-heave all across Liam's desk.

Liam stalks over from where he had been standing by the window, watching for our guest to arrive, spins me in the chair until I face him, then squats, resting his hands on my thighs. "You don't have anything to be nervous about, Lucky. This is a good thing. Attorney Truman is coming to help."

I absently chew on my bottom lip—a habit I have never been able to break no matter how many times I try to be conscious about not doing it.

A familiar heat flares across Liam's gaze, and even though the tension permeating the room is heavy enough to suffocate us, he grins.

That slow, quick tilt of his lips that first drew me to him.

I quickly release my lip, knowing full well what's going through his head after the warning he issued me about my lip before.

"After the meeting."

He pushes up and presses a searing kiss to my lips that's far too intense and inappropriate for the setting—maybe intentionally to try to get my mind off what I have to do.

It works.

The McBride Timber office melts away.

All that exists in this moment is his mouth moving over mine, his hands sliding into my hair and tugging me to him.

When he finally pulls away, he rests his forehead against mine. "I promise, it'll be okay, Bluebell. Killian knows him and has used him for multiple things in the past. His firm is incredibly reputable. If anyone can help us figure this out, it'll be him."

I release a shaky breath and nod. "Okay."

It's the same thing he's been saying to me for the past several weeks, since I came clean with him and confessed everything, since he relayed the information to his brothers so that I wouldn't have to look them in the eye and tell the story again.

Which is exactly what I'm going to have to do today.

The McBrides would love to believe they can control everything, that they can snap their fingers and throw around their name and any threat just *vanishes* instantly. But this isn't something simple that can be solved overnight, nor can it be "fixed" by them alone.

That's frustrating as hell for all three of them, but it's nothing compared to the spine-tingling sense of dread settling over me now as we wait for the man who is supposedly going to save my ass with some sort of elaborate legal maneuvering.

Footsteps sound on the porch outside, and Liam turns toward the door. When it opens, Killian walks into the office, his jaw locked so tightly that a muscle there jumps, followed by a man in an impeccable dark suit carrying a briefcase. Connor trails behind him, closing the door once they're all inside and offering Liam a hard look I can't quite decipher.

What's wrong?

The man in the suit gives me a smile that makes my skin crawl slightly. When Killian described working with Attorney Truman in the past, I had imagined an older man, more of a fatherly figure. This guy is younger, maybe in his early thirties, and his slick style immediately puts me on edge.

He steps forward and extends a hand to Liam first. "Hi. I'm Attorney Julian Snow."

Liam's back stiffens along with mine, and his gaze cuts to Killian, who gives a slight shake of his head.

"Umm, hi. Liam McBride." Liam shakes his hand, then glances at me with as much confusion in his gaze as everyone seems to be sharing. "This is Lucky. We were expecting Attorney Bill Truman."

Attorney Snow gives us another smile, then steps over to offer his hand to me. "Nice to meet you, Lucky. I do apologize, but Bill couldn't be here. I've worked with him for several years, and he sent me instead of cancelling the meeting or having to reschedule. He said it was time sensitive and filled me in on the basics."

I swallow thickly, unease tightening my chest.

This isn't the man Killian knows and has worked with.

I'd prepared myself mentally for that—not for *this*.

Liam turns back to me and squats again, offering me a reassuring smile that can't quite hide the uncertainty in his mossy eyes. "You can do this. He can help. It'll be okay."

This man works with Truman.

He came to help me.

The only way he can do that is if we have a very difficult conversation.

I have to keep reminding myself of that.

Because we can't go on like this.

Constantly looking over my shoulder is exhausting.

Secluding myself away from everyone up on the mountain and making the McBrides live on the razor's edge wondering when my past might show up isn't fair to them.

This isn't really living.

It's barely surviving.

Killian grabs a chair from behind his desk and drags it over to the front of Liam's. "Please, have a seat, Attorney Snow."

The man who now holds my life in his hands settles into it, crosses an ankle over his knee, and pulls out a legal pad and pen from his briefcase. "So"—he glances around the room— "Bill tells me that you've gotten yourself into a bit of trouble."

I can't help the snort that comes out at his description of my predicament, and I shake my head. "'A little' would be an understatement."

Liam pushes to his feet and moves behind me, resting his hands on my shoulders and offering me his strength the only way he can right now without me physically sitting on his lap and allowing him to hold me.

Snow gives me a tight smile. "Well, I've already heard bits and pieces from Bill that were apparently relayed to him previously, but in order to really get an assessment of how we will proceed with this, I need to hear the full story from you directly."

Which is exactly what I have been dreading since Killian first came up with this idea.

I understand the situation I'm in and that no attorney will ever be able to negotiate any kind of deal on my behalf if they don't know what they're working with, but that doesn't make it any easier.

Liam squeezes my shoulder, and Killian and Connor offer me reassuring looks from where they lean against the wall behind Attorney Snow, watching and waiting for me to proceed.

Coming clean to Liam and telling him everything was hard enough, but now having to do it in front of his brothers and a total stranger is pure agony.

I draw in a long inhale and release it, squeezing my eyes closed as I brace myself for the judgment I know is coming.

You can do this.

One more time.

"It started a year ago..."

I open my eyes to Snow nodding, jotting something down on his notepad before he glances up expectantly, waiting for me to continue.

"I was in Columbia, South Carolina, and I met a man named Brad."

One of his dark brows rises. "Last name?"

"The one he gave me was Ryan. Bradley Ryan."

Attorney Snow's jaw tightens almost imperceptibly, and he scribbles on the paper. "Where did you meet?"

"He came into a retail shop where I was working for a while —a small clothing store. Mom and pop type place. We chatted for a bit, and he asked me to join him for lunch. It was all very organic." A little mirthless laugh slips from my lips. "Or so I thought."

That volatile mix of embarrassment and anger that always surges through me when I think about how easily I was deceived comes back full-force, and I tighten my hands into fists on my lap.

It was all a game.

It was all one giant fucking game to him.

And I lost.

I release a shaky breath, refusing to give in to the burn of tears. "He always seemed to have a lot of money, which I attributed to the fact that he told me he was an investment consultant. He drove a nice car, had classy clothes, a great watch, and he was sweet, funny. Attentive." My throat tightens. "He *showered* me with attention, and I let him..."

Because I was an idiot.

As someone who spent their entire life having to read people, having to be able to see what someone's true intentions were so I could protect myself or my foster siblings from them, the way I so easily fell for Brad's level of bullshit is mortifying.

Was I that lonely?

That desperate?

I find myself glancing back at Liam.

Because I *need* to see him. I need to see if anything in his gaze alters when he hears this again. I need to witness the moment I lose him, which is still hard to imagine won't happen. But his reassurances that nothing will ever change echo through my chest and remain shining in his eyes, urging me to continue.

Clearing my throat, I refocus on Attorney Snow, who waits patiently. "Nothing was unusual for quite a while. A few months. We became romantically involved."

Liam's hand tightens on my shoulder, but I know it isn't because he's angry or jealous about me being with someone else; it's because he knows where this story ends.

His distress is *mine*.

His frustration tied to the fact that he can't do a *thing* to the man who hurt me so badly.

Attorney Snow jots down a few more notes, then raises a brow again. "When did things become 'unusual,' as you put it?"

Shifting restlessly under his assessment, I think back on those days I've tried so hard to forget to ensure I get it right. "When he started hanging around more and more at the store I was working at. It was right along a very busy street, across from a bank."

"What bank?"

"Columbia Savings and Loan."

He keeps writing, expecting me to proceed with the story.

And I have to, no matter how painful it is to recount being blindsided so badly by someone I had trusted.

"I thought he just wanted to spend time with me." I shrug. "We weren't super busy most of the time, so he could hang out while I worked, and we would chat."

Though, it was never anything important.

Superficial, at best.

Nothing like the long, deep conversations I have had with Liam about my life, my past, my fears, and his own.

Because deep down, I *knew* there was something off about Brad.

"He started asking me questions about the bank hours and what time I brought over the deposits. He said he was worried about me doing it alone at night in the dark, and he insisted he wanted to start coming with me. I didn't think anything of it." I release a little sigh at my own ignorance. "I thought it was kind of sweet." My throat tightens at how naïve I was, at how easily I fell for the act. "I'd never met a guy who was like that before. I never had anyone want to *protect* me like that."

Liam's hand shifts to the back of my neck, and he lightly brushes his thumb across the skin there, settling me as I reach the part of the story where it all went to shit.

"He started coming with me when I made deposits, and it became a daily thing."

Attorney Snow nods. "How long did this go on?"

"Maybe six weeks?" I shrug, the timeline melting together. "Eight weeks?"

Intense dark eyes watch me expectantly. "And then what happened?"

"And then I helped him rob the bank."

LIAM

I don't know why I believed hearing this for the second time would make it easier somehow. It was delusional to think knowing everything Lucky went through might make standing here as she relays it again—to a total stranger who might be her only chance of getting her life back—break me less.

The pain definitely isn't any better.

If anything, the second go-around is worse, like having acid thrown into an already open, gaping wound that was created the day Lucky revealed the truth.

It takes all my will power to retain a neutral expression as Attorney Snow's eyes narrow on her with her confession.

My gaze flicks up to meet Killian and Connor's. While they've both heard the story from me so we could prepare a game plan, having Lucky tell it in her own words is rough for them, too.

They're both always so stoic, internalizing their emotions and only letting them out when they've been contained so long that they finally have to explode.

And now, they're both tense.

Jaws locked.

Arms crossed over their chests.

Backs ramrod straight.

But it isn't because they're angry with Lucky.

They want to kill the bastard who did this to her—just like I do.

Because they've grown to love her, too. The past several weeks, she's become one of us—a McBride. Not bound by blood, but something strong, something that means *more*.

Feeling the way her body trembles under my hands and how terrified she is to be revealing all this to a complete stranger is enough to make me want to pull her into my arms and end it immediately.

I ache to whisk her away to the top of the mountain, where we can hole up again in the cabin and shut out the world. But weeks of doing just that haven't changed anything.

And until this is resolved, Lucky will always have one foot on the road, ready to run.

Attorney Snow can't help her if he doesn't know what happened, if he doesn't have all the facts, no matter how agonizing it might be for her to speak these words again.

Lucky sucks in a sharp breath that makes her whole body shake, and I reach over her and open the bottle of water on my desk, handing it to her. She takes a long sip from it, using the short reprieve to gather her thoughts and courage.

Attorney Snow seems to sense she needs a moment,

focusing on whatever he's writing, giving her a moment to compose herself.

I lean down and brush my lips against her ear, inhaling that eucalyptus scent of her shampoo that I've become so addicted to. "Are you okay?"

She nods, setting the water on the desk with a quivering hand. "I have to do this, right?"

Her distress claws at my chest, and my gaze flicks back up to Killian and Connor, who have tried to get me to talk for months while I've resisted and resisted—over and over again—because it would be too painful.

It wasn't fair to them or Willow, who, of all people, could probably understand what I have been going through. But I wasn't prepared to suffer that agony. Wasn't ready to confront it.

My meltdown on the mountain the other day put a crack in that dam, but it's still hard to let it fall fully. Allowing all those emotions I've bottled up since learning the truth about my father to filter out slowly rather than in a deluge of anger and fear feels so much safer.

But Lucky doesn't have that option.

It's all or nothing.

I'd much rather take her home, lay her out on the bed, and give her a reason not to think about it for hours, but I nod and feather a kiss to her temple. "You do. But I'm right here. I'm not going anywhere. I've got you, Bluebell."

She clears her throat, her hands tightening in the material of her shirt, as if she needs something physical to ground her during this. "I didn't know what was happening. I was"—she releases a little huffed laugh—"naïve, I guess. The day it happened, I went to go make my deposit right before the bank closed. The street was always fairly deserted at that time, but that day, there were two dark SUVs parked in front of the bank, their windows tinted so you couldn't see in. Brad walked across the street like normal, with my free hand in his." Her voice wavers, and she takes another sip of water. "But instead of moving right to the bank door, he banged on the window of one of the vehicles. The doors flew open, and eight men climbed out of them, dressed in black fatigues with masks covering their faces. One of them grabbed my arm and put a gun to my head, shoving me toward the bank—"

A sob slips from her lips, and she presses her hand over her mouth as I wrap my arm across her chest from behind her, trying to hold her the only way I can through this.

I need the connection as much as she does.

It seems to settle her after a moment, and her unsteady, hitched breathing slows.

"I tried to fight them, to pull away, but they were strong." She shakes her head, as if trying to clear the memory. "And they had so many guns. They told me they would shoot me if I tried to resist, if I didn't help them."

She squeezes her eyes closed, several tears sliding down her cheeks, and I can feel the tension radiating from her body, as if she is struggling to contain a full-on breakdown.

I press my hand directly over her thudding heart, and she reaches up and entwines our fingers.

"They...used me as a hostage. Told the teller to get everything out of the vault, which they had open to move in everything at the end of the day. Which Brad *knew* because he'd been watching how they did things every day for the past two months. Because he'd come in with *me*." Her blue hair fans around her face as she shakes her head again. "Everything happened so fast. We weren't in there more than two minutes, and then they walked me out and shoved me into the SUV where Brad was waiting."

She exhales another shuddering breath.

"I-I thought they were going to kill me. I asked what the fuck just happened, what was going on, and he told me to shut the fuck up. I looked at him, and I was looking into the eyes of somebody I didn't know."

I cringe, remembering how I looked into my own father's eyes that day. How I saw my own face and my eyes. How I saw who I could become.

It's been impossible to look in a mirror since then without seeing him.

Attorney Snow continues to scribble notes before he looks up. "What happened after that?"

"They went to a warehouse, where they unloaded the money. They removed die packs and split it into other bags. It was a well-oiled machine. They knew *exactly* what they were doing." Her voice levels out slightly. "This had been planned meticulously. None of the other men ever took their masks off when I was there. Only Brad."

Because they were smart.

They kept their identities concealed.

"Brad put a gun to my head, and he was going to kill me." She shudders. "I saw it in his eyes. He was prepared to pull that trigger."

And I could have lost Lucky before I ever found her...

My chest tightens, the pain so real, it's like someone is strangling the life from me. Which is what will happen if she's ever taken from me, if this doesn't work.

Attorney Snow offers a sympathetic look. "Then what happened?"

I try to prepare myself for what's coming, trying to *brace* myself for the impact of the words I know she's about to say, but they still almost drop me to my knees.

Lucky releases a shaky breath. "He pistol-whipped me, and everything went black."

Killian and Connor wince, both of them shifting uncomfortably where they quietly wait across the room.

"When I came to, I was secured inside an old locker of some

sort. Metal with slats at the top that let in a tiny bit of light." She swallows thickly. "My head was spinning and hurt. I didn't know what had happened, why he hadn't shot me...until I realized I couldn't get out."

Trapped.

She was *trapped.*

Left to die in an old, abandoned building that no one would have entered until it was too late.

Maybe Brad didn't shoot her because he was afraid the sound would draw attention to them from anyone nearby, or perhaps he didn't want to leave a bullet that could be traced and tied to other crimes he used the gun in. Or maybe he couldn't pull the trigger while looking into Lucky's soft blue eyes...

Another sob crawls up her throat, and she forces it back, the motion heaving her chest under my hold. "My hands were tied."

"How did you get free?"

If her story wasn't agonizing enough, the answer I know is coming to Attorney Snow's question would be enough to shatter anyone. I brace myself for it, knowing full-well the tears and rage will come anyway.

She squares her shoulders, gathering her strength. "I learned how to get out of restraints at a very young age. There's a trick to it. As soon as I got free, I managed to kick the door and bend the metal enough to get it open. The warehouse was deserted. They hadn't left a single thing. It was as if they were never there..."

"And you never told this to anyone? Didn't call the police?"

She glances up at me. "Not until I told the McBrides."

Snow raises a brow. "Why didn't you go to the authorities?"

It's the same question I asked her, the same Killian, Connor, and Willow did as soon as I told them everything.

And the reason exemplifies the type of life Lucky has had, what she's had to suffer.

"Would they have believed me?" She asks it incredulously, the hint of annoyance in her voice. "I have a record from when I was still a juvie. I was living on the streets, and I had to do things to survive. I stole. This isn't a big step from that. Not really." She shakes her head. "And I got a job across from the bank. I walked one of the robbers into that bank every night while he cased it. I would have been tossed behind bars before I even *told* them my story. And they wouldn't have believed a word of it if they had listened."

Attorney Snow's jaw hardens, and I see the look in his eyes that confirms she's one hundred percent right.

He wouldn't have believed her.

I'm not even sure he believes her now.

"It was only a matter of time before the police found me since the tellers who were there that night knew me. I stumbled home, grabbed my bag, and what I could carry along with Gizmo, and I've been moving ever since then. Hitchhiking my way north. Mostly walking, though. Doing odd jobs here and there to make cash when I could." She peeks up at me, offering me a tentative near-smile. "The longest I've ever stayed anywhere is here, in McBride Mountain."

Attorney Snow releases a heavy breath, clipping his pen to the pad and settling back slightly in the chair. "Well, obviously the goal will be to try to keep you from being charged as an accomplice in this, because you're right. It will look like you were casing the bank with him and only pretended to be a hostage when you were actually in on the whole thing, especially since you disappeared. But we have to be able to give them something. Some information that could lead them to the arrest of the men who were actually responsible, if we have any chance of that happening."

Lucky nods. "Then it's a good thing I know Brad's real name."

The shoulders under the silk suit tighten slightly, and Snow tilts his head. "And how do you know that?"

"Because he wasn't as careful as he thought he was. I can identify him. And that might lead to other members of his crew, too."

A slow smile spreads across Attorney Snow's face.

It should be reassuring, but a chill rolls down my spine instead.

"Well"—he nods slowly—"that certainly *is* something."

17

LIAM

I ease open the cabin door to complete silence.

It may seem empty, but Lucky's scent permeates the air, her presence very real in the space, even if I don't see her or hear her.

The living room and kitchen stand unused, despite having encouraged her to come down and eat or read by the fireplace.

Which means she probably hasn't moved since I left to go talk to Killian and Connor over an hour ago.

We needed to debrief after the unexpected meeting with Snow instead of Truman, to regroup after the man told us—in no uncertain terms—how precarious Lucky's situation really is.

I shouldn't have left her...

Worry burns a hole through my stomach as I climb the stairs to the loft and find Lucky sitting in the chair in the corner with Gizmo curled up next to her, petting him almost absently as she stares straight ahead at nothing—not down at the book she told me she was coming up here to read.

In all the time I was gone, she hasn't turned a single page.

Her other hand still rests spread out across it, holding the book open in the same place it was when I kissed her goodbye and she insisted she was okay.

Which she definitely is *not.*

She's a million miles away.

That glassy look in her eyes doesn't fade as I watch her. She doesn't even see me here or react when Giz lifts his head and wags his tail, excited for my return and anticipating my approach.

The fact that she's practically catatonic is likely the only reason he didn't already leap from the chair and bolt down to greet me at the door the moment I opened it.

I draw in a heavy breath, then walk over and close the book, setting it on the table beside her.

Lucky glances up at me, her eyes clearing. "What'd you do that for?"

"Because you weren't reading it, anyway."

I glance at the title I hadn't bothered to check when she grabbed it from the shelf down near the fireplace earlier, cringing slightly at her choice of reading materials.

Othello...

A story about manipulation and deceit of someone who trusts you wouldn't be high on my list of options for her right now, but I doubt she even read the spine when she took it or glanced down at the first page.

I hold my hand out to her. "C'mon."

Her brows rise slowly. "Where are we going?"

"Away from here. You've spent too long cooped up in the shop, in this cabin, and on this homestead. And after today, you need a change of scenery."

Hopefully, one that can help her snap out of this downward spiral she seems to be stuck in.

Things should be advancing, getting better, but Snow

reminded us that nothing actually moves fast when it comes to the government, especially back-door plea negotiations.

That has left all of us hanging in the wind again.

Waiting.

Like I am now for her to take my proffered hand.

Lucky considers me, and for a second I think she might actually say no, might cave in on herself and give in to those old instincts, but she finally slides her hand into mine and allows me to tug her up from the chair.

Giz jumps down and stares up at us expectantly.

I glance down at him. "He's coming, too."

Her brow furrows. "Where are we going?"

There are so many things I've wanted to show her on the mountain, so many places I've wanted to share with her since she arrived, but with all the uncertainty building around us, I didn't want to push her.

My greatest fear has been doing *anything* that might make Lucky run, but now I see that forcing her into a tiny box doesn't help, either. It's no better than what that fucker Brad did to her.

"You'll see."

The hesitation and uncertainty still lingers in her gaze as I lead her down the steps and to the front door with Giz hot on our heels.

I point to the hiking boots I bought her several weeks ago. "You're going to need those."

They're an absolute necessity on the mountain. She might have been able to get away with wearing her favorite Chucks while she was walking down paved roads and on city streets, but up here, they're more for appearance than utility. That doesn't mean there isn't a line of them in six different colors now waiting next to the boots, but they won't be useful today.

Tossing me a narrowed look, Lucky does as she's told, sliding them on and tying them as I go to the closet and grab two of my hiking packs. Her eyes follow me to the kitchen where I toss a few snacks and bottles of water into them before I meet her back at the door.

She shifts on her feet, eyeing the packs. "Should I be... worried?"

I shake my head. "No."

If anyone should be worried, it should be *me*.

This could backfire big time, but I have to do *something* to try to distract her.

"Let's go."

The entire trip down the mountain, I can feel her eyes on me and sense how badly she wants to demand that I tell her where we're headed. I can't say I blame her for being a little wary after we've spent weeks trying to keep her locked away and hidden from pretty much anyone else.

It might have been in her best interests, to protect her, but despite Lucky essentially always being alone, the isolation hasn't done her any good. Regret about that sits heavily on my chest, so does the uneasiness about where we're heading—given her history.

When we reach the road at the bottom of the mountain, I turn left, heading toward town, but we don't go far before the turnoff for the falls appears.

I slow to make the turn down the narrow, gravel road, my hands tightening on the wheel as I peek at her out of the corner of my eye.

Hers widen. "We're going to the falls?"

"I've always wanted to bring you here, so you can see it in all its glory and how beautiful it is—when it's not pitch-black outside, and you're not stressed out and worrying."

Like she was the night she slept out here—alone and on the run without an end in sight and with no one to have her back.

She gives me a reproachful look that requires no explanation.

A tiny laugh slips out, and I slide my hand over hers and

squeeze it. "Okay, so you're *still* stressed out and worrying, but you're going to see it with completely different eyes now. That's something."

That night was filled with uncertainty, panic, fear, and darkness that she only kept at bay with a damn flashlight. Then she lost Gizmo and spent the next morning frantically looking for him and running around accusing people of stealing him.

My hope is that all those feelings can be placed squarely in the past.

If not today, then soon.

She offers me a soft smile that tells me she isn't so sure, and we ride in silence until we make it to the small parking lot that's really nothing more than packed dirt where people have parked for so long that no grass grows anymore.

On such a hot summer afternoon, the place should be packed with swimmers trying to cool off in the crystal-blue water of the swimming hole at the base of the falls, but the building clouds and threatening thunderstorm have kept everyone away today. Which means we have the place completely to ourselves.

That might be a good thing given how jumpy Lucky is after her conversation with Sheriff Briggs earlier this week and the awful one this morning.

She needs the space and time to reorganize her thoughts, to see the world the way *I* do—starting here.

I park and help her climb out. Giz jumps after us and immediately races toward the water's edge, sniffing around, ignoring us in favor of all the exciting smells nature has to offer.

Lucky remains tense as I grab the backpacks, hoisting the larger, heavier one onto my back and giving the other to her. She slips it on, and I take her hand as we pick our way over uneven ground down to the swimming hole.

The mountain cliff towers above us almost two hundred feet, so high that we have to crane our necks to see the top of it. Water from the same river that meanders across McBride Mountain cascades down the sheer face, crashing into the pool below. A few stray rays of late afternoon sunlight filter through the building clouds, causing a prism of rainbows to flash in the wet spray.

Lucky's lips curl up into the first real smile I've seen in a long time. "Wow..."

I squeeze her hand. "I told you."

She stares at it for several minutes, her eyes getting glossy with tears that—for once—aren't sad. "It really is beautiful."

"It is..."

But I'm not looking at the waterfall anymore.

Seeing Lucky here, in this place where we used to come so often growing up, that is so important to our lives and those of everyone in McBride Mountain, feels like another puzzle piece clicking into place.

These are the moments I've been trying to savor and concentrate on. The *good* ones. Rather than getting lost in the bad memories and the nightmares created by the unsettling truths I've learned about myself, I want to create new ones with her.

This woman who learned about the darkness that runs through my veins and wasn't deterred...

This woman who has never flinched when it's come to staring down my demons, even as she runs from her own...

This woman who has held my heart from the first moment we met has the ability to destroy me with a single look and unravel me with a simple touch.

And the way she looks at me when she glances over her shoulder makes me weak in the knees.

Her gaze that was so clouded by her internal storm only a few hours ago has cleared, replaced by a warm crystal blue that makes me want to dive into it and break free from the tempting waters.

All I want in this moment is to latch onto it and keep it alive —to keep her in this place where she can forget about the fact that there are still things beyond McBride Mountain that can hurt us.

I tug on her hand, urging her to follow me around the pool to the left, toward the thickest part of the forest. "I have something to show you."

Her gaze narrows on the trees. "Where are we going?"

After warning her about what lives on the mountain, her slight agitation as we near the darkness created by the canopy isn't completely unwarranted.

"You'll see."

I squeeze her hand as we push into the trees, making our way down a familiar barely-there path no one would even see if they didn't know it was here. But I recognize it and know it by heart.

Because I made it with Killian and Connor.

We walked it so many times, we could probably do it blindfolded.

Gizmo trots along beside us, dodging around our feet and disappearing off to the sides to explore everything around us.

A few raindrops hit us, and Lucky flinches, glancing up at the trees arching overhead, toward the darkening sky barely visible between the branches and leaves.

"We're going to get rained on, Liam."

I grin at her. "Trust me."

I've said those words so many times to her over the past month, made demands of her that probably weren't fair, considering everything she had been through.

Trust is earned, and Lucky, of all people, has *every* reason to never trust *anyone* again.

But things have changed.

We have changed.

A light rain starts to fall, trickling through the leaves, the sound soft and soothing as I draw to a stop just in time.

Lucky glances around at the thick trees. "Why did we stop here?"

I pull her up against me, pressing my body to hers and feathering a kiss across her lips. "You didn't think that I would let you get soaked out here, did you?"

Her brow furrows, and I look up.

She follows my line of sight, her eyes widening. "What *is* that?"

I grin at her. "That is one of the McBride brothers' secrets. Something I've never shown anyone else. Our very first building project."

LUCKY

If Liam hadn't pointed it out, I would've walked right past it without even noticing it.

The structure blends into the trees the same way his cabin does up on the mountain, the beams and floorboards the same color as the limbs around them, supporting them as if the trunk itself grew specifically for this purpose.

"Is that a *treehouse*?"

He grins as the rain picks up and starts seeping through the canopy harder. "It is. Come on."

His hand tightens around mine, and he pulls me to the massive tree where slats of wood appear to be screwed into the trunk to act as a ladder. "You first."

I stare up at how high it is. At least twenty or thirty feet up. "You...*can't* be serious."

Heights have never scared me, but the thought of climbing

up the side of a tree on old pieces of wood that have probably been here for decades makes my stomach drop out.

He nods, kissing my cheek. "I am. I'll bring Giz."

Sitting at our feet, Gizmo tilts his head, looking up as if trying to determine what the hell is happening.

I glance over my shoulder at him. "It can't be safe, Liam…"

"It is."

"Even after all these years?"

He nods. "We built it to last, and I stop by to check on it every once in a while, to replace any boards that need repair."

If there is one thing the McBrides know, it's how to handle wood. They've built so many beautiful things, and he has never led me astray before, but it's the rain starting to fall in earnest, soaking into our clothes, that finally forces me to grab the first rung.

"All right."

With a grin, Liam scoops up Giz and puts him into his backpack, his head sticking out as he tries to watch what's happening.

I heave myself up, and Liam's hands find my ass as it reaches his eye level. He nudges me slightly—and completely unnecessarily—and I look back and grin at him.

"I appreciate the boost."

He winks, waggling his eyebrows. "Anytime, Bluebell."

That easy-going, playful smile and relaxed demeanor that first drew me to Liam seeps into me now the same way the rain does, helping wash away some of those lingering feelings our meeting today left me with.

I cautiously make my way up the makeshift ladder, my hands tightening around the old wood, testing each rung before I put my full weight on it. The higher I climb, the harder the rain falls, so by the time I reach the top and pull myself up through the small opening cut into the floor of the structure, it's coming down steadily.

Liam's head appears in the gap a moment later, and he reaches back and snags Giz out of the backpack to lift him into the treehouse, giving him room to squeeze his broad shoulders through the narrow hole.

Giz immediately begins searching and sniffing around the small space.

In here, the rain makes a different sound as it hits the wooden roof only about five feet above us.

It isn't tall enough for us to stand up inside, though it would have been when the McBrides were children, and visions of the three of them as small boys up here draws a grin across my face.

Liam sits across from me, a smile playing at his lips. "So, what do you think?"

I scan the small space that can't be any bigger than five by five. "How old were you when you built this?"

He looks at it wistfully. "I think Killian was twelve? And Connor would've been...nine? I was six or seven."

I laugh. "And your mom let you come down here and do this?"

He nods, the affection for her glowing in his gaze. "My mom gave us a lot of leeway to be boys and to explore and really enjoy the mountain. When she had to be at the lumber yard, she'd let us come over here and mess around. Where do you think we got all the materials to build this in the first place?"

My heart aches at the longing in his voice. He clearly misses her, and after everything I've heard about her from literally *everyone* I've spoken to since I arrived on the mountain, I can see why.

Connie was the type of mother I always dreamed of but never got. Someone to love me unconditionally and give me a safe place where I never had to worry about what happened inside the walls, where even the world outside them wasn't so scary because she was there.

"She sounds like a wonderful mother."

He offers a sad smile. "She was. I wish you could have met her." His warm gaze roams over me. "She would have loved you, the same way I do."

My eyes start to fill with tears, and I try to blink them away but fail. For the first time in weeks, I feel like I can breathe. Like sitting up here in this treehouse, surrounded by nothing but the forest and the falling rain, my past is being washed away, wiped clean. Like maybe, everything really is changing. "Thank you for bringing me here."

"Of course."

Gizmo makes a snuffling sound, something in the corner making him dig at the wood slightly, and I crawl toward him and discover carvings in the walls.

I trail my fingers over several of the words and images, making my way around the entire structure, taking them all in. "Did you do all these?"

He shakes his head. "A lot of it was Killian, a little bit Connor."

Some of them are initials, some names of people I assume were friends of theirs during childhood, but I pause at one that makes me smile, dragging my fingers over the familiar peak.

"This is McBride Mountain."

He scoots next to me and nods, doing the same with his own calloused fingertips. "Yep. Killian did that one. He has it tattooed on his chest, too."

Of course, I've seen it as he's worked in the hot summer sun around the homestead the last few weeks, but I never asked him about it.

Truth be told, the other McBride brothers unnerve me.

Not because they haven't been anything but welcoming to me in their home, but because of the intensity with which they do *everything.*

Especially Killian.

"He'll never leave."

Liam shakes his head. "No, he won't."

"What about Connor?"

He sighs slightly and leans back on his hands. "I don't think he will, either."

"I know Killian has Willow and Niall, and the lumber yard and now Willow's shop, but what keeps Connor here? He doesn't seem particularly friendly with anyone in town."

Liam issues a low chuckle. "Have you been reading Raven's articles?"

I duck my head slightly, embarrassed at being called out for reading the McBride Mountain gossip. "Yes, but my own personal observation, too. He hasn't said very much to me..."

Scooching closer, Liam offers me a sympathetic look. "He isn't mad, you know? About what happened. That's just how he is. He's more quiet. More reclusive. Even more so than Killian."

"And what does he do?"

"What do you mean?"

I shrug, staring at the art, thinking about both Killian and Liam's workshops on the homestead. "Well, Killian has his family and his carvings. You have your chairs—"

"And you and Giz."

Giz climbs into my lap and settles, sufficiently done with his exploration as the sound of the rain increases above us, now pouring down so hard it's difficult to imagine how we'll get back to the truck without being soaked unless it lets up soon.

Liam's words make my throat tighten, the ease with which he says them and the intensity and surety in them.

"But what does Connor have?" It's something I've asked myself multiple times over the last few weeks, when I've seen his dark eyes get a faraway look. "It just seems like he's missing something in his life."

"I agree with you." His coppery-red head bobs slightly. "And believe me, we've had conversations with him about it over the years, tried to get him to open up more, but he just prefers to be alone. Spends most of his time in his cabin doing whatever it is he does."

"Has he ever had a girlfriend?"

Liam shakes his head. "Not that I know of."

"That sounds...lonely."

He nods. "It is."

Only he isn't talking about Connor anymore; he's talking about himself. About what his life was like before I came to McBride Mountain. And he's worried about what it will become if I have to leave.

If *we* have to leave.

What he said the day of the opening has been weighing heavily on my shoulders ever since, his promise to leave with me, to start over somewhere new if we have to.

He would do that for me.

And that meeting with the lawyer this morning rattled me.

While Snow assured me that he thinks he can speak with the FBI agent in charge of investigating the bank robbery, to come up with some sort of proffer agreement that would permit me to give information in exchange for their guarantee that I won't face any charges, we all know it won't be so simple.

Not once I revealed Brad's true identity to Snow and he recoiled slightly.

Because it's a name people beyond McBride Mountain would recognize.

One that means those men who robbed that bank are capable of so much worse.

I saw it in their eyes through the slits of their masks, in the way they so easily pointed the gun at me, at the tellers.

They were killers.

Stone-cold ones.

And they expected me to die in that warehouse.

The fact that I got away makes me a loose end.

One they might want to tie up if they ever figure out I'm still alive and talking.

"Where'd you go just now?"

I shake my head to clear it and refocus on Liam, his brows drawn low over his eyes in worry. "I was just thinking about what we discussed the day of the opening."

"About leaving McBride Mountain?"

"I don't want to." I run my hands over Giz, using the familiar motion to soothe the disquiet I'm feeling about Liam's promise. "I don't want you to have to leave your brothers, I don't want to have to leave these people. I don't want to leave this."

I motion upward absently as the sound of the rain drowns out the rest of the world.

"Then we won't." Liam says it so definitively, as if there isn't a shadow of a doubt. "If that's what you want, we *won't*. I told you I would run with you, and I still mean it. But if what you want is McBride Mountain, then no matter what happens, we'll stay and fight." He pushes up and shifts over to me, pulling my face to his. "I'll fight for you, Lucky. For *us*. For *this*. So we can always stay on the mountain."

18

LIAM

By the time we step into the cabin, night has fully fallen and we're soaked and trembling. We waited it out in the treehouse for as long as we could, hoping the rain would let up enough for us to hike back to the truck without becoming completely drenched, but as the sun started to fall— along with the temperatures as the cold front moved in fully— we eventually had to make a break for it.

Even the long drive up the mountain with the heater running full-blast did little to warm us or dry off our clothes that now cling to our shivering bodies.

Gizmo bolts inside, racing for his favorite spot in the loft chair, annoyed with the events of the day that left him wet.

I nudge the door closed behind me, water instantly dripping off me onto the hardwood floors. It pools under Lucky, too, after the short run from the truck to the safety of the cabin was enough to undo any good the reprieve of the drive offered.

She turns to me, laughing, a smile spread across her face,

even as she wraps her arms around herself and shivers. "Well, that was certainly an experience..."

Her good humor despite our current predicament makes me grin as I grab the hem of my wet t-shirt.

It worked.

I succeeded in my original goal when taking her to the falls —getting her mind off everything else. Even cold, wet, and physically miserable, the light has returned to her eyes. "We need to get warmed up."

Lucky nods her agreement and reaches to pull off her wet shirt as I remove mine. I toss it onto the mat near the door, trying to save my floors from the worst of the water, and she does the same.

I'm immediately distracted from getting fully undressed by the way her wet bra clings to her breasts.

I swallow thickly as I struggle to drag my gaze from her nipples pebbling under the damp fabric. My cock hardens, straining against my already too tight jeans.

Fuuuuck...

This wasn't what I intended when I took her out of the cabin today.

Because it wasn't what she needed.

Distracting her with orgasms only goes so far, and it would have felt wrong, given the mental state she was in.

And it never even crossed my mind until this moment.

We sat, cuddled together in the treehouse talking for hours, listening to the rain pound on the roof, inhaling the smells of the damp forest around us, and just enjoying being together, being *away* from it all.

And it was probably the single best day I've spent with her since we met.

But seeing her like this now...

I can't deny the way my body craves her, how badly I want

to warm her up and watch her come apart over and over again in my arms.

Clearing my throat, I force myself to reach down and untie my boots. I feel her gaze on me while I toe them off and remove my wet socks, but I don't dare look in her direction as she strips out of her clothes, too.

Not until I can get my baser instincts under control.

I tug the wet denim free of my legs, tossing it onto the growing pile, leaving me completely nude and still hard as hell. Goosebumps pebble across my damp skin in the chilly air of the cabin, and I finally turn to face her again, my cock jutting out and still aching despite my best efforts to get myself in check.

Lucky stands before me in only her bra and panties, her arms wrapped around herself as she watches me. Her eyes drift over my naked skin, drifting to my cock, and her tongue darts out across her lips.

All I want is to move toward her, but I make my bare feet move in the other direction, to the fireplace to get us warmed up.

My hand shakes as I strike the match and get the waiting logs and kindling going, both from the chill in the air against my damp skin and because I know she's watching me.

Waiting for me to turn around.

Waiting for me to do or say something.

But I'm suddenly tongue-tied.

A tension permeates the cabin, and I face her again, unsure what I'll find or what I should do about it.

She stands shivering in the same place I left her, as if she, too, has been frozen in place by the intensity of what happened today and what's happening now.

We've learned so much about each other over the past several weeks, but how we talked stuck in that treehouse felt

like something else. A cataclysmic shift that we both experienced and don't know what to do with.

It was the decision to stay and fight.

For her and for us.

No matter what.

My cock aches, my body desperate for her in a way that
terrifies me now more than it did our first night together.

I move forward and grab the fluffy blanket from the couch.
Lucky's gaze stays locked on me as I approach her and wrap it
around her. She groans at the contact of the warm, soft material, and the sound does nothing to help alleviate the strangle-
hold I'm currently trying to maintain on my control.

She leans into me, her warm breath fluttering across my
cool skin, and I scoop her up into my arms, my hands digging
into her fleshy bare thighs. The fire crackles behind us, the heat
already starting to flood the cabin along with the wonderful
smell it creates.

Lucky wraps her legs around my waist, burying her face in
my neck and dragging her hot core along my length.

My hips jerk at the contact, and I issue a low growl of warning. "Lucky..."

She lifts her head back and gazes at me in a way I've never
seen before. I've asked for her trust over and over again, and
she's handed it to me. But the way she looks at me now is something different.

It isn't just trust.

It isn't just want or physical need.

What I see in those pale blue depths is precisely what I feel
when I look at *her*.

Instead of taking her upstairs to the loft, to our bed, I walk
us in front of the fire and lower her down onto the bear skin
rug in front of it. She gazes up at me with her blue hair spread
out beneath her, damp and wild and unruly, a smile curling her
lips as she trails her fingers down my chest.

"This is kind of romantic, you know."

I chuckle and feather my lips across her cheek. "What is? Getting stuck in the rain and then having to drive up the mountain before we freeze to death?"

She laughs and shakes her head. "No. You starting a fire like this and laying me down on a bear skin rug in front of it. It's very mountain man of you."

I drag my head back and raise a brow. "Isn't that what I am?"

Her returning grin matches the spark in her eyes. "I guess you are."

"What does that make you?"

She chews on her bottom lip, contemplating the question for a moment as her hand travels lower and lower, across my abs, making my entire body tense in anticipation of where it'll go next.

Her palm wraps around my cock and I groan, my eyes drifting closed at the feel of her touch.

"I...don't know."

The hesitation in her voice is enough for me to open my eyes again, and I take her cheek in my palm, dragging her face up until my lips meet hers. They tremble, as if she's afraid of the answer.

"I know exactly what you are, Bluebell. Mine. That's all that matters."

She whimpers against my lips, and I kiss her fiercely, crushing my mouth to hers and dragging my tongue along the seam until she opens for me. Until she accepts everything I'm willing to give her and have been trying to over the last month.

If she hasn't figured out exactly what she means to me after everything that's happened, and after everything we've said to each other, then I'll have to find another way to show her.

Every second of every minute of every hour of every day, I

will make Lucky see how important she is, how much she means to me, and how impossible life would be without her.

That's my mission now.

To give her all those things she never had—including the confidence that this isn't a dream and I'm not going to disappear.

She wraps her legs around my back and guides me to her slick core. The feel of her arousal, knowing she's so ready for me, makes my cock ache to drive into her, has my brain begging me to bury myself so deeply inside that I'll never leave that spectacular place. But I hold my hips steady. I keep myself back as I raise myself up on one elbow.

Lucky watches me, breathless and with a furrowed, soft brow. "Why'd you stop?"

"Because I need to taste you first."

Her cheeks darken, the flickering firelight casting shadows across her body as I slowly work my way down it. I pause to pay special attention to her breasts, sucking one nipple between my lips and flicking my tongue across it, then doing the same to its partner until she writhes under me, her body seeking what I'm holding back.

But not because I want to tease her.

Not because I want to make her wait.

Not because this is some game.

Simply because I need her to know that this thing between us isn't just sex.

It isn't merely a sizzling physical attraction we've both felt since the moment we met.

It isn't a fling that's going to fizzle out once it has lost its excitement and luster.

It isn't any of those temporary things.

It's *everything*.

And that's what I plan on giving this woman.

Everything I have, along with my heart and soul.

Alternating between kissing her skin, grazing it with my teeth, and dragging my tongue over the sensitive flesh, I move lower and lower, and by the time I bury my face between her legs and finally taste her sweet cunt, we're both ready to explode.

Her arousal coats her pussy, glistening in the flickering light from the fire, and I can't get enough of it. Every glide of my tongue fills me with her taste, and every flick across her clit makes her arch into me like an offering from God spread out before me on an altar of fur.

Those little mewls, moans, and gasps as she threads her fingers through my hair mingle with the crackling of the now-roaring fire beside us, the perfect soundtrack for losing myself in this woman and what she's brought me.

Hope.

Joy.

Belief in something I wasn't sure existed for me anymore— a happy ending.

Her body undulates under me, her fingers tightening in my hair, nails scoring my scalp as she grinds against my face.

Taking what I give her.

Taking what she *needs*.

I suck her clit into my mouth and swirl my tongue over it viciously, making her twist and buck, then back off slightly, alternating between long, slow explorations of every inch of her and faster movements that have her hips bowing up.

By the time I slide two fingers into her slick cunt, she's already so close that her entire body is rigid, poised to be pushed over that cliff to plunge into the bliss waiting below.

I slide my other my hand underneath her ass, grasping her and holding her in place while I feast on her relentlessly.

Until she's breathless.

Until she's gasping and moaning my name and begging for release.

When she finally tenses, her pussy rippling along my fingers and grinding against my seeking mouth, I'm so close to coming myself that I almost do with her.

Because seeing Lucky come undone, watching her unravel, seeing the pieces of those walls she's built break away, is enough to get me off, even without her touch.

This is all I need.

Just us.

I may love this mountain. I may love my family. But if it came down to it, I would choose her every time.

LUCKY

With the heat of the roaring fire beside us and flames of ecstasy still licking across my skin after my orgasm, I watch Liam with half-lidded eyes as he climbs over my body and takes my mouth with a soul-claiming kiss.

And he can have it.

It's his.

I don't know the exact moment I lost it to Liam McBride, whether it was when he saved Gizmo, when he laughed at my theft accusation, when he helped me clean up my mess at the diner, when he walked me home to ensure I got there safely in what is undoubtedly one of the safest places in the world, when he first kissed me in the store, when he stopped me from running, or when he learned the truth and nothing in the way he looked at me changed.

There have been so many times I've been spellbound and left speechless by this man, and this is one of them.

Any words I might have said are swallowed by his mouth on mine, lost in a flood of desire for him.

I groan against his lips, my fingers tangling in his hair, my body arching up to pin his hard cock between us as he kisses me like the only thing that exists in this moment is the two of us.

Giving in to it is so easy.

So natural.

As if right here with this man is where I was always meant to be.

My mind spins with that possibility and with everything that happened today. The crazy juxtaposition over only a handful of hours that led us to this cabin, in this storm, with this fire going beside us and our bodies now slick with sweat and desire instead of cool rain.

A horrible morning filled with reliving some of the worst moments of my life was somehow turned into something else completely. He's taken me from the dark place I was in after, to this bright, happy, contented one, where the promise of all those things I never had overwhelms me instead of fear of what's coming.

His mouth still moving over mine, Liam reaches between us and guides his cock to my entrance, sliding into me on a long, languid glide that makes me tip my head back on a groan.

My pussy ripples and clenches around him, and I score my nails across his back, arching into him and giving myself to him completely.

He buries himself in me all the way to the hilt, a deep rumble moving through his chest and mine. "Fuck, I love you, Bluebell."

The heated words murmured against my skin send as much pleasure coursing through me as being with him like this does. Because it isn't bullshit. He isn't another man like Brad, telling me what I want to hear and making promises he never intends to keep.

He's the real deal.

And he's mine.

Just like I'm his.

That single word from earlier was enough to shatter the last of my defenses, to allow me to break down those final bricks I tried to hide behind. It washed away any sort of regret for anything that got me here to Liam.

Because I've never been anyone's anything before.

Instead of feeling controlled by his possessive statement, by the way he has me pinned beneath him, by the feral look in his eyes, it feels like being branded with a mark I never want to lose.

Liam captures my hands and pushes them above my head, holding my wrists together and keeping me in place. His eyes never leave mine as he drags his hips back and slowly pushes into me again, the rhythm he sets so slow, so sensual, that it truly feels like being taken completely by this man.

Like I'm *his*.

Unable to control my own reaction, the tears start to pool in my eyes.

He dips his head and kisses them away before they trickle down my temples to the soft rug beneath us. "Please don't cry."

I made so many promises to myself that I wouldn't again, but since arriving in McBride Mountain, they've all vanished like the mist does as the sun rises over the mountain. Burned away by the bright sunlight that overtakes the darkness the same way Liam's shining heart forced away the darkness I've lived with for so long.

But these are happy tears.

The type I can't remember ever crying before...

"I'm sorry."

He shakes his head, the intensity with which he looks at me while he moves so slowly and deliberately inside me enough to make me suck in a sharp breath. "Don't ever apologize to me for anything, Lucky."

It's hard to break myself of that habit learned at a young

age. Whenever anything went wrong in one of my temporary homes, apologies were self-preservation. Sometimes, the only thing that could be done or said to prevent things from getting worse.

And there are so many other things I want to say to him.

Words that have sat on the tip of my tongue but that I've been too damn afraid to say.

But even if I could manage my fear, my ability to speak them is stolen by the power of his strong, hard body driving into me at such a torturously slow pace.

He pulls back abruptly, using his grip on my wrists and his other arm around my body to drag me upright with him, so I'm sitting on his cock with my knees on either side of him.

Chest to chest.

Face to face.

Not a single inch of space exists between us.

And it feels like two halves of a whole clicking together.

He pushes so deep into me that I drop my head onto his shoulder and bite into the flesh. His hips buck, and he grasps my ass, slowly lifting me, dragging me up and down his cock and helping my movements as I kiss every inch of him that I can reach—his shoulder, his chest, his cheeks, his mouth.

The fire crackles and burns beside us. The soft rug beneath us brushes my skin. His cock splitting me wide. Our shared breaths. All the sensations are too much, so overwhelming that the tears keep flowing despite me trying to rein them in.

But it's a cathartic release I've needed so badly.

For the first time in a long time, it feels like there's hope for a future. Not just for me, but together with him in this place that has somehow felt like home even when I knew I couldn't stay.

I have to trust that Attorneys Truman and Snow will find a way out of this quagmire and that those who hurt me will get what's coming their way. I have to believe that we're safe here on McBride Mountain, that the arms wrapped around me won't ever let me fall.

And I finally do.

We move together fluidly, Liam's kisses sending my head spinning wildly, even as heat builds in my core that matches the fire. Every nerve in my body flares as brilliantly as the flames, and I come hard, bucking on his lap, clenching around his cock, screaming down his throat.

He issues a groan of approval and continues to move me on top of him when I lose the rhythm, keeping us going until I finally sag against him. But he isn't done with me yet. Liam lifts me off his hard cock and turns me quickly, settling me onto my shaking hands and knees on the rug while holding me up with his strong arm around my waist.

And then he's entering me again from behind, driving so deep my strangled gasp echoes around the cabin.

His free hand slides down to find my hyper-sensitive clit, and I jerk on him at the slightest brush of his fingertips. He overwhelms me in every way possible.

Lips on my neck.

Breath on my skin.

Fingers playing my clit.

Cock moving inside me in harsh thrusts.

"You can come again for me, Bluebell." He grazes his teeth over my ear. "I want you to as I come inside you. We do this together."

Together.

He doesn't have the experience to understand what he's asking from me, to fully comprehend what he's trying to coax out of my already wrung-out body. But as he alters the angle of his hips slightly, and the head of his cock catches that perfect spot inside of me, that flash of heat that warns of an impending orgasm ignites again.

My body is in his control.

His thrusts become more erratic, his hold on me tighter, and he buries his face in my neck, the strain of his rigid muscles against me as he tries to hold back, tries to wait for me long enough for me to finally let go.

This one blindsides me, hitting me with the force that the cascading river does the pool at the base of the falls. Pleasure courses through me, and my pussy clasps around him, giving him exactly what he wanted.

Liam's hips jerk, and he drives in impossibly deep, his teeth digging into my shoulder as he comes inside me.

Held up only by his arm around me, I start to sag as he does, and he rolls us onto our sides on the rug, tugging the blanket over us as he buries his face against my neck.

We lie motionless for an eternity.

Listening to the sounds of the fire, the rain, and our labored breaths.

Feeling our sweat-slickened skin pressed to each other.

Knowing things have changed.

Then he slowly pulls his half-hard cock free and turns me toward him, fully wrapping me in the warmth and safety of his arms and his home—this beautiful place built with so much hard work and filled with so much love.

He brushes hair from my face, trailing his fingertips across my temple, then down across my cheek to my lips. "What are you thinking about?"

"This place."

One of his coppery brows arches. "McBride Mountain?"

I shake my head. "No. Your cabin. How much I love it. How absolutely perfect it is."

He grins at me. "You know we can change anything you *don't* like."

The offer returns tears to my eyes, but I pull his hand to my mouth fully, pressing my lips to the calloused palm. "There isn't anything I don't like. I love everything about this place...and about you."

It's the first time I've said those words to him—to *anyone*—and his gaze flashes, as if he hadn't expected them despite what we've shared.

"I love you too, Bluebell." His hand slides to my lower back, drawing me even closer, and he uses the other to take my cheek and draw my mouth to his for a sweet brush of his lips. "Welcome home."

Those two words...

Ones I have longed for my entire life.

No one ever said them to me.

And nowhere else felt like one.

They were places I stayed with people who were sometimes good to me and oftentimes indifferent. They were physical roofs over my head that offered me shelter but no warmth. They were temporary stopping-off points that moved me forward in time but not in life.

But it now means something here with him, in this place.

Because after twenty-two years without one, I've finally found a home in Liam McBride.

19

LUCKY

Something wakes me from the warm, safe place I've been floating in.

Liam's scent fills my breaths—pine, warm spices, mixed with the rain that soaked us and the mountain.

The soft crackling of what's left of the fire fills the otherwise silent room, and I groggily blink my eyes open, listening, trying to figure out what dragged me from my blissful sleep.

A few seconds later, it comes again.

The low growl...

Goosebumps immediately break out across my skin, my body tensing in Liam's arms. Those last lingering vestiges of the dream world I could have stayed in forever evaporate because I know that sound all too well.

I had hoped to never hear it again.

It's usually a precursor to Giz completely losing his shit, and it isn't one I've heard often—or at all, really—since I've been up here on McBride Mountain.

He isn't the biggest fan of Killian or Connor and gives them a wide berth and dirty looks when they cross paths, but as long as they leave him alone and don't piss me off, he lets them exist in peace.

This is different.

Something isn't right.

I push myself up and scan the room. Nothing seems amiss inside the warm cabin, and darkness still looms outside the windows, the only light coming from the remaining embers of the fire.

It crackles low behind me, the soft pop of a log making me jump, already on guard.

Given the wildlife on the mountain that Liam has repeatedly warned me about and the evidence I've seen of its presence on the homestead over the past several weeks, I know better than to believe we're ever truly alone up here.

We're just visitors who have invaded this paradise Mother Nature created for *them*, and there's every chance it's a bear or coyote wandering near the cabin that caught Gizmo's attention.

It could be something passing by on its way to the river or out hunting some late-night prey. But as Giz releases another low growl from where he stands at the base of the steps with his hackles raised, my gut tells me otherwise.

Oh, God...

I glance down at Liam where he sleeps soundly beside me, spread out across the bear skin rug with the blanket draped over him, his tattooed chest rising and falling gently. He looks so peaceful, the same way I was lost to the world only a few minutes ago.

Completely content in the safety of his home, where he never thought anything bad could ever touch him.

I'd give anything to be able to snuggle back up against him and ignore Giz. To tell him to go back to bed so I can do the same and pretend that there aren't *worse* things than the wildlife on the mountain that could be outside stalking us.

That isn't an option, though.

Not when I know the kind of danger I brought with me when I came here. Not when all those instincts developed over all the rough years of my life are screaming that danger lurks just outside the door—of the human kind.

The kind I should have seen for what it was from the moment it walked into the store and flashed that too-perfect smile.

Bradley Ryan wasn't who he pretended to be.

And he wasn't just some random dude who decided to rob a bank.

I might not have fully understood the seriousness of what getting free from that locker meant...

If I hadn't found that single slip of paper at my studio apartment when I was scrambling to pack and get out of town.

If I hadn't seen his real name in black and white on something he thought he had thrown away the last time he was there and recognized it—or at least, the last name.

Lorell...

Everyone on the eastern seaboard knows that name for the same reason—because they're one of the most notorious and ruthless criminal organizations in existence today.

RICO cases against them have crumbled countless times as witnesses vanish. The list of their alleged crimes has grown and grown until they now rival the five families in New York in both size and power all along the southern coast.

And he is one of them.

Somehow connected to the crime network powerful enough to make people disappear, and to rob a bank like it was a simple walk through the fucking park without leaving a single shred of evidence.

Except me.

I'm the loose thread.

One they won't hesitate to cut if they find me.

Which is why I *know,* deep in my gut, that it isn't a *wild* animal outside. It's the *worst* kind of animal.

I nudge Liam as my panic grows, my ribcage tightening and making it difficult to breathe.

He shifts somewhat restlessly, wrapping his arm around my waist and squeezing me against him, trying to draw me across his warm body. "Mmm...come back to bed."

Shit.

I shake him harder, pushing on his shoulder until he finally lifts his head groggily, blinking as he tries to wake up.

Those mossy eyes attempt to focus on me, his lips turned down slightly. "What's wrong?"

Tugging the blanket up around myself against the sudden chill, I glance toward Giz and the door where he still stands sentinel. "I don't know. Giz heard something."

As if on cue, he releases another low growl.

Liam's entire body stiffens as he pushes himself fully up, now wide awake and alert. His typically soft eyes flash hard, dark emerald. "Stay here. Don't fucking move."

I can hear it in his voice, the confirmation that he doesn't think it's merely a wild animal outside, either. Giz has adjusted to life on the mountain, to the sounds and smells, and his reaction now is unlike anything we've witnessed since he's been up here.

We were kidding ourselves to believe it would be so easy to hide from a man like that, from a family with those kinds of connections and that vast of a reach. I could have hitchhiked to California and they probably could have found me without much difficulty, if they were looking.

That it took *this* long suggests he believed I was dead, that I had been injured badly enough by his strike and that he had bound me securely enough that I eventually died in that locker.

How did he find me now?

The question rattles around my brain as Liam climbs to his

feet and inches toward the front door, his muscles bunching and flexing with each step in the faint glow from the fire. He doesn't seem to care that he's naked and completely exposed, his sole focus what might be lurking outside.

He peeks out the window, glances back at me, and shakes his head, indicating he doesn't see anything, then moves to the one on the other side of the door and does the same.

Several seconds pass as he waits there, watching, listening, and Giz growls again.

Even if Liam can't see the threat, it's there.

Something we both seem to realize at the same time.

He holds a hand out to me, indicating for me to stay where I am, then quickly races up the stairs and comes back a minute later with a stack of clothes in his hand.

Stopping beside me, he tosses me some of them and then tugs on a pair of jeans and a t-shirt himself, the whole time eyeing the door, never putting his back to it.

Every muscle in his body vibrates as he moves over to the corner of the cabin where his shotgun leans against the wall. He grabs a box of shells from the cabinet next to it and shoves some into his pockets, then opens the drawer next to it and pulls out my handgun.

He comes over to me and squats as I hastily finish getting dressed. His lips brush against my ear. "Take this. It's loaded. Lock the door behind me. Don't open it for anyone but me, Killian, Connor, or Willow, you hear me? *No one* else."

I nod, but as he starts to rise, I grab his arm, keeping him down.

"Please don't go."

The thought of him stepping out into the darkness of the mountain alone, not knowing what waits for him out there, makes bile climb my throat. My fingers tighten around him, as if that will keep him here when we both know he has to go.

The look he gives me tells me he doesn't want to. That

leaving me and walking away right now is the last thing he would do if he had a choice. But he trusts Gizmo as much as I do, and a warning like that isn't one that he'll ignore.

He kisses me fiercely. Like it's our last kiss. Like we may never see each other again.

And my heart shatters.

This is my fault.

All of it.

He pushes to his feet, then moves over to the door, sliding on his boots and quickly tying them while he keeps his eye on the windows.

Giz stands at the base of the stairs, hackles still up, growling low in his chest.

Liam glances at him. "Stay here. Protect her."

Giz tilts his head slightly, and Liam cautiously turns the knob on the front door. It doesn't make a sound as he eases it open while standing to the side, where his body is protected by the massive wooden beam.

He peers out, scanning the area in front of the cabin. After a few seconds, he looks back at me, mouths "I love you," then slips outside, pulling the door closed behind him softly.

The mechanism clicking into place rings loudly in the silence, and it sets me in motion like a starter's gunshot.

I launch to my feet and race across the room, throwing the deadbolt he didn't bother with when we got home earlier in place.

Pressing my ear against the heavy wood panel, I strain to hear anything happening outside, and Giz rushes forward to stand beside me, staring up, still intently focused on whatever might be outside.

My legs tremble.

A strange, tingling coldness seeps into my limbs, making them feel numb.

I tighten my grip on the gun and reach down to scoop

Gizmo up in my arms, hoping to quiet him so he doesn't draw any unnecessary attention to us as I move to the window in an effort to see anything outside.

Darkness still envelops the mountain, but the rain finally subsided, the heavy storm giving way to allow stars to twinkle and the moon to shine between passing wisps of the remaining few clouds.

The single bulb above the porch directly outside the door remains off like we left it when we raced inside earlier, and all I can make out are the vague shapes of some nearby trees.

They sway softly in the breeze that still carries the scent of rain, and it's peaceful in a way only McBride Mountain has ever been for me.

That tightness in my spine relaxes slightly.

Only for a split-second, though.

A flash of movement draws my attention to the far side of the road that leads to our cabin, near the barn Liam uses as a workshop and for random storage on the homestead.

And that isn't Liam.

By now, I know him and the way he moves. The confident way he carries himself as he stalks across the property. And this is different.

Someone dressed in all black...

Attempting to blend into the shadows of the night...

The threat that Giz sensed.

The one that Liam just walked out to face.

Alone.

LIAM

They move like the shadows they try to blend in with, creeping in and out of the darkest places on the homestead, avoiding any open spaces where the moonlight might give them away.

And they're good.

They know what they're doing and came prepared for a stealth mission in one of the most remote places imaginable.

But I know the homestead, I know the land and every rock in this place, better than they do their own faces.

Even in the dark, I can see them.

At least three I've spotted so far—men dressed in all black and carrying semi-automatic rifles. Who look more than prepared to use them. The way they move seems almost military. Precise and deliberate.

These are the men who robbed the bank.

Somehow, they've found us.

They've discovered McBride Mountain and come for her, to tie up the loose end and destroy the only evidence of their crime.

My stomach pitches violently, my hands tightening around my shotgun as I inch along the exterior logs of the cabin to where I can peek around the corner and get a better view of the barn.

One of the men pulls open the main door, the sound of the metal rollers moving across the track loud in the unnatural stillness, and pauses, waiting for any sort of response to the sudden noise.

I hold my breath until he disappears inside, releasing it slowly as I scan the surrounding area to try to locate the other men. They must be clearing the homestead, checking to ensure there aren't any surprises before they hit the cabins and take us all out.

Fuck. Fuck. Fuck.

If Giz hadn't woken Lucky, we might have been fast asleep when they finally barged in shooting.

We would have been defenseless, and I wouldn't have had any way to protect Lucky like I promised her I would.

There isn't any way to warn Killian and Connor or call the sheriff since our cell phones don't work up here and the only sat phone is in the main cabin.

Killian, Willow, Niall, and Connor are sitting ducks—or sleeping as it may be.

I have to get to them before these guys do...

But the only way to do that is go right past the barn, completely exposed under the moonlight, or to go *through* it, where I might stand a chance of coming out on the other side, and sticking to the shadows to pick my way back down the ridge.

It's really the only option.

And it isn't good.

These men are trained killers. They work for the Lorells, and that family has no qualms about removing people in their way.

I've never had to use this gun on anything but bears and other wildlife up here, never even considered *having to* before Lucky told me the truth about who Brad was and I realized the depth of the danger she was in.

Which means the only chance I stand of beating them is by using the thing that they're lacking—my knowledge of this mountain and everything on it—to my advantage.

I scan both directions, searching the trees I know so well for any shadows that don't belong, then quickly bolt across the small open space toward the small back door of the barn.

Pressing my back against the worn boards, I hold my breath, waiting and listening for any sounds that would suggest anyone might have seen or heard my approach.

But an eerie silence that feels completely wrong hangs over the mountain.

Almost as if the animals can sense intruders and know

something is wrong and have gone quiet to allow me to hear better, to give me a fighting chance.

I slowly ease open the door, cringing at the creak the old metal hinges make.

Freezing again, I wait for a response or any sound that might tell me where the man who slipped in here might have gone.

My gaze flicks back to the cabin one final time, wishing I didn't have to leave Lucky like that, wishing there were any other way...but one thing I have learned about her in our short time together is that she's stronger than I gave her credit for.

She would have shot Connor that day if he were a threat.

She would have stood her ground and done what was necessary even if she regretted it afterward.

I just have to remember that as I force myself to look away and slip inside, allowing my eyes to adjust.

It's even darker in here, without any hint of the light the stars and the moon provide outside now that the rain has passed. To anyone who doesn't know the building, it would almost be impassible.

Tools and equipment scattered across the main open space.

Stalls filled with other various other items lining the sides.

Plenty of obstacles for whoever snuck inside before me.

But I quickly and silently move around each item in my way, making my way deep inside and toward the open main door where I can sneak out and move down to warn Connor and Killian and get their help.

My feet move almost silently on the familiar old floorboards, and I sidestep the ones that creak without even thinking about it. Moving stealthily, like one of the mountain predators in the night.

Only, I've never considered myself one.

At least, not until I learned about my father...

Now those same feelings simmer in my blood, the agony of

discovering who he was and what he had done, not only to Willow but to the woman who risked her life to give me this one.

The heat of it spreads through me, threatening to consume me with the shame and fear that what runs through my veins matches what does in the man who shares my face.

He took my mother's life so easily.

Holding this gun in my hands, I hope it won't be easy for me, that if I have to pull the trigger, it will only be because I don't have any other option in order to protect what I love— this place and the people in it.

A hint of moonlight filtering in through the open main door starts to lighten the way ahead.

Almost there.

Once I'm out on the other side, I can go to Connor's quickly through the trees and send him to warn Killian.

Then I can get back to Lucky...

She'll be okay...

Those words echo in my head as a heavy boot falls on the hardwood somewhere to my left.

I whirl toward it, leveling the shotgun in that direction, but the blow doesn't come from there.

Something hits me from behind, knocking me forward and causing my only weapon to fly from my hands.

Pain shoots through my head, warm blood spilling down my neck, and my chest slams into the floorboards, knocking the air from my lungs in an agonizing rush. Despite being disoriented and struggling to breathe, I turn my head to the side, gasping for air and try to push up, to regain my feet.

A boot presses against my back between my shoulder blades, forcing me down, and the barrel of a rifle presses into my face.

"Where is she?"

Lucky...

Her face flashes before my eyes. The way she looked at me tonight when she told me she loved me. When she said the words I wasn't sure I would ever hear. Ones I didn't know I needed so badly until I heard them and absorbed them into my heart like a balm that soothed all the wounds I've carried for almost a year.

I struggle against the hold, throwing all my weight back, but he hits me with the butt of the gun again, sending me sprawling at his feet with bright flashes in my vision as pain explodes through my head.

"Where the *fuck* is she? Which cabin?"

He doesn't know...

A flicker of hope ignites in my aching chest, and I clench my jaw to keep myself from showing him just how badly he hurt me while I swallow the blood in my mouth.

"There's no way in fucking *Hell* I would tell you that."

The man dips his head lower, his hard eyes close enough for me to see them, even in the darkness. "We'll find her with or without you. She was stupid to think she could ever hide from me."

From me.

Me.

The word flashes through my head.

This isn't just some nameless, faceless goon working for the Lorells. This is "Brad." Brent fucking Lorell.

In the weeks since she told me all of this, Killian, Connor, and I have done our own digging into the family. Even Raven got involved after Willow and the rest of us swore her to secrecy.

And what we found would have stopped anyone else from looking further.

These are not the people you want to fuck with.

Anyone who does isn't around long enough to regret it.

Yet, Brent is the one who fucked up by leaving Lucky alive.

He underestimated her the same way everyone in her life had until she came to McBride Mountain. And that mistake is going to be what assures his failure now.

I crane my head back to look at him more fully, to gauge his size and what he might be capable of physically while I buy myself a moment for my head to stop spinning and to gather my strength. "You shouldn't have underestimated her."

He recoils slightly at my comment.

"That was your first mistake."

His dark laugh fills the barn. "Believe me, I'm regretting it more and more every day. I let myself get sentimental for a split-second, but it won't happen again, believe me."

"It won't matter. Because you fucked up even worse than leaving her alive. It's the second mistake that's going to end you."

Lorell sneers. "Oh, yeah." He tilts his head, leaning in closer, pushing the barrel to my cheek. "What was my second?"

"Fucking with the McBrides."

The moment the words are out of my mouth, I spin my left arm back against his rifle, knocking him slightly off balance as he tries to maintain his grip on it.

Get up.

My body protests the rapid movement, the damage to my head making my thoughts sluggish and cloudy. Acid roils in my stomach, the pain threatening to make me gag as I manage to push myself up onto my knees before he regains control, but the barn spins around me, my already narrow vision in the dark blurring, making it impossible to focus.

Fuck...

I press my left hand against the blood pulsing from my temple, hoping it might help me get my bearings, but he drives the butt of the gun into my ribs to get more space between us so he can use it.

It doubles me over, the searing pain and loss of all the air in my lungs enough to make everything go black, but I refuse to go down again, kicking out blindly toward him.

My boot connects with his leg, and I hear him stumble as I force myself to my unsteady feet.

Everything spins, a cascade of agony and terror combining into a volatile mix that has my body battling between giving up and going under and digging to find the last few shreds of strength I have left.

Lucky...

Giving in to the darkness isn't an option.

I have to stop him.

My unsteady legs wobble as I prepare to lunge for him to try to disarm him before he regains his footing, but rushed footsteps sound behind me.

I roll toward the sound, but it's too late.

Searing-hot pain hits me, knocking me backward at the same time the sound of the gunshot shatters the ominous quiet of the night.

20

LIAM

I slam against the floor, agony exploding through my shoulder, and it takes a second for me to process what just happened.

That I'm bleeding.

That I was shot.

Fuck!

I clamp my hand over the wound in my left shoulder and try to struggle to my feet, but Lorell is right in front of me, pointing his gun at me again. The goon who shot me stands behind him with a smug look on his face.

Maybe with reason.

The struggle to stay conscious, to fight and breathe through the pain is getting harder, but I refuse to give up.

They'll have to kill me.

Lorell offers me a grin. "I do commend your spirit. You must really like her." He squats in front of me. "I can understand that. She was a good fuck."

This motherfucking son of a bitch!

I growl and try to push up, but he just chuckles as I collapse back against the dirty floorboards, all the energy zapped from my body as blood starts to pool under me.

That isn't good.

None of this is.

It isn't at all how it saw it happening—them coming here and infiltrating the mountain. I thought we'd have some warning, some hint that this was coming before they arrived.

I never thought I'd fail so miserably.

My eyelids grow heavy, the barn darkening even more, but the sound of a familiar growl makes my eyes fly back open.

A flash of white appears, and Gizmo flings himself toward Lorell, latching onto his arm with a vicious, snarling attack.

Giz!

If he's here...

Lucky shifts into my line of vision, the revolver pointed at the man who destroyed her life and sent her running.

"No—"

Before I can stop her, tell her to run to Connor's and seek his help, Lorell manages to send Gizmo flying across the barn with a yelp and turns toward her.

Lucky stands her ground, unwavering. "Thanks for the compliment. At least one of us had a good time."

Good God.

Even terrified, staring down this man who abused her trust and tried to kill her, she's fucking stunning. And seeing her here, so close to this kind of danger, helps clear some of the fog of pain from my head.

Enough to help me push it to the side and focus on what's right in front of me—my axe leaning against the wall only a few feet away.

Almost within reach.

The head glints in the moonlight, and my hand itches to

hold its familiar weight, to swing the blade straight into the man threatening everything I love.

Gizmo releases a whimper, and Lucky's eyes dart to where he landed.

That split second is all it takes for the second armed man to sneak up behind her and pull the gun from her hand before she can get off a shot.

"No!"

She screams, kicking back, trying to get out of his hold, but he keeps her there, pressing his hand over her mouth as Lorell snarls at her and stalks toward them, his chest heaving.

"You fucked up everything!" His sinister gaze cuts to where Gizmo lies, barely moving. "You and that fucking dog!"

That fucking dog just saved my life—again.

Though, the reprieve is temporary.

Sticky blood seeps from my shoulder and head, the wooziness making any clear thinking more and more difficult.

I have to get to her—

Lorell advances toward them, one hand still clutching his weapon, the other fisted at his side. "I always knew it would come in handy to have Julian Snow on our payroll, and I was right. He led me right to you, you fucking bitch."

Her eyes flare wide, as if she's watching her own worst nightmare come for her, because she is.

That's precisely what this night has become.

A worst nightmare for both of us.

Crack. Crack. Crack.

The sound of gunshots echoes across the homestead, splintering the night air for the second time, and Lorell's head whips in that direction. He grabs Lucky from the other man's hold. "Go see what happened."

Connor...

Killian...

Willow and the baby...

Terror seizes what little air is left in my lungs, but I can't give in to it.

There are other men out on the homestead. Other men who could have snuck into Connor's and Killian's cabins. But I also know my brothers, and they won't go down without a bloody battle.

I inch toward my axe slowly, dragging myself while Lorell still has his back turned and his focus on Lucky. She strains in his hold, refusing to stop fighting the man who has been the source of all her fears for so long.

Fuck, I love her...

So fucking much.

My fingers curl around the axe handle and I stagger to my feet. But the blood on my hand makes it slide from my grip, clanking loudly, the sound reverberating through the barn like thunder.

It takes half a second for Lorell to start to turn, but by then, I'm already lunging toward him, the only weapon I had now out of my reach. I slide my good arm around his neck and pull, using every bit of strength I have to wrench him backward.

Lucky bucks out of his hold, stumbling away, her eyes locking with mine over his shoulder.

"Get out of here, Lucky! Go back to the cabin."

She could run for Connor's or Killian's, but if the other men out there see her, they won't hesitate to shoot. My cabin is closer, and at the very least, she can lock herself inside and search for another weapon.

A knife from the kitchen, the fire poker, literally *anything* would be better than standing here, watching this, remaining in harm's way.

"No." She shakes her head, watching me as I struggle with him. "I won't."

I'm bigger and stronger than Lorell, but I'm also badly injured.

Something he seems intent on taking advantage of.

He reaches up with one hand to claw at my arm around his throat, then uses the other to dig his fingers into the gaping wound on my shoulder.

Searing hot pain makes me gag and almost black out, but I somehow hold on, wrangling him through sheer will alone, staggering across the barn.

He bucks wildly, refusing to give in even though my grip on his neck is tight enough that I've been cutting off his airway.

It doesn't seem to be enough to stop him.

I don't let go until my back slams into the wall of the barn.

The old wood creaks, threatening to give way with the force of our impact, but I shove him forward, onto the ground, digging in my chokehold even tighter. This position gives me better leverage, an advantage I will need if I have any chance of winning this fight.

He throws his head back, and I move a split second too late, the impact hitting my cheek and knocking my vision from me momentarily.

It's enough time for him to turn under me, to reach up and land another blow to my temple.

Lights flash across my otherwise dark vision, my head whipping to the side as the taste of blood fills my mouth, but I'm still on top of him. Still have the upper hand if I can just manage to gain control of him somehow.

I slide my hands down around his throat, trying to restrict his breathing, trying to keep him from getting to his feet.

Visions of my nightmares flash before my eyes, his face morphing into my mother's, mine becoming my father's, but I force them away, even as he continues to try to swing at me.

Another gunshot sounds somewhere on the property, this one closer, and Lucky recoils, backing away and scanning the barn, searching for anything that might help me.

I struggle with the man under me, absorbing his blows and

trying to maintain my grip as it slips with the blood rolling down my arm.

Until heavy footsteps pound on the ground outside.

Lucky snags something from the ground and whirls toward the noise, and the glint of one of the axes I keep in the workshop catches the corner of my eye just as Connor rounds the corner, shotgun in his hand.

For once, Giz doesn't growl or bark at him, but runs toward us as if trying to lead him to where he's needed.

"Liam!" Connor's voice echoes through the small space and he races over toward us, but I've lost the upper hand now, all my strength draining from me quickly, and Lorell manages to get a hand between us and shove hard enough to push me away a few inches then throw me onto my back.

He pins me down and reaches for a knife from his boot, pulling it out and pressing it to my neck.

But before the blade can bite into the skin, the sound of something whooshing through the air fills my ears and his eyes widen as he collapses on top of me, my ax embedded into his upper back.

Connor stands there, his own chest heaving as he stares down at us.

He grabs Lorell and rolls him off of me, then squats and presses his hand over my shoulder.

"Shit, are you all right?"

I try to regain my breath. "Lucky?"

He glances up. "She's okay."

I crane my neck, trying to see her, and she drops onto the floor beside me, tears streaming down her face.

Gizmo barks.

"We heard gunshots."

Connor nods. "I killed three other ones, but I don't know how many more are out there."

"Killian?"

He inclines his head. "In the cabin with Willow and Niall."

I nod.

"Good." The world starts to go even darker around the corners of my vision. "Good."

"Liam, stay with me." Lucky's hand tilts my face toward her, and I hear the franticness of her words, feel the way she trembles, but I can't lift my arm anymore to try to hold her or comfort her. "You promised me."

I did.

So many promises I intended when I said them.

So many I won't be able to keep.

"I'm so sorry."

It's the last thing I say before the whole world goes black.

LUCKY

In the months since the robbery, I've imagined a thousand different horrific scenarios, had nightmares about what would happen if Lorell ever found me, what he would do if he ever realized I had survived and came to hunt me down. But in all of them, it was always me in the crosshairs.

It was always me he was targeting.

Never innocent people.

Never people who just wanted to help.

Never someone I *loved*.

As Liam's eyes drift closed, my scream cuts through the barn. "Liam, no!" I take his face between my palms, the blood on them from his shoulder smearing across his face. "Stay awake, Liam."

But his eyelids don't flutter.

He doesn't respond at all.

Connor pushes to his feet. "Fuck. We have to get him to the

hospital. Even if we called for a helicopter, by the time it came from Asheville and returned, we could have gotten him there faster."

I glance over my shoulder at him, tears blurring my vision.

He scans the barn in the darkness. "Fuck. I don't know if there's anyone else out there. How many men he might have brought with him." Scrubbing his hands over his face, he turns back to me. "If we try to carry Liam out to the truck, we wouldn't be hard targets for people like them."

Panic laces his words, but he's trying to tamp it down.

For both our sakes.

I press as hard as I can on the wound in Liam's shoulder, desperate to stem the bleeding. "What do we do?"

Connor grabs his shotgun from the floor where he dropped it to grab the axe now embedded into Lorell's back. "Stay with him. Keep pressure on that."

"Where are you going?"

His hard, dark eyes meet mine, the unease in them making them almost onyx. "I'm going to get the keys for Liam's truck from his cabin, then get it over here."

Shit.

That means going out where anyone could be waiting, concealed in the trees, for one of us to appear to take us out.

But we don't have any other options.

Not if we have any chance of saving Liam's life.

He's already lost so much blood.

The dark crimson is smeared across the axe handle, along the wall where he was propped up, and all over the floor, currently pooling under him.

It coats my hands where I press into the wound, which seems to be doing very little to help the situation.

We have to hurry.

"Be careful."

Connor kicks the axe over to me without comment, but he doesn't have to explain.

If anyone comes in, it will be the only way I have to defend myself.

He disappears out the back door closest to the cabin, leaving me with Liam bleeding and unconscious in my hands.

Gizmo nudges me, whimpering softly.

He's hurt, too.

The way Lorell flung him across the barn...

"I'm so sorry, buddy." Tears stream down my face. "We'll get you to the vet, too. You'll be okay. He'll be okay. Everyone will be okay..."

Everyone will be okay...

Everyone will be okay...

That's what I have to keep telling myself because the alternative isn't possible.

I *can't* lose him.

He can't die because of me, because of my mistake.

He can't die because he loved me.

The only person in the world who ever did...and now he's paying for it.

A sob tears from my chest, my tears coming harder, my breaths hitching more and more as the seconds tick by, then minutes that feel like hours until the sound of a truck hits my ears.

And it's the most beautiful sound I've ever heard.

It means there's a glimmer of hope.

"You hear that, Liam? It's Connor." I brush a kiss across his lips, hoping he can hear me, hoping he knows that I'm here with him. "You're going to be okay."

You have *to be.*

Heavy footsteps approach, and Connor reappears. He holds out the shotgun. "Take this while I carry him."

My hands tremble, and I nod, reluctant to take the pressure

off his wound, but I grab the gun and step back. Connor squats and lifts Liam's limp body from the floor.

I have to look away from all the blood that pooled underneath him, the blood smeared all across the space where he fought with Lorell.

My stomach turns, and I swallow back the bile rising in my throat.

Connor situates Liam in his arms, straining under his weight, and moves toward the main barn door. He locks eyes with me as we reach the sliver of moonlight streaming in. "Shoot anything that moves out there. You understand me?"

I nod, using the back of my hand to wipe away the tears quickly so I can see through them enough to actually aim if I have to. Despite my entire body shaking, my palms being slick with blood, I raise it and keep it steady with my finger resting just above the trigger.

To protect Liam.

To protect the McBrides.

To protect myself...

I'll pull it without even blinking.

Giz trots along with us, limping slightly but keeping up.

Connor peers around the edge of the door. The truck sits only a few feet away, engine running, but the lights are off so as not to draw more unwanted attention this direction.

"I'm going to get him into the back. You climb in with him."

I nod, readying myself to move quickly.

"On the count of three." Connor breathes in deeply. "One. Two. Three."

Those three seconds feel like an eternity when I know each one is one more Liam's life hangs in the balance. Every one is wasted time we could be using to get him to someone who can help him. It's time the wound continues to bleed without any way to stop it.

But then we move with hurried footsteps to the truck.

I shift the shotgun to my left hand to open the back door for Connor.

The interior lights remain off—probably because Connor was smart enough to hit that little button that ensures they won't come on when the doors open. Something that would give away our position as much as the sound of the engine does.

Connor struggles to get Liam in. He's nothing but dead weight—and a lot of it. His bulky muscle, well-earned through hard manual labor around the mountain his entire life isn't doing any good right now.

And Liam doesn't react at all to the movement, to Connor jostling him to try to get him arranged, spread across the crew cab seat.

I try not to think about the fact that no reaction means he's so far gone that he doesn't feel it.

A blessing and a bad sign...

But I have to focus on what I'm supposed to be doing.

I scan the darkness around us. My gaze flicks toward the faint light, barely visible, further down on the homestead, coming from the single bulb that hangs above the porch on Killian's cabin. "What about Killian and Willow, the baby?"

Connor takes the shotgun from me and motions for me to climb in the backseat with Liam. "Don't worry about them. Killian can handle it."

That man can handle just about anything.

There isn't a doubt in my mind about that.

It doesn't stop the worry though, the feeling like I might never see any of them again.

I bite my lip to keep another sob from slipping out, then slide in and settle Liam's head on my lap. Connor shuts the door and races around to the front. He scoops up Giz and sets him on the passenger seat as he closes his door.

Giz immediately turns and looks over the center console at us, his eyes darting between me and Liam.

He knows what's happening.

Somehow he does.

I can see the intelligence in his eyes.

He's always been my protector, my constant companion, and now he loves Liam as much as I do. He leaped on Lorell like a damn military attack dog instead of the tiny, pudgy couch potato he usually is. He went full Gizmo to protect his friend. And now he feels Liam's pain and my own.

I don't think it's possible to love this dog any more than I do in this moment...

As Connor throws the truck into drive and tears down the narrow gravel road, I glance on the floor and find a duffel bag. Leaning down, I rummage through it and grab a stack of clean clothes Liam must keep back here. Pressing the fabric over Liam's wound, I pray it will slow the blood loss enough to keep him alive.

Please, God...

I can't lose him.

It isn't the first time in my life that I've prayed.

I did it so many times as a child, begging to be adopted, begging to be placed with one of the incredible foster families I knew were out there, but my prayers just seemed to float off into the ether.

Unanswered.

Maybe unheard.

I wasn't even sure I believed in God until I walked into McBride Mountain and saw something only a divine hand could have created.

Now, I need Him to hear me.

I need this *one* thing from Him.

As we finally reach Killian's cabin and the main clearing, the front door opens and he steps out with his shotgun.

Connor opens his window and slows, coming to a stop at the bottom of the porch steps. "We have to get Liam to the hospital."

Killian's eyes flare wide for a second, his brow furrowing. "Is he...?"

The middle McBride brother gives a little shake of his head and Killian's jaw hardens.

Connor glances through the windows at what's visible of the homestead from here. "There may be more of them."

Killian nods. "I already called the sheriff. He's on his way."

Which means we'll probably cross paths with him somewhere on the narrow mountain road.

Connor inclines his head. "Stay safe."

Killian glances into the backseat, his eyes meeting mine, and he simply gives me a tight smile and nods before he disappears back into the cabin. The door hasn't even closed when Connor takes off again, kicking up gravel with the spinning tires.

The dense trees soon swallow us up, the night that was already so dark becoming impenetrable.

We drive a minute or two in pitch black. No headlights. Nothing to guide the way down the long, narrow, winding road that will take us to the base of the mountain.

But I remember what Liam told me the night he brought me up here, that he could drive this road with his eyes closed.

Connor can no doubt do the same.

Still, I hold my breath until, a few miles from the homestead.

He flicks the lights on, illuminating the steep decline through the forest that offers our only potential salvation. But even once we get to the bottom, it's still hours to the nearest major hospital.

Too much time we don't have.

Too much time that Liam might not have.

I bury my face against his, the rough scrape of his growing beard against my cheek somehow reassuring. All I want is his familiar scent that always soothes me, but it's mingled now with the tangy scent of blood.

His.

"I'm so sorry." My sob tears through the cab of the truck. "This is all my fault."

"Lucky..."

I glance up at Connor's voice, and he peeks over his shoulder at me before focusing on the drive. "It *isn't*. Someone tipped them off."

I swallow another sob lodged in my throat. "It was Snow."

His head whips back toward me again briefly. "What?"

"Lorell said Snow was on their payroll." I shake my head, the events of the night coming in violent flashes of information my brain doesn't want to fully process. "I don't know what happened to Attorney Truman, but Snow told them where I was, probably told them everything that I confessed this morning and that I could identify him."

"Fuck." Connor slams his hand against the steering wheel. "That fucker is as good as dead."

The promise in his voice that they'll handle the man responsible for sending that death squad after us should ease some of my fears, but it doesn't.

Not when Liam's life hangs in the balance.

Not when I could lose the one thing I've always wanted and finally have.

Not when I might lose him.

21

LUCKY

I pace the length of the small hospital room and back, the same route I've followed continuously for the last several hours. The soles of my Chucks squeak on the linoleum floor, the sound mixing with the steady beeps of the monitors lined beside Liam's bed.

It feels like being a caged animal...

Worse than being locked in that box meant to be my coffin.

Because it isn't *my* life I'm worried about anymore.

I would give it up now if it meant Liam would wake, would open his eyes and give me that easy, smooth smile that always melts away any pain or worry I might have.

It's what drew me to the youngest McBride in the first place. The way he so easily laughed off my accusation about stealing Gizmo in the diner that morning. How quickly he smoothed my ruffled nerves.

He's always been an unmovable rock.

So solid.

So reliable.

But now that he hasn't moved, it's all I want.

I watch for it, never tearing my gaze off him.

It never comes.

Not a twitch.

Not a sigh.

I keep my eyes locked on him where he lies in the bed, eyes closed and thick lashes spread out across his cheeks, and despite all the machines telling me he's alive, this vise wrapped around my chest won't loosen.

It only seems to grow tighter as the minutes tick by and nothing changes.

All that exists now is this endless waiting and doom pacing.

Even when I paused it to change into the clean clothes Willow and Killian brought from the cabin, my body vibrated with the need to keep moving. As if it will somehow make him wake up quicker.

I turn and start another lap across the room, wrapping my arms around myself, as if that will somehow hold me together and prevent me from completely falling apart.

Again.

When we finally got to the hospital and they wheeled him away on the gurney, only Connor's arms around me kept me from collapsing onto the ER floor.

Only his murmured assurances that they would do everything they could for him kept me from screaming his name.

Only his whispered promise that Liam would be all right kept me from dying right there.

But he isn't here now to placate me.

And the longer it takes for Liam to wake up, the less those words mean anyway.

People say a lot of things that aren't true. That horrible reality was proven to me at an early age. I didn't believe anything anyone said until I met Liam. Until he proved to me through his actions that he meant every single promise made.

Which is why his final words to me keep slashing at my heart like a knife.

I'm so sorry...

He took a bullet protecting me, yet he apologized because he thought he had failed. But Liam McBride never failed me.

I failed *him.*

By not leaving McBride Mountain the moment I knew what a problem he was going to become for me, I failed him.

And as my feet move over the floor, back and forth, in the tiny room, that truth strangles my ability to remain rational and calm.

Willow steps in, her soft gray eyes flicking over to Liam before landing on me. "Hey..."

My feet stop, but my body feels like it's still moving, like it has to keep up with my racing heart that won't seem to slow. "Hi."

Her dark brows rise. "No change?"

I shake my head, fighting back a sob that threatens to slip out. Clamping my hand across my mouth, I turn away from her, squeezing my eyes closed and doubling over so this feeling of being torn apart might ease.

Willow's arms loop around me, and she presses her cheek to my back, holding me tightly and letting me completely lose it. "The doctor said it might not be until tomorrow."

"I know, but—"

Another sob catches in my throat.

She turns me in her arms, and I let my eyes open to meet hers. Her gaze holds so much wisdom even though she's only ten years older than me, and despite everything she suffered, the warmth there has never faded.

The past two years could have crushed her, could have turned her into a miserable, damaged woman who hated the world and everyone in it, but she didn't let it.

Her hands tighten on my upper arms. "*Don't*. He'll be okay. The surgery went well. The doctor said he's fine, right?"

I nod.

That *is* what the surgeon told us.

But after watching him fight with Lorell, after seeing so much blood, after being helpless when he passed out and not being able to rouse him, after that race down the mountain with his head on my lap in the backseat, waiting any longer is the worst type of torture.

All those worst-case scenarios won't leave my head.

All the guilt and regret won't stop choking me.

Willow reaches up and wipes the tears from my face. "When he does wake up, you don't want him to see you like this, right?"

Shit.

I clear my throat. "Right."

The last thing he needs when he finally comes out of this is my out-of-control emotions.

I try to force a smile and hope that it looks like one instead of the grimace it feels like.

Willow returns it, but hers actually lights up her face with the hope we're all clinging to right now.

She glances over her shoulder toward the open door to the hallway, where Killian, Connor, Raven, and several other people I don't recognize have been talking for what feels like hours. But I've mostly lost track of time related to anything but how long it's been since I heard Liam's voice and those mossy green eyes found mine.

Whatever is going on in that hallway, I can't think about it right now.

There *will* be fallout from what happened on the homestead.

People are dead.

People connected to a very dangerous and powerful criminal empire...

There will be consequences.

All because of me.

The guilt that sits like a thousand-pound boulder in my gut only grows heavier and heavier with each passing moment, as the future that might have been so bright with Liam in McBride Mountain is overshadowed by the very dark reality of what I've set in motion.

"Hey..." Willow squeezes my shoulders. "I know what you're thinking, and you have to stop."

"What am I thinking?"

She releases a little sigh, shoving her hands through her long hair. "When I was taken, I thought it was my fault. Because I left Killian instead of going back to talk. I kept thinking that if I had just never tried to leave McBride Mountain, none of it ever would have happened."

"What?" I gape at her. "Of *course* it wasn't your fault! Earl was unhinged, completely out of his mind. How could you ever think you caused any of that?"

Her slender shoulders rise and fall. "The same way you think you somehow caused any of *this*."

I recoil slightly at her words, the force of them rocking my feet back a step. "I don't—"

She nods. "You do blame yourself. And you have to stop doing that." One of her hands waves absently around the room. "All of *this* was caused by *one* person—Brent Lorell. *You* were an innocent victim in all of this, just like I was with Earl."

"But—"

"No." She shakes her head. "I know you blame yourself because you think you should have seen through him and his game, but wanting to believe in someone, in something good, isn't a fault, Lucky. It isn't something you can *blame* yourself for or see as a weakness." Her eyes glisten with tears. "It will ruin everything good in your life if you keep seeing it that way."

I don't know how to process what she's saying, how to reconcile the guilt and regret in my heart with what is true in my head.

It's all too tangled up with my worry for Liam and what might be coming for all these people—including the woman standing in front of me who has become such a good friend.

She pulls me back into her arms, tightening them around me. "It will all work out. Maybe not the way we all imagined it, but the way it was meant to be."

I hope she's right, and for a moment, I allow myself to just absorb her warmth and the confidence she has that I'm not sure I can share.

When she pulls away, she gives me a small smile. "Let me know if you need anything. I'll be right out there."

What I need is Liam to wake up...

Once that happens, there might be a chance of being able to sort through everything else, but until I hear his voice again, this wicked spiral I seem trapped in will just keep spinning downward.

Willow slips from the room, and I stare down at my hands, still tinged with Liam's blood that won't completely come out, even after scrubbing them raw when they took him back for surgery.

His blood is literally on my hands...

My legs wobble, another breakdown threatening, and I stumble over to the chair beside Liam's bed to collapse into it before I hit the floor.

I pull his hand into mine, trying to ignore the discoloration.

The rough callouses on his palm rub against my smooth skin, and all I want is for him to squeeze back. For him to acknowledge that I'm here. For him to wake up and smile at me and call me Bluebell again.

Lowering my head, I brush a kiss across his cheek. "Please wake up for me."

I don't know if he can hear me or not, but it helps to talk to him, to think that he can and that it might somehow draw him away from whatever place the lingering medications in his system have him trapped in.

The machines next to the bed beep.

His chest rises and falls.

And I lower my face against it, carefully avoiding his ruined shoulder so I can feel his steady heartbeat beneath my ear.

That familiar rhythm that has lulled me to sleep so many times starts to calm me the longer I stay like this.

Each thud a reminder that he's alive and there's hope.

I close my eyes, trying to bring myself back to those moments in front of the fireplace, or talking in the treehouse yesterday. The beautiful moments spent together before everything went to shit when I had hope that there may be a way out that didn't end like this—

Liam's hand twitches in mine.

That tiny movement hits like a bolt of lightning slamming into me and restarting my heart.

I jerk upright and search his face. "Liam?"

His brow furrows.

His eyes slowly flutter open.

Glassy.

Unfocused.

Confused.

He blinks a few times.

That mossy green gaze finally meets mine.

"Oh, my God!" I scramble to press the call button at the side of the bed for the nurse, then take his face in my hands, leaning over him. "Liam. I'm right here. Can you hear me?"

The tiniest flicker of a smile pulls at his lips.

I glance toward the door. "Willow!"

My scream comes out a little unhinged, but after waiting for so long, after feeling like I wasn't breathing since the moment his eyes last closed, I can't contain the emotions bubbling inside me any more.

A second later, she pops her head around the corner, her eyes wide with concern. "What?"

Tears stream down my cheeks as I release a choked laugh and smile at her. "He's awake!"

LIAM

Footsteps move away.

I blink a few more times, trying to clear away the dark fog enveloping my mind.

Slowly, bits and pieces of memories filter through it.

Lucky waking me...

Giz growling...

Movement outside...

The men in black with guns...

Pain...

Fear...

It hits me now, flooding back in.

But Lucky's face appears above me, those warm blue eyes filled with tears somehow soothing the panic almost instantly.

"Hey!" Her soft hands cup my cheeks and she smiles, but it's such a contradiction to what I see in her gaze. "Welcome back."

Back?

The low, constant beeping sound at my left slowly registers.

A hospital.

I'm in the hospital...

And then *that* memory returns.

The gunshot.

The blinding, searing agony in my shoulder.

Fuuuck...

As my brain fully comes back online, the dull ache there registering now, even through the haze of drugs they must have given me.

Lucky's fingers drift across my cheeks, as if she needs to feel me to really believe I'm here. "How you feeling?"

I groan, shifting slightly in the bed, trying to find a more comfortable position, but moving isn't a good idea. Pain spikes, and I grit my teeth. "Like I got shot."

It's meant to be funny, but the small laugh it brings only makes my shoulder hurt more. I wince, instantly regretting it.

Joking is bad...

Noted.

Tears stream down Lucky's face, and she bites her trembling lip, trying to keep from completely breaking down.

"Hey..." I lift my hand, to reach for her, but something tugs at it. The IV cords prevent me from raising it too high. I manage to get my palm around her wrist and squeeze. "Don't cry. I'm... okay."

At least, I think I am.

The pain sucks, as does this feeling that I'm missing something.

A giant gap in my memory that ends with my axe in the back of the man threatening all of us...

"What happened, Bluebell?"

She sniffles, finally releasing my face to swipe away the tears from her cheeks. "Don't worry about that right now. Everyone is safe. The nurse will be here soon."

I shake my head, trying to push myself up slightly despite the pain it causes, needing to be closer to her. "I don't want the nurse. Just want you."

Lucky is the only thing I can even think about in this

moment. Holding her. Soothing her distress. Feeling her pressed against me and knowing she's all right.

But she gently places a hand on my right shoulder, nudging me down. "I'm not going to let you hurt yourself."

She leans in, kissing me softly, letting her lips linger over mine in an assurance that she can't voice. When she pulls away, her gaze has cleared a little. Some of that panic and worry has melted away, but enough lingers there that I can already tell what she's going to say before she does.

"I'm so sorry, Liam. For everything. They could have killed you. They could have—"

I squeeze her wrist, tugging her hand from me to twine our fingers together. "I'm okay. Please tell me what happened after I passed out."

Lucky releases a heavy sigh. "Connor and I brought you here while Killian called the sheriff and dealt with what was left at the homestead."

"What about Gizmo?"

Her lips curl, relief in her gaze. "He's okay. Elaine came and took him to the vet to get checked out. He's with her right now until we can go home."

Home.

The mountain.

The place that has always meant safety and security.

All that was shattered last night.

That evil man tried to destroy it, tried to demolish what we have, what we've built. He tried to take Lucky from me.

Anger rises, tightening my grip on her. "He's dead, right?"

I don't need to clarify which *he* I'm asking about.

Lucky nods. "He is."

A relieved breath rushes from my lungs. "Thank God...did you talk to the sheriff?"

She shakes her head and glances nervously toward the hall-way. "Not yet. They've been keeping him out of the room because they knew I wasn't in any mindset to speak to him while I was waiting for you to wake up."

I nod, trying to imagine how frantic she must have been, given how I know I would feel if anything had happened to her. "Probably a good thing."

Tony Briggs is an excellent sheriff, committed to his job and role, but he's also an incredible human being. A friend to the McBrides for a very long time.

He wouldn't push to talk to Lucky if he knew she needed time, which she clearly did. Even now that I'm awake, she's still trembling, still barely clinging to her composure, trying to keep it together for me.

She releases a heavy sigh and buries her face against my chest. "I'm just so glad you're all right."

I wrap my good arm around her and hold her there, letting her cry, letting her release everything she's been trying to hold in this entire time for my sake.

Lucky doesn't need to hide anything from me.

She has never had to.

Certainly not now, after she saved *my* life. Lorell would have killed me in that barn if she hadn't ignored my order to stay in the cabin. If Gizmo hadn't come in and attacked him, and if she hadn't had the strength to face him, Connor wouldn't have had time to get to us. And I wouldn't be here.

Her quiet sobs fill the room, and I run my fingers through her hair gently, trying to soothe her the only way I can right now. "I'm not going anywhere, Bluebell."

Ever.

It would literally take death to rip me away from this woman.

Movement in the doorway catches my attention, and I glance up to see Tony walk in, followed by Killian, Connor, and Willow, who holds a sleeping Niall against her chest.

The sheriff grins, inclining his head toward me. "Glad to see you awake."

Lucky lifts her head, swiping at her tear-stained cheeks.

I offer Tony a returned smile. "Good to be awake."

Killian, Connor, and Willow all look like they're fighting back the same emotions overtaking Lucky and me right now.

Tony pulls off his hat, his gaze locking with Lucky's. "The boys have filled me in on everything that's been happening the last several weeks." It flickers over to me. "I wish you two would've come to me. Would've told me the situation."

The admonishment in his tone is overshadowed by the hurt that we didn't come to him.

Killian leans against the door jamb, arms crossed over his chest, his jaw hard. "You're too good at your job, Tony. You would've brought her in on the open warrant and handed her over to the FBI."

Which is why Lucky was so terrified of having a conversation with him, despite the fact that Tony is a good friend.

She knew the clerks from the bank would tell the police about her involvement, even if they believed she was truly a hostage. And once she ran...that only made her look more guilty and gave them reason to suspect her.

He nods slowly. "You're right. I probably would have. But at least I could have prevented *this*"—he spreads out a hand toward me—"from happening."

Maybe he's right.

If we had gone to him after Lucky came clean to me, if she had been taken into custody and held while the FBI investigated her story, that death squad never would have come for her. McBride Mountain and the homestead wouldn't have ended up on the Lorell family's radar or hit list. But the thought of her being alone, terrified, in some cell somewhere, wondering if she had been abandoned by me, by us, after we promised to protect her, never would have allowed me to take that route. Especially because there was a very real chance she wouldn't be believed.

"What happens now?" My question comes out shaky, barely a whisper. "With Lucky...with...*everything*."

Connor cringes and looks away, and Willow offers a sympathetic look.

The sheriff locks his gaze with Lucky. "I spoke with Agent Michaelson from the local Columbia FBI field office. He's in charge of the investigation into the bank robbery and flew in to manage what happened at the homestead as soon as I contacted them. He's there now, collecting evidence and assisting the Charlotte FBI officers. I've told them what I know, but"—his eyes shift over me with an apology in them before they move back to Lucky—"you're going to have to meet with them—today—to give them any information you have about those men up there and what happened with the robbery."

I tighten my grip on Lucky's hand, swallowing thickly. "Is she going to be arrested?"

He shrugs. "I honestly don't know what they plan to do, but I'm not going to arrest her now. I know she's not going anywhere. Not as long as you're here." He points to me, then offers Lucky an apologetic smile. "I'll leave you guys alone."

As he says the words, a nurse bustles in, glaring at everyone congregated just inside the door. "All of you need to get out."

Lucky's grip tightens on my hand, and she shakes her head. "I'm not leaving."

I can't fight the smile that pulls at my lips, despite my growing discomfort the longer I'm awake. "She's not leaving."

The nurse releases an exasperated sigh. "Fine." She swings an arm toward Connor, Killian, and Willow. "Everyone else though—*out*."

She closes the door behind the rest of them and comes over to the machines to my left, checking the various readouts. "How are you feeling?"

Instead of looking at her, I watch Lucky to see how she's doing after that conversation with the sheriff. She appears surprisingly calm, considering that the FBI will show up soon and whisk her away for an interview—and potential arrest if they don't get the warrant that was issued after the robbery vacated.

"I'm okay."

"I can see that..."

I glance over at the nurse, and she offers a little half grin, her gaze dipping to where my hand is still clenched around Lucky's.

"How's the pain?"

Terrible.

But I don't want Lucky to worry about me any more.

It isn't anything I can't deal with.

I swallow thickly. "Okay."

The nurse gives me a reproachful look. "You know you don't have to lie just because she's here."

Lucky narrows her eyes on me, squeezing my hand. "If you're in pain, you need to tell her so she can help you."

There's a plea in her voice, to stop being tough or trying to protect her and to think about myself for once—even if she won't say it out loud.

I chuckle at how intense she glares at me and wince. "Okay, it's not great."

Lucky immediately flinches, her body tensing with the knowledge that I'm in pain, and I can see it in her eyes, the *guilt* she's going to allow to overwhelm her.

"I would do it again, Lucky. Anything to keep you safe." I tug her gently until she leans closer to me, until I can release her hand and draw her face to mine, pausing just before our lips touch. "You are now. No one will ever threaten you again."

Tears brim in her eyes. "Everything horrible in my life that led me to McBride mountain led me to you. I know you would do anything for me. Even if I don't deserve it."

The reservation in her voice, the fact that she might actually believe those final words, hurts more than the gunshot did. "You deserve everything, Bluebell. You deserve the entire world."

She kisses me softly. "I don't need the entire world, Liam. I just need you to get better and get to sleep. You need your rest."

I shake my head. "Not until you promise me something."

"What's that?"

Cupping her face, I hold her in place, ensuring she can't look away. "You're done running."

Tears spill down her cheeks, and she nods. "I'm done running. The only place I'm ever going to run again is into your arms."

EPILOGUE
TWO MONTHS LATER

LIAM

The vast, endless mountain sky spreads above us, millions of stars twinkling against the utter blackness. A high, full moon casts shadows from all the trees around the cabin, but I've finally forced myself to stop looking into them for lurking danger.

At least, beyond the natural ones that have always existed here on McBride Mountain.

But I've never feared them.

Only respected the animals who were here long before us.

I sit back in the new chair on the porch and stare up at the sky, like I often do, letting the vastness of it overwhelm me and make me feel like a tiny speck in the universe.

There was a time when I thought disappearing would be a good thing for me, for everyone around me, when I believed that the taint that had been brought by my father could lead me to do something as awful as he had. When I thought there would be no escaping who I was in my blood.

But one woman changed all of that.

I never could have sat here, in *this* chair, or even *finished* it, if she hadn't pushed me to move past my fears and embrace what's right in front of me.

This wood may remind me of what happened that day up on the mountain and of what my father did to Willow, but it also serves as evidence that something horrible can lead to something beautiful.

Willow and Killian's new life with their son.

Mine with Lucky.

It might not have happened if I hadn't been in that mental state that night. If I hadn't waited downtown, lingering because I didn't want to spend another evening with my nightmares. I might not have driven on that road at that exact time and found Gizmo...and ultimately *her*.

Lucky pushes out of the cabin with a glass of amber liquid in her hand and grins at me as she slides into my lap, handing it to me as she examines the chair. "You finished it."

I nod, running my free hand over the arm of it. "I did."

"It's beautiful." She laughs, grinding into my lap. "And sturdy."

"Very."

Raising the glass to my lips with my left hand, the familiar twinge hits my shoulder and I wince, allowing Lucky to take the drink. I roll my shoulder slightly, trying to work out the discomfort the work I did today caused.

Her gaze narrows on me. "You all right?"

I nod. "I'm good."

She takes a sip of her bourbon, then hands it back to me, looping her arms around my neck. "Are you lying to me?"

Not about that.

It doesn't feel good after pushing myself so hard this afternoon to finish the chair, but it will be fine—eventually.

And I had to do it today.

There wasn't any other option.

I grin at her and take a sip, letting the warm, spicy liquid coat my tongue and burn down my throat into my belly. "You know I would never lie to you."

Her warm blue eyes search mine. "I do know that."

After all this time, she finally believes it. She finally understands that every promise I made to her, I would die to fulfill.

I almost did.

She feathers her lips over mine, then settles her head against my good shoulder and stares up at the sky with me. "It's beautiful tonight."

I nod, loving the weight of her body pressed against mine. How perfectly we fit together like this.

The sounds of the evening float around us.

All the normal ones the mountain at night always provides.

Its own symphony.

What happened here only a few months ago is finally gone from it, even if it isn't from our memories.

Today was the first time I walked into the barn and didn't see the red stain. Even though we washed it and painted over it months ago, I could still *see* it the same way I felt the taint in my blood knowing about my father.

Until today.

Lucky pushes up and turns toward me, her brows narrowed over concerned eyes, locked on me. "You sure you're all right?"

I nod and kiss her, trying to distract her worry, but she can read me too damn well.

"Did something happen at work today?"

My hand tightens around the glass, and I take a long sip before I answer, swallowing the liquid courage. "I didn't go to work today."

"What?" Her brows fly up. "Where were you?"

I clear my throat, bracing myself for her reaction. "I went to see my father."

Her entire body stiffens, her palm coming to rest against my chest, directly over my heart. "Why didn't you tell me?"

The deep concern in her voice is one of the reasons I love her so much.

She understands what it means for me to go see him, to face the man I've been so worried about looking like and coming from for so long.

I raise my hand and cup her cheek, her soft skin like silk beneath the rough calluses of my thumb as I brush against it. "Because I knew you'd worry."

A little mirthless laugh floats from her. "With good reason. Liam, I don't understand."

"I had to do it. I had to look in his eyes one more time. I had to talk to him."

Her brow furrows. "Why?"

"So that I would know for sure."

"You would know what?"

I offer her a smile I finally feel. "That I'm not a Byers. I'm a McBride."

Lucky's gaze softens. "What did you say to him?"

Probably not enough.

There were so many things I planned in my head over the past two years, so much I *wanted* to say and questions I wanted to ask if I were ever face to face with him, but all of that went out the window as soon as he opened his mouth.

I take another sip as I consider our conversation from earlier today at the state mental hospital where he's been locked up for almost a year now. "I'm not even totally sure he knew who I was. They've been medicating him, but ..." I shake my head slightly, my jaw tensing. "I told him Willow was my sister-in-law, and that I was his son. There was a flicker, a second where I thought maybe he understood everything, but —" I release a heavy sigh, the pain of that moment hitting me hard again. "But then, it was gone. I think *he's* totally gone at this point. But seeing him was good because I don't see myself anymore when I look at him."

She smiles, with nothing but love and affection glowing in her gaze. "Good, you shouldn't."

"I saw a broken man who's been broken for a very long time, who had everything to live for—a wife and a child—and instead became a monster. I won't let that happen to me, to us."

She leans into me, burying her face in my neck. "I know you won't. I'm glad you went and saw him."

I press my lips into the top of her head, inhaling that eucalyptus scent. "Me, too."

"But I wish you would've told me."

The pain in her voice makes regret sit heavy on my chest.

"I needed to do it on my own."

She pushes up and nods. "I understand that."

"Good, because it's the only thing I want to do alone. For the rest of my life, it's you and me...and Giz."

He pops his head up from the other chair beside us at the sound of his name, scanning to see why I said it, and then instantly slumps back down, returning to his evening nap when he discovers he isn't getting any snacks or attention.

Lucky runs her hands through my hair. "Good. While you were gone today, I got a call."

"From who?"

"Agent Michaelson."

My back immediately stiffens. "Why didn't you tell me right when you walked out the door?"

She gives me a sly smile. "Because I didn't want you to worry."

"Using my own words against me, huh?"

A grin plays at her lips. "If that's what it takes."

"What did he have to say?"

"A lot."

LUCKY

I've been dreading having this conversation all day, but after what Liam just revealed to me about going to see his father, there doesn't seem any point in keeping it from him.

Not when we've been waiting for this news for a long time.

"I was going to tell everyone at breakfast tomorrow..."

His body tenses under mine. He's anticipating the blow because that's what it seems like has been happening over the last several months since the attack on McBride Mountain.

The Lorells set a series of crazy legal maneuvers in motion, trying to twist what happened in any way that would give them the upper hand in their battle against the people trying to bring them down.

They tried to argue it was some giant conspiracy to frame one of the youngest members of their family and cover up a murder committed by the McBrides. All orchestrated by me—the mastermind bank robber.

It was ludicrous.

And of course, Agent Michaelson didn't buy any of it, nor did the U.S. Attorney's office.

But we've still had to jump through hoop after hoop, give statements, attend interview after interview and retell the same story dozens of times.

Yet it has felt like everything has been stagnant.

There was no moving forward until today.

I smile at him. "It's good news."

A little of the tension in him releases. "What did he say?"

Settling back onto his chest, I rest my head on his good shoulder. "He said that their legal tactic has changed."

"How so?"

"They weren't going to get anywhere, trying to prosecute a

RICO case using the robbery with almost all of the crew dead. Finding out who the other few were would have been nearly impossible, let alone tying them to the larger criminal enterprise. So, they came to an agreement with Brent's uncle."

He raises the glass and takes a long pull from it, like he needs the alcohol to settle his nerves. "What kind of an agreement?"

"One I think we can all live with."

At least, I hope we can.

I still don't *fully* trust it. I don't think I can ever *fully* trust anything having to do with that man or his family after what he did to me, what he did to us. But he's long dead now and buried. And this is the fallout we have to deal with.

It's going to be messy, no matter what.

There are no tightly wrapped, pretty bows around boxes that contain it.

I snag the glass from Liam and take a sip of the bourbon, staring up at the stars. "He said that the Lorells are agreeing to stop pursuing any legal action against any of us for Brent's death, if the government agrees to stop any potential prosecution of anyone in their organization."

"What?" Liam's entire body stiffens again, and he tugs my face up to look at me, searching my eyes. "But they tried to kill you. They almost killed me."

I bite my bottom lip. "I know, but they don't want the government breathing down their necks. They don't want to be constantly fighting this battle. So, if I disappear quietly, if this story remains under wraps..."

Which it mostly has, thanks to the people of McBride Mountain understanding how essential it was, and to Raven being able to keep her mouth shut for once.

"It'll all just go away, Liam." I shrug. "They told Agent Michaelson that if Brent was involved in the robbery, he acted alone and outside their structure. I don't know if that's true. It's hard for me to believe he would do that, but there's no way to prove otherwise. If the FBI leaves it alone, leaves them alone, then they'll leave *us* alone."

It seems like such a simple concept.

Almost *too* simple.

Which is why it's impossible to really trust it, but I don't know how else this ends.

Liam drags my head down, pressing his lips to my forehead and holding me there for several moments as the night settles around us. "You're really okay with this?"

I release a heavy sigh.

No one is going to pay for what happened.

No one is going to pay for what was done to me and the McBrides.

At least, that's what I initially thought, but as the day has gone on, I realized that the person responsible already has.

He's gone.

The man who did this to me, the man who hurt me, never can again.

And the one who brought me back to life, who *gave* me a life, now has his arms wrapped around me, and he continues to be my rock, my safety, my everything every damn day.

"This is all I need, Liam." I raise a hand vaguely toward the sky. "This right here. You and McBride Mountain and this beautiful sky. Everything beyond it could vanish as far as I care."

He kisses my temple, tightening his hold on me. "That's the same way I feel about this place and about you. And if you're okay with this resolution, then the rest of us will be."

"Are you sure?"

The fallout from the attack on the homestead has been more than just legal.

Since doing what he had to that night, since killing those men, Connor has been untouchable. He's holed himself up in that cabin and barely left, only coming down to eat, where he barely touches his food and hardly says a word. He sits in the office at his desk, staring absently at the wall or a paper I know he isn't reading, going through the motions without really interacting with anyone or enjoying anything.

Liam, Killian, Willow, and I have all tried to talk to him.

We've all tried to get through.

He doesn't want to talk—the same way Liam never did about what he was dealing with—but the crushing weight of it is really starting to wear down on him.

"I'm worried about Connor."

Liam nods. "We all are."

"You really think he'll be okay with this?"

"He doesn't have a choice. We all have to be..."

And that's the real lesson—that sometimes in life we don't have a choice. Sometimes things happen to us, and all we can do is deal with them and live with the fallout.

It's taken me a long time to realize that what happened with "Brad" wasn't my fault, though there are times when I look at the giant scar on Liam's shoulder and remember how close I was to losing him, that I have to force myself to hear Willow's words over and over again assuring me of that.

"You really think he'll be okay?"

Liam nods. "I do. Eventually."

A door slams somewhere on the property, and I jerk up slightly, glancing at Liam, whose eyes narrow through the darkness.

We both listen as familiar voices float through the night air.

I glance at him. "Is that Connor?"

He nods.

"And *Raven*?"

His jaw tenses. "Sure sounds like it."

And though I can't make out the words, the tone is unmistakable.

"What are they arguing about? What is she even doing here?"

Liam shakes his head. "I don't know, but it can't be good."

He isn't wrong. The way they bicker and the glares they toss at each other when they're in the same room is enough to make everyone else leave it.

But I refuse to let whatever is going on with them interfere with this moment, when so many things have finally come together.

This right here, wrapped in Liam's arms, staring at the night sky above McBride Mountain, is home.

I'm done running.

I hope you enjoyed *Beyond the Mountain Sky.* Continue your visit to McBride Mountain with *Bigger Than the Mountain Sky,* the final book two in the McBride Brother Lumberjacks Series!

Available from your favorite retailer:
books2read.com/BiggerThanTheMountainSky

And check out five other broody, sexy lumberjacks with the Lumberjacks in Love Series, complete and ready for you to binge now! Each is a complete standalone!

https://www.gwynmcnamee.com/lumberjacksinlove

ABOUT THE AUTHOR

Gwyn McNamee is an attorney, writer, wife, and mother (to one human baby and two fur babies). Originally from the Midwest, Gwyn relocated to her husband's home town of Las Vegas in 2015 and is enjoying her respite from the cold and snow. Gwyn has been writing down her crazy stories and ideas for years and finally decided to share them with the world. She loves to write stories with a bit of suspense and action mingled with romance and heat.

When she isn't either writing or voraciously devouring any books she can get her hands on, Gwyn is busy adding to her tattoo collection, golfing, and stirring up trouble with her perfect mix of sweetness and sarcasm (usually while wearing heels).

Gwyn loves to hear from her readers. Here is where you can find her:

Website: http://www.gwynmcnamee.com/

Shop: http://www.gwynmcnameeshop.com/

Facebook:https://www.facebook.com/AuthorGwynMcNamee/

FB Reader Group: https://www.facebook.com/groups/1667380963540655/

Newsletter: www.gwynmcnamee.com/newsletter

Instagram: https://www.instagram.com/gwynmcnamee

Bookbub: https://www.bookbub.com/authors/gwynmcnamee

Tiktok: https://www.tiktok.com/@authorgwynmcnamee